Walter Mosley is one of America's best loved authors. He is the author of the internationally bestselling Easy Rawlins series, and his novels include *Devil in a Blue Dress*, which was made into the acclaimed film of the same name starring Denzel Washington and Don Cheadle. His books have been translated into 23 languages and have sold more than 3.5 million copies to date. He lives in New York City.

www.waltermosley.com

Also by Walter Mosley

THE EASY RAWLINS MYSTERIES

Devil in a Blue Dress

A Red Death

White Butterfly

Black Betty

A Little Yellow Dog

Gone Fishin'

Bad Boy Brawly Brown

Six Easy Pieces

Little Scarlet

Cinnamon Kiss

Blonde Faith

Little Green

Rose Gold

Charcoal Joe

THE LEONID MCGILL MYSTERIES

The Long Fall

Known to Evil

When the Thrill Is Gone

All I Did Was Shoot My Man

And Sometimes I Wonder About You

THE FEARLESS JONES SERIES

Fearless Jones

Fear Itself

Fear of the Dark

OTHER FICTION

Always Outnumbered, Always Outgunned

The Man in My Basement

RL's Dream

DOWN THE RIVER UNTO THE SEA

WALTER MOSLEY

WEIDENFELD & NICOLSON

First published in Great Britain in 2018
by Weidenfeld & Nicolson
an imprint of the Orion Publishing Group Ltd
Carmelite House, 50 Victoria Embankment
London EC4Y 0DZ

An Hachette UK Company

1 3 5 7 9 10 8 6 4 2

A CIP catalogue record for this book is
available from the British Library.

ISBN (Hardback) 978 1 4746 0866 4
ISBN (Export Trade Paperback) 978 1 4746 0874 9
ISBN (eBook) 978 1 4746 0868 8
ISBN (Audio) 978 1 4091 7962 7

Printed in Great Britain by Clays Ltd, St Ives plc

www.orionbooks.co.uk

For Malcolm, Medgar, and Martin

DOWN THE RIVER
UNTO THE SEA

1.

LOOKING OUT FROM my second-floor window onto Montague Street is better than the third-floor view. From here you can almost make out the lines in the faces of the hundreds of working people moving past; people who, more and more, have no reason to walk through the doors of the fancy shops and banks that have made their claim on that thoroughfare. These new businesses are like modern-day prospectors panning for gentrified, golden customers who will buy the million-dollar condos and fancy clothes, eat in the French bistros, and buy wine for a hundred dollars a bottle.

When I took this office, almost eleven years ago now, there were used-book stores, secondhand clothes shops, and enough fast food to feed that displaced army of workers in Brooklyn Heights. That's when Kristoff Hale offered me a twenty-year renewable lease because another cop, Gladstone Palmer, had overlooked his son Laiph Hale's involvement in the brutal attack on a woman; a woman whose only offense was to say no.

Three years later Laiph went to prison for another beating, one that got bargained down to manslaughter. But this had nothing to do with me; I had the lease by then.

My maternal grandmother always tells me that every man gets what he deserves.

Thirteen years earlier I was a cop too. I would have tried to put Laiph in prison for the first assault, but that's just me. Not everyone sees the rules the same. The law is a flexible thing—on both sides of the line—influenced by circumstance, character, and, of course, wealth or lack of same.

My particular problem with women was, at one time, my desire for them. It didn't take but a smile and wink for me, Detective First Class Joe King Oliver, to walk away from my duties and promises, vows and common sense, for something, or just the promise of something, that was as transient as a stiff breeze, a good beer, or a street that couldn't maintain its population.

For the last thirteen years I have been somewhat less influenced by my sexual drives. I still appreciate the opposite, sometimes known as the fairer, sex. But the last time I acted on instinct I ran into so much trouble that I believed I was pretty much cured of my roaming ways.

Her name was Nathali Malcolm. She was a modern-day Tallulah Bankhead, with the husky voice, quick wit, and that certain something that defined the long-ago starlet. My dispatcher, the same Sergeant Gladstone Palmer, called via cell phone to give me the assignment.

"It should be easy, Joe," Palmer assured me. "It's basically a favor for the chief of Ds."

"But I'm on that portside thing, Glad. Little Exeter always makes his move on Wednesdays."

"That means he'll be doin' it next Wednesday and the one after that," my sergeant reasoned.

Gladstone and I had come through the academy together. He was white Irish and I was a deep shade of brown, but that never affected our friendship.

"I'm close, Glad," I said, "real close."

"That may very well be, but Bennet's in a hospital bed with a punctured lung and Brewster messes up two out of every five collars. You need a point or two on your sheet this year anyway. You spend so much time at the docks you don't make half the arrests you need to keep your numbers up to snuff."

He was right. The one place the law was not flexible was in statistics. Criminal arrests and convictions, the retrieval of stolen property, and competent investigation that leads to crime solution were what our professional careers hinged on. I had a big case in front of me, but it might be a year before I could wrap it up.

"What's the offense?" I asked.

"GTA."

"Just one cop for a chop shop?"

"Nathali Malcolm. Stole a Benz from Tremont Bendix of the Upper East Side."

"A woman car thief?"

"Order came from up top. I guess Bendix got friends. It's just a single woman lives alone in Park Slope. They say the car is parked in front of the brownstone. All you have to do is ring the bell and slap on some cuffs."

"You got paper on her?"

"It'll be waiting for you at the station. And, King..."

"What?" Glad only used my middle name when he wanted to make a point.

"Don't mess it up. I'll send you a text with all the details."

The purple Benz *was* parked in front of her place. It had the right plates.

I looked at the front door, flanked by full-length windows that were swathed in yellow curtains. I remember thinking that was the easiest arrest I'd ever been sent on.

"Yes?" she said, opening the door maybe a minute after I rang.

Her tan eyes seemed to be staring through a fog at me. She had red hair, and the rest, pure Tallulah.

My grandmother likes old movies. When I visit her in the Lower Manhattan retirement home, we watch the old love stories and comedies on TCM.

"Ms. Malcolm?" I said.

"Yes?"

"I'm Detective Oliver. I have a warrant for your arrest."

"You're what?"

I took out the leather fold with my shield and ID. These I showed her. She looked, but I'm not sure she registered anything.

"Tremont Bendix claims you stole his car."

"Oh." She sighed and shook her head slightly. "Come in, Detective, come in."

I could have grabbed her right there, put on the restraints while reciting her rights as the Supreme Court detailed them. But this was a soft arrest and the lady was feeling tender, vulnerable. Anyway, Little Exeter Barret

6

had already connected with the captain of the *Sea Frog*. The shipment of heroin wouldn't be in for a few more days.

I was a good cop. The kind of officer who had yards of patience and lost his temper only when threatened physically by some suspect. And even then I took no joy in beating him after he'd been subdued and restrained.

"Would you like some water?" Nathali Malcolm asked. "The good stuff's all been packed away."

The living room was filled with boxes, bulging duffel bags, and piles of books and electronic equipment, along with clusters of potted plants.

"What's going on here?" I asked, as if reciting a line that had been written for me.

"This is what Tree calls me stealing his car."

She was wearing a sheer and shimmery green housecoat with nothing underneath. I hadn't paid close attention at first. When I got there I was still intent on the job.

"I don't understand," I said.

"For the past three years he's paid my rent and left me the Benz to use as my car," she said. Her tan eyes had turned golden under electric light. "Then his wife threatened to divorce him and he told me to get out and bring his car back to his uptown garage."

"I see."

"I have to move, Detective . . . what's your name again?"

"Joe."

When Nathali smiled and shifted her shoulders, the structure of our temporary relationship changed from potential handcuffs to definite bedsheets.

7

*   *   *

Nathali was very good in bed. She knew how to kiss and that is the most important thing to me. I need to be kissed and kissed a lot. She intuited this necessity, and we spent the better part of that afternoon and way into the evening discovering new and exciting ways and places to kiss.

She was a victim. I could see that in her eyes, hear it in her deep voice. And the arrest warrant was wrong. A man leaving his car at a girlfriend's house, a house he paid the rent on, had no expectation of her returning that automobile to his garage.

The next morning I'd make my report...and get back to the docks, where the real crime was happening.

When I opened my eyes, Monica Lars, my wife at the time, was already awake and making breakfast for her and Aja-Denise Oliver—our six-year-old daughter. I awoke to the smell of coffee and the memory of Nathali kissing my spine in a place I could not reach. I'd left her when my shift was over. I'd showered and changed at the station and got home in time for a late supper.

Drowsing for the last time in my morning bed, I took in a deep, satisfied breath; then the doorbell rang.

The bedroom of our Queens home was on the second floor, and I wasn't due in to work until the afternoon. I was naked and very tired; anyway, Monica knew how to answer a door.

I stretched a bit, thinking how much I loved my little family and that a promotion to captain was not an impossibility once I single-handedly busted the largest heroin ring to ever exist within the borders of the greatest city on earth.

"Joe!" Monica yelled from the entrance hall, which was downstairs and all the way at the front of the house.

"What?" I bellowed.

"It's the police!"

The one thing a cop's wife never says is, *It's the police.* That's what criminals and victims of criminals say. Sometimes we said it about ourselves while pointing a service revolver at the back of some perp's head. The mayor called us *the police* and now and then the newspapers did, but a cop's wife saying *it's the police* would be like my black-skinned grandmother calling out to my ex-sharecropper grandfather that *it's some Negroes at the do'!*

I knew there was something wrong and that Monica was trying to warn me. I had no idea that that would be her last loving act in our marriage or that her call heralded the end of any kind of normal life I could expect.

After the arrest, my union-supplied lawyer informed me that the prosecutor said there was a small sign posted next to the front door of the Park Slope brownstone. It read, PROPERTY UNDER ELECTRONIC SURVEILLANCE, so I had no expectation of privacy.

"Ms. Malcolm said that you presented her with the choice of either going to jail or performing fellatio," Ginger Edwards explained.

I'd been at Rikers for only thirty-nine hours and already four convicts had attacked me. There was a white adhesive bandage holding together the open flesh on my right cheek.

I broke the slasher's nose and knife hand, but the scar he gave me would last longer.

"That's not true," I said to Ginger.

"I saw the tape. She wasn't smiling."

"What about when she was kissing me?"

"Nothing like that."

"Then the tape was doctored."

"Not according to our guy. We'll look deeper into it, but the way it stands they got you on this."

Ginger was short with light brown hair. She was slender but gave the impression of physical strength. In the middle of her thirties, she had a plain face that wouldn't look much different in twenty years.

"What should I do?" I asked the diminutive white woman.

"I'd like to float a plea with no jail time."

"I'd lose everything."

"Everything but your freedom."

"I need to think about this."

"The prosecutor intends to bring rape charges."

"Come back day after tomorrow," I said. "Ask me about a plea then."

Ginger's eyes were also light brown. They opened rather wide when she asked, "What happened to your face?"

"Cut it shaving."

I decided to take my chances with the system. In the next two days I got into half a dozen fights. They'd given me a private cell, but on the fourth morning of my incarceration, a crazy-looking fellow named Mink splashed a bucket of urine through my cell door. Mink was gray-eyed with olive skin and kinky blond hair.

The guards didn't have anyone clean my cell.

It was in that stink that I became a murderer-in-waiting. The next time Mink passed my cell door he leaned forward, pretending to get a whiff of me. He miscalculated by five inches and I got him. Before the clown-man knew it, I had him in the chokehold I'd used against many of his peers. I'd kill him and anybody else who even thought about putting a hand on me. I'd be in prison for the rest of my life, but everybody from Mink's friends to the warden would know better than to ever get within reach again.

The guards got to us before I could kill the ugly, piss-slinging convict. They had to open the door to pry me loose from my victim. Then the peacekeepers and I had one hel-luva fight. I never knew what it was like to be pummeled with a truncheon; you don't feel the blows through the rage, but that night the bone bruises hurt like hell.

Just a few days and I'd switched allegiances from cop to criminal. I thought that was the worst thing...but I was wrong.

The next afternoon, when I had grown accustomed to the smell of piss in my clothes, a group of four guards ap-proached my cell wearing head-to-toe riot gear. Someone hit the switch to pop the door open and they rushed me, pinning me to the floor and chaining my wrists and fore-arms around the waist and to the leg irons on my ankles. Then they dragged me down one hall after another until I was tossed into a room so small that three men wouldn't have been able to play blackjack at the miniature metal table that was soldered to the floor.

I was chained in a metal chair to the table and the floor.

Many a suspect had been tethered before me like that while I interrogated them. I had never really understood how they felt or how anyone could expect someone to have any kind of revelatory conversation while being hog-tied in that manner.

I struggled against my bonds, but the pain from the previous day's bruises was too great and I had to stop.

When I quit moving, time congealed around me like amber over a mosquito that had taken a small misstep. I could hear my breaths and feel the pulse in my temples. It was in that moment I understood the phrase *serving time*. I was that servant.

Just as I gave up hope, a tall and, some say, handsome Irishman walked into the room.

"Gladstone," I uttered. It might have been a psalm.

"You look like shit, your highness."

"And I smell like piss."

"I wasn't gonna mention that," he said, taking the metal chair across the table from mine. "They called and told me that you put a convict in the hospital along with three guards to keep him company. You broke one dude's nose and another guy's jaw."

The grin on my face was involuntary. I could see my pain reflected in Gladstone's eyes.

"What's wrong with you, Joe?"

"It's like a crazy house in here, Glad. I been beat, cut, and showered in piss. And no one even gives a damn."

Dispatch Sergeant Gladstone Palmer was lean and mean, six foot one (two inches on me), with a mouth that was always smiling or getting ready to do so. He stared at me and shook his head.

"It's a shame, boyo," he said. "They turned on you like a pack of dogs."

"Who signed the papers on the girl?" I asked.

"It was an e-mail from the chief of Ds, but when I called his office they said that they never sent it."

"I didn't force that woman."

"It would help if your dick wasn't so big and black. Just looking at her look at it, you could imagine how scared she was."

"What about the rest of the video?"

"The only camera was in the living room. That's all it showed."

I remembered then that she wanted to go up to the bed after the first movement of our tragic opera. It was a plan.

"They framed me, Glad."

My friend winced and shook his head again.

"They framed me!"

"Look, Joe," he said after a full thirty seconds of silence. "I'm not saying they didn't. But we all know what you're like with the ladies, and then there's that other thing."

"What thing?"

"If it's a frame it's airtight. From the video to the girl's testimony, they've got you as a predator. You were pulling her by the hair, for chrissakes."

"She asked me to," I said, realizing what those words would sound like in front of a jury.

"No audio on the tape. It looks like she was begging you to stop."

I wanted to say something but couldn't find the right words.

"But it's not that that's the problem," Gladstone said. "The problem is you got powerful enemies who can reach in here and snuff you out."

"I need a cigarette," I replied.

My only friend in the world lit a Marlboro, stood up from his chair, and placed it between my lips. I took in a deep draw, held it, and then blew the smoke from my nostrils.

The smoke felt wonderful in my lungs. I nodded and inhaled again.

I will never forget the chill in that room.

"You got to be cool, Joe," my dispatcher said. "Don't be talking about a frame in here, or to your lawyer. I'll look into this and I'll talk to the chief of Ds too. I got a contact in his office. I know a couple of people here too. They're going to take you out of gen pop and put you in solitary confinement. At least that way you'll be safe until I can work some magic."

It's a terrible fall when you find yourself grateful to be put in segregation.

"What about Monica?" I asked. "Can you get her in here to see me?"

"She don't wanna see you, King. The detective on the case, Jocelyn Bryor, showed her the tape."

My gratitude for getting solitary didn't last long. The room was dim and small. I had a cot, a hard-edged aluminum toilet, and two and a half paces of floor space. I could touch the metal ceiling by raising my hand six inches above my head. The food sometimes turned my stomach. But because they fed me only once a day I was always ravenous. The fare was reconstituted potatoes and corned beef jerky, boiled green beans and, once a week, a cube of Jell-O.

I wasn't alone because of the roaches, spiders, and bed-bugs. I wasn't alone because the dozens of men around me, also in isolation, spent hours hollering and crying, some-times singing and pounding out rhythmic exercises.

One man, who somehow knew my name, would often regale me with insults and threats.

"I'm gonna fuck you in the ass, and when I get outta here I'm'a do the same to your wife an' little girl."

I never gave him the satisfaction of a response. Instead I found an iron strut that had somehow come loose from the concrete floor. I worried that little crosspiece until finally, after eight meals, I got it free.

Nine inches of rusted iron with a handle torn from my threadbare blanket. Somebody was going to die behind that shard of Rikers; hopefully it would be the man who threat-ened my family.

Never, not once, did they take me from that cell. In there I craved a newspaper or a book...and a light to read by. Bunged up in solitary confinement, I fell in love with the written word. I wanted novels and articles, handwritten let-ters, and computer screens filled with the knowledge of the ages.

During those weeks I accomplished a heretofore impos-sible feat: I gave up smoking. I had no cigarettes and the withdrawal symptoms just blended in with the rest of my suffering.

The other prisoners' complaints became background noise like elevator music or a song you'd heard so often but never knew the words.

I clutched my cell-made blackjack at all times. Somebody

was going to die by my hand—after two weeks it didn't much matter who.

I had eaten eighty-three nauseating meals when, while I was asleep, four riot-geared officers came into my cell and shackled me. I fumbled my blackjack because the sudden light from outside my crypt-like cell blinded and disoriented me.

I yelled at my captors, demanding they tell me where they were taking me, but no one answered. Now and then someone hit me, but those were just love taps compared to what they could have done.

They deposited me in a pretty big room, attaching my bonds to steel eyes that were anchored to the floor. I sat at the butt end of a long table. The fluorescent light burned my eyes and gave me a headache. I wondered if someone was going to come in there and kill me. I knew that this was still America and that people who worked for the law did not execute without the will of the courts, but I was no longer sure of that knowledge. They might execute me because they knew I had become an unrepentant murderer behind their prison walls.

"Mr. Oliver," a woman said.

I looked in the direction the voice came from and was amazed to see that she had made it into the room without my notice. Behind her stood a hale black man uniformed in a blue that was new to me. I hadn't heard them come in. Sounds had taken on new meanings in my head, and I couldn't be sure of what I heard.

I yelled a word at her that I had never used before, or since. The man in the blue suit rushed forward and slapped me ... pretty hard.

I strained every muscle trying to break my restraints, but prison chains are designed to be greater than human sinew.

"Mr. Oliver," the woman said again.

She was fair-skinned, tall, and slender, with salt-and-pepper hair and a pants suit that was muted navy. She wore glasses. The lenses glittered, obscuring her eyes.

"What?"

"I am Underwarden Nichols and I am here to inform you that you are being released."

"What?"

"As soon as Lieutenant Shale and I leave, the men that brought you here will remove your bonds, take you to a place where you can shower and shave, and then give you clothes and some money. From there on your life is your own."

"What about—what about the charges?"

"They've been dropped."

"What about my wife, my life?"

"I know nothing about your personal dealings, Mr. Oliver, only that you are to be released."

I saw my face for the first time in months in the polished steel mirror next to the small shower where I cleaned up. Shaving revealed the vicious gaping scar down the right side of my face. They didn't always offer stitches at Rikers.

When I got off the bus at the Port Authority on Forty-Second Street I stopped and looked around, realizing how hollow the word *freedom* really was.

2.

"ARE YOU THINKING about prison again, Daddy?"

She was standing at the door to my office. Five nine and black like the Spanish Madonna, she had my eyes. Though worried about my state of mind, she still smiled. Aja wasn't a somber adolescent. She was an ex-cheerleader and science student, pretty enough not to need a regular boyfriend and helpful enough that other teenage girls with boyfriends knew she was the better catch.

Her black skirt was too short and the coral blouse too revealing, but I was so grateful to have her in my life again that I picked my battles with great care.

Monica, my ex-wife, spent years trying to keep us apart. She took me to court to try to get a judgment against my ever seeing Aja-Denise and then sued me for failing to pay child support when she had drained my accounts and I didn't have two nickels to my name.

It wasn't until she was fourteen that Aja forced her mother to let her stay with me on a regular basis. And now that she was seventeen she said that either she worked in my office or she'd tell any judge who would listen that Monica's new husband, Coleman Tesserat, would walk in on her when she was in the shower.

"What?" I said to my child.

"When you look out the window like that you're almost always thinking about jail."

"They broke me in there, darling."

"You don't look broke to me." It was something I said to her one morning when she was a little girl trying to get out of going to school.

"What's that you got?" I asked, gesturing at the bundle in her hand.

"The mail."

"I'll get to it tomorrow."

"No, you won't. You never go through it until the bills are all late. I don't know why you won't let me put your bank account online so I could just pay them all myself."

She was right; I kept thinking that some false evidence would come in the mail and send me back to that roach-infested cell.

"I have to go out on that Acres job," I explained.

"Take it with you and go through it while you wait. You said that ninety-nine percent of the time you're just sitting in your car with nothing to do."

She held out the bundle and stared into my eyes. There was no mistaking that Aja-Denise had fought with her mother because she knew I needed her.

I reached out for the package and she grinned.

"Uncle Glad called," she said when I was sifting through the bills, junk mail, and various requests from clients, courts, and, of course, my ex-wife. There was also a small pink envelope addressed by an ornate hand and post-marked in Minnesota.

"Oh?" I said. "What did Gladstone have to say?"

"Him an' Lehman, War Man, and Mr. Lo, are playin' cards down the street tonight."

"That's Jesse Warren," I said, "not War Man."

"He told me to call him that."

I didn't like Gladstone's friends very much, but he kept them away from the office most of the time. And I owed Glad; he had saved my ass more than once since the arrest.

Getting me put in solitary rescued me from becoming a murderer, and then later, when I couldn't raise enough money for rent and child support, he came up with enough cash for me to start the King Detective Service. He even guided the first few clients my way.

But the best thing Gladstone Palmer ever did for me was to broker my severance with the NYPD. I lost my retirement and benefits except for medical insurance for Monica and my daughter. Magically, there was no blemish on my record either.

For the past week or so I'd been reading the nearly hundred-year-old novel *All Quiet on the Western Front.* There was a character in there who reminded me of Glad; Stanislaus "Kat" Katczinsky. Kat could find a banquet in a grave-yard, a beautiful woman in a bombed-out building. When the rest of the German army was starving, Kat would show up to his squad with a cooked goose, ripe cheese, and a few bottles of red wine.

You couldn't question a friend like Kat or Glad.

"I told him you were on a job," Aja said.

"You're my angel."

"He said he'd try to stop by before you left."

The letter from the heartland intrigued me, but I decided to put off reading it.

"How's your mother?" I asked.

"Fine. She's writing you to give money for her and Tesserat to send me to Italy for this youth physics conference they're having in Milan."

"That sounds nice; like an honor."

"There's a hundred kids and only four from the U.S., but I don't want to go. So you could tell her you'll help but you won't ever have to pay."

"Why don't you want to go?"

"Reverend Hall is having a special school in this Bronx church where good science students teach at-risk kids how scientists do experiments."

"You know you really have to start doing some bad things," I said with a little too much gravitas in my tone.

"Why?" Aja asked. She was really worried.

"Because as a father I have to be able to help you at least some of the time. With great grades, a good heart, and the way you bully me over the mail I feel like I have nothing to offer."

"But you did do something for me, Daddy."

"What? Buy you a Happy Meal or a hot dog?"

"You taught me to love reading."

"But you never read except for homework, and you complain about that."

"But I remember spending those weekends with you when I was little. Sometimes you'd read to me all morning, and I just know that I'll do that when I have a little girl."

"There you go again," I said, mostly covering the tears

in my voice. "Being so good that it makes me feel useless. Maybe I should start punishing you every time you get something right."

Aja knew when the conversation was over. She shook her head at me and turned. She walked from the room and I was, for a brief moment, relieved of the fall from grace foisted upon me by somebody in the NYPD.

Before I could turn to the pink envelope from the Midwest, Aja returned with a big brown envelope in her hands.

"I almost forgot," she said. "Uncle Glad left this for you."

She handed me the package and turned away before I could tease her more about her perfections.

3.

AFTER AJA RETURNED to the outer office desk, I was at sea there for a while. My life since those ninety-odd days in Rikers had been what I can only call vacant. I didn't feel comfortable in the company of most people, and the momentary connection with my daughter, or the few friends I had, left an aftermath of isolation. Human connection only reminded me of what I could lose.

Being an investigative private detective worked out perfectly because my interactions with people were mostly through listening devices and long-distance camera lenses. The few times I had to actually talk with people I was either playing a role or asking cut-and-dried questions like "Was so-and-so here on Friday night after nine?" or "How long has Mr. Smith worked for you?"

The buzzer sounded.

Half a minute later Aja-Denise said, over the intercom, "It's Uncle Glad, Daddy."

"Send him in."

*　　*　　*

The door opened and the tall, athletic, eternal sergeant walked in. He was wearing a straw-colored sports jacket and trousers so dark green that they might have passed for black. The white shirt and blue tie were his mainstay, and that smile lived equally in his eyes and on his lips.

"Mr. Oliver," he hailed.

"Glad."

I rose to shake his hand and then he lowered into the seat across from me.

"This office smells like a prison cell," he said.

"I got a cleaning lady come in and lay down that scent every other week."

"What you need is an open window and less time moldering behind that desk."

"Aja told me about the poker game tonight. I'd like to join you, but I got a man needs following."

Glad's eyes were cornflower blue. Those orbs shone on me, accompanying his *that's too bad* smile.

"Come on, Joe. You know you got to get outta this funk. It's been a decade. My son is off to college. My little girl is working on a second grandchild."

"I'm doing fine, Sergeant Palmer. Detective work suits me. That's the way I roll."

I had always been envious of Gladstone, even before my life hit the rocks. Just the way he sat in a chair made you think that he had a handle on a life that was both a joy and deeply meaningful.

"Maybe you could roll your way into better circumstances," he suggested.

"Like what?"

"I know a guy who might be of some help. You remember Charles Boudin?"

"That crazy undercover cop? The one that got into his cover so much that he bit an arresting officer to get in good with the Alonzo gang?"

"And which one are you?" Glad replied. "The pot or the kettle?"

"What about Charlie?"

"I was gonna get you drunk on this new seven-hundred-dollar bottle of cognac I got," Glad said. "You know...win all your money and get you singing. Then I was gonna tell you that C.B. is now a lieutenant in the Waikiki PD. He says he could get you in there in a wink."

That was the first inkling of the great transition before me. Glad had been angry that I was treated with disrespect by our brothers in blue. He wanted every cop to have the best. He really was my only close friend, with maybe one exception, who wasn't also blood.

"Hawaii? That's five thousand miles from here. I can't leave Aja like that."

"After a year you'd be a resident, and the university at Manoa has an excellent physics department. A.D. could get a BS there and move on, or she could stay and get a PhD. It's a real good school and the cost is almost nothing."

He'd done his homework.

"Are you trying to get rid of me, Glad?"

"You need to get back up on the horse, Joe. There's no charges pending against you and the department is legally prohibited from saying what you were suspected of. I know three captains would give you glowing references."

"And Charlie already said he'd get me in?"

"They need experience like yours out there on the island, Joe. You were one of the best investigative cops New York ever had."

"Aja might not want to go so far away."

"She would if you were there. That girl idolizes you. And she'd do it just so that you stop brooding in here like some kind of lovesick walrus."

"What if it came out?" I said. "You know...what they say I did? What if I upended my life and then the whole thing falls apart under my feet? I'd have moved Aja, with no money and no way to come home."

Without missing a beat Glad said, "You remember that time Rebozo was shot up in East Harlem?"

"Yeah?"

"Two gunmen with semiautomatics and Officer R. on the asphalt hemorrhaging like a motherfucker. You take them on with just your sidearm, wound them both, cinch Paulo's wounds, and make it home in time for supper."

"And still they set me up like a goddamned tenpin."

"Fuck them," Glad said with barely a smile. "If you could stand up to armed gunmen, then why would you be afraid of five thousand miles?"

It was a good question.

4.

IN MY LINE of work you need a car; to follow people, yes, but also to get from place to place without having to wait for, and pay for, taxis and limos, Ubers and gypsy cabs. That is unless you like climbing down into subway tunnels like a rat or roach passing through some forgotten prisoner's cell.

New York is not a car-friendly city and so I decided to buy the Italian-made Bianchina—a microcar that's so small it almost brings its own parking place with it. It looks like a full-grown sedan that got shrunk down until almost a toy. I had mine painted dull brown to make it a little less likely to be noticed.

At 6:16 I parked down the block from the Montana Crest apartment building near Ninety-First Street and Third Avenue. While waiting for my quarry I intended to sift through the mail that Aja-Denise gave me.

Before I tore open the first envelope I thought of what life might be with no winter and a job as a cop again. I'd be so far away that no one would know my story. Maybe that was all I needed to break out of my ten-year funk.

That got me thinking about my daughter again.

Aja was not my daughter's given name. When she was still small she learned how to spell the word for the continent in school and then saw the letters *A-J-A* graffiti-scrawled on a wall somewhere. The idea that two differently spelled words sounded exactly the same tickled the little girl and she took on the name because, she said, "Sometimes I'm happy and sometimes I'm sad but I'm still the same person anyway."

I started with the package that Gladstone had dropped off.

Therein I found four NYPD-generated documents that followed the path of a file-based investigation.

These records told me that the fingerprints lifted from the discarded water bottle of the woman identifying herself as Cindy Acres actually belonged to someone named Alana Pollander. Ms. Pollander had been born Janine Overmeyer but changed her name after being convicted for check kiting in her home state—Ohio. Armed with this new name, she went to work for a man named Ossa James, a political "researcher" from Maryland.

With the use of the iPad my daughter made me buy I was able to see that Ossa James had recently signed an exclusive contract with Albert Stoneman—candidate for the congressional office in the same district where I was waiting for Representative Bob Acres. Bob Acres who was married to a Cynthia I'd never met.

Representative Acres, when he was in New York, was extremely punctual. He usually returned home between 6:30 and 7:05. So at 6:25 I put away the records and iPad and turned on my boom box because the Bianchina radio doesn't have the best speakers.

That day I played a CD I'd burned featuring my favorite musician since getting out of Rikers—Thelonious Monk. Before my arrest I loved old jazz: Fats Waller and Louis Armstrong among many others. My father, Chief Oliver, wanted to name me King so that no one could denigrate me by using my first name as if I was some kind of servant or something. He also loved Louis Armstrong's mentor, King Oliver, and wanted to make a memorial to him with my naming. But my poor, luckless mother, Tonya Falter, was raised in Chicago and thought the other schoolkids would make fun of a fancy name like King. Chief respected Tonya's opinion and named me Joseph, King Oliver's given name, and used King as the middle appellation.

My christening being so close to jazz, I naturally leaned in that direction. But once I got out of jail I no longer felt the smooth riffs of the earlier musicians. Monk always had a good group of talented musicians with him, but while they played deep melodies, he was the madman in the corner pounding out the truth between the fabrications of rhythm and blues.

"Round Midnight" was playing when Bob Acres got out of a cab in front of the Montana Crest. He was wearing a light brown suit, dark shoes, and no hat. He didn't wear a tie either, his political career being based on brotherhood rather than superiority. He liked talking with his constituents and, if I was to believe the press, he represented their concerns as closely as any politician could.

For two hundred and fifteen dollars a day I shadowed Acres's nighttime activities as the woman calling herself his wife had asked. She told me that she was sure he was having an affair and wanted proof so that she could force him into an amicable settlement for the divorce.

On the surface all this made sense. The *New York Times* had printed a small article on the separation of Cynthia and Robert Acres. She'd moved back to her home state, Tennessee. The one blurry picture of her looked enough like the woman who'd come to my office—if that woman had lost some weight and dyed her hair blond.

Before my frame and arrest I would have believed the woman calling herself Cindy Acres, but after my downfall I always questioned what I was told. Therefore I took the fingerprints from a water bottle she'd used and got Glad to run them.

This was only the second week that Bob was in town. He'd spent most of his time down in D.C. working on legislation and political strategies.

The first week I followed Bob he'd gone out three times: once to dinner with a young man who might have been his son; once to a fund-raiser at the Harvard Club; and lastly to what appeared to be an illegal card game on West Twenty-Seventh. But this last week all that changed. He came home every evening by 7:00, went to his fourth-floor apartment, and turned on the light. Then, each night, the light went off at 10:17 and came on again at 6:56 the next morning.

Four days in a row Bob's light went on and off with military precision. I wondered who had tipped him off that he was being watched and where he was going that he needed an automatic system on his lights.

The night before, I waited in the alley near a doorway alcove at the side of the Montana. At 8:34 Bob Acres, dressed in a sweat suit, came out. He walked two blocks west, where he was met by a black Lincoln Town Car.

Twenty-four hours later I was ready.

The moment he walked through the front door of the Montana I drove to the block where he'd met the black car. There was another limo parked at the far corner.

There I waited.

Thelonious had moved on to "Bright Mississippi." While he played that fairly traditional number I took out the pink envelope from Minnesota, sniffed its mild scent, and tore it open.

Dear Mr. Joseph K. Oliver,

Pardon my intrusion into your life but my name is Beatrice Summers and I believe that I have very important information for you. We are not unknown to each other. When you met me I was going by the name Nathali Malcolm. I fooled you into believing that I was the victim of a cruel man, seduced you, and then blamed you for sexual assault. You have always been in my mind since that time. I was forced to entrap you by a policeman named Adamo Cortez. He came to me after I'd been arrested with a large amount of cocaine and I was facing a long prison sentence. But since then I moved to Saint Paul, got off drugs and into a Christian community that knew my sins and forgave them. I am now married with two beautiful children and a wonderful husband from whom I hide nothing. We, Darryl and I, discussed what I had done to you and we agreed that I should write and offer to come back to New York and testify on your behalf. We were both sinners, Mr. Oliver, but I believe that you have paid for your transgressions while I have not. Below you will find my home phone number. I am a stay-

*at-home mother and housewife these days and there's an
answering machine. I hope to hear from you soon.*

Yours in Christ,
Beatrice Summers

Reading that letter I felt both numb and jittery. I knew,
of course, that there had been a conspiracy behind my arrest, but it was so well done and I had come so close to
being locked in a cell forever that I let that truth fade until it was almost completely hidden behind the memory of
those prison walls.

But here was an answer to a question that I was afraid to
ask; afraid because I didn't want to go back into that cell. I
didn't want to, but there was the evidence right there in my
hand...right there.

The unstable mixture of rage and fear caused me to raise
my head just as Representative Bob Acres was opening the
back door of the hired transport.

I am a lifelong Democrat, as my father and his father
had been. Bob Acres was a dyed-in-the-wool Republican,
but I would have cast my ballot for him right then. His
appearance purged the past for a moment, allowing me to
concentrate.

The limo made its way to the West Side Highway and then
through to the Holland Tunnel. We crossed the state line
somewhere under the Hudson River, but it was a short trip.

Exiting in Jersey City, New Jersey, the limo took the first
right and pulled into the parking lot of the Champagne
Hour Motel on Clarkson. I stopped across the street and

snapped pictures with my high-resolution digital camera. The first-floor rooms' doors opened onto the parking lot. Through the high-powered lens I saw Acres entering room number thirty-nine.

The limo drove off.

I waited seven minutes, then drove into the lot, parked, and went to the glass-encased office, which had a high pink desk, turquoise walls, and a ceiling paved with glittering red tiles. Behind the high counter stood a lovely young black woman with thick braids of dark brown and cherry red. Her face was broad, but there was no smile attending her beauty.

I had my go bag at my side. It might have been a travel bag.

"Good evening," I said.

"Hello," she replied without a hint of welcome.

I was glad to see her despondence. Happiness rarely wants to do business with a man in my trade.

I put a hundred-dollar bill down on the desk and said, "I have fond memories of rooms thirty-seven and forty-one."

"That ain't enough," she said, sneering at the bill. "It's a hundred eighteen dollars a night."

"That's for you," I said, putting two more C-notes next to the one I'd already dropped. "This is for the room."

She smiled, said "Forty-one is free," and I secretly cheered for my country, where, over and over again, the almighty dollar proves its superiority.

There were a few sounds coming through the wall from thirty-nine. I opened my bag and took out a small hand drill with a one-eighth-inch bit. The device was almost silent, and when I just tapped the diamond-crusted bit every second or so against the locked door that connected the two rooms, there was hardly even a whine.

My room was dark, and when the light of thirty-nine shone through I took the surgical fiber-optic lens from my bag, connected it to the all-purpose digital camera, and then attached the camera to my iPad. I threaded the laser-wire lens through the hole and an image of what can only be called matchless debauchery filled the screen.

The pair of transgender prostitutes must have been waiting for him. The three of them were already naked and erect. I watched the play closely, mostly to avoid thinking about the intelligence that Beatrice Summers had bestowed.

The T-girls were good at their job. They played feminine very well.

Bob, for his part, was passionate and very, very happy.

I got about three and a half hours of video before the alcohol- and drug-induced mini-orgy was over. I waited until everyone from room thirty-nine had showered, dressed, and departed; then I went to bed with the most important item in my detective's bag of tricks—a small silver flask filled with twenty-year-old hundred-proof bourbon.

My dreams were of solitary confinement and the iron rod I dropped while being dragged from that cell. In the nightmare I was beating Mink's face in with the most powerful, the most satisfying blows I had ever delivered.

5.

I WOKE UP at 11:07 by the digital clock next to the bed. The hangover was mild considering what it might have been. The room wasn't spinning; it merely shook. And my head ached only if I moved it too quickly or looked directly into the light.

It was at least ten minutes before I even remembered Beatrice/Nathali's letter. But there was no time to think about that. I got up so late I had to hurry if I wanted to get to the Gucci Diner in time.

My cell phone sounded halfway through the Holland Tunnel. I put it on speaker and said, "Yes?"

"Daddy?"

"Aren't you supposed to be in school, A.D.?"

"It's passing period and I wanted to tell you that I made an appointment for you and a woman named Willa Portman for four o'clock today. I sent you a text, but sometimes you don't read them."

"What's the meeting about?"

"She wants to hire you to do some investigative work."

"What kind?"

"She didn't say, but she seemed nice."

"On the phone?"

"Uh-uh. She walked in."

"Okay. I'll be there."

"See you then. I love you, Daddy."

Between the headache, midday Manhattan traffic, and trying to compose the speech I had to deliver, there wasn't much time to consider Beatrice Summers and the danger her confession might pose.

The Gucci Diner was pretty far over on the east side of Fifty-Ninth Street. It was a family-owned restaurant that had been there for decades. I knew the place because my father liked going there when he and my mother were still a couple. The patriarch, Lamberto Orelli, had the foresight to buy the three-story building, and so far no big-time real estate offer could buy them out. I parked my car in a lot and went to a bus-stop bench across the street—there to sit and wait. I wondered if I could somehow forget the letter, Beatrice, and Adamo Cortez (whoever he was). Maybe if I waited long enough, the rage and fear would subside again, leaving me to help raise my daughter and follow upstanding perverts back and forth across state lines.

There was aspirin in the go bag, bottled water too, but I preferred to feel the discomfort. It seemed an appropriate response to who and what I was.

Bob Acres showed up at exactly a quarter past one. He went to his usual table and sat down with the *New York Times, Wall Street Journal,* and *Daily News.*

I allowed him to order and be served before jaywalking to the front door of Gucci's and through to the politician's table. I sat without invitation and looked into my quarry's eyes.

"Yes?" he said.

"Who told you that you were being followed?"

Acres opened his mouth but did not speak.

"I mean," I said, "that's the only reason you'd put your lights on a timer just this week."

I liked Bob. He was a deviant and a Republican to boot, but we all had our dark sides. I would have been a murderer if I hadn't fumbled that iron rod.

"Who hired you?" Bob asked.

Instead of answering I took out the iPad, played around a bit, and handed him a screen showing a full page of thumbnail stills that I'd sorted out while he got fucked.

He worked his way through the photographs, studying each one. There was no expression I could read. This made me think that he'd probably won at that poker game he attended.

"Who hired you to take these?" he asked, looking up.

I liked the guy.

"She said her name was Cynthia Acres," I replied.

That made his eyelids tighten.

"Cindy?" He might have been a child registering his mother's first betrayal.

"That's what she said, but when I looked into it I found out she was a ringer sent in through a third party to gather dirt on you for Albert Stoneman."

"So it wasn't my wife?"

"No. Not love, but politics as usual."

"So Stoneman hired you."

"Probably hired me. A man named Ossa James employs the woman posing as your wife. Ossa is a paid political adviser to Stoneman."

Acres put his right hand up with the palm confronting his face; then he rubbed the center of the palm with the fingers of his left hand.

"I don't understand," the congressman said. "Why would they have you bring the evidence to me instead of making it public? Why would they allow you to identify them?"

"The dollar is my master, but I ain't no slave," I replied. It was something my father used to say. "When I realized that the woman who hired me wasn't your wife I got kinda mad. I once had a woman lie about me and I didn't like it one bit."

Acres put both his palms flat on the table.

"Is this man bothering you?" a burly man asked Bob. By his white uniform I thought that maybe he was a cook. The authoritative way he asked the question meant that he was either a thug or a member of the Orelli clan.

"No, Chris, this is an aide of another member of Congress come to deliver a message."

Chris turned his grizzled gaze upon me. He had more muscle but I probably had better training. I had a license to carry too, but I usually left the hardware at home, or in the trunk of my Bianchina; this because of the memory of that iron rod in my calloused hand.

After the self-appointed bodyguard left, Acres asked, "So what do you want? And what's your name?"

"Whoever told you about me didn't give a name?"

"No. She just said that there was a detective following me."

She.

"I don't need a name for this talk, Congressman Acres. And what I want is not a physical thing."

"I will not resign," he said.

"Look, man, I'm a Democrat and an ex-cop. Three people in a motel room in New Jersey don't mean a thing to a cop, and you bein' a right-winger doesn't mean much either. I'm here because a halfway-decent detective could watch you, follow you, and get pictures like those without even having to work hard at finding a way in.

"I figure it like this—either you want to get caught or you're just so hungry for it you kind of lose your mind sometimes. If it's the first I know a good therapist. If it's the second I know a woman named Mimi Lord. For a competitive rate she will set up rendezvous that Sherlock Holmes could not pierce."

"That's it?" Bob asked when I didn't continue.

"I'll call the second Cindy and tell her I couldn't find anything. They've already paid me for half the work. I'll tell her she's wasting her money, that she doesn't need to pay the rest. But you have to do something for me."

"How much?"

"Not money. I need to know who told you about me."

Acres had walnut eyes to go with the golden sports jacket he wore that day. Those orbs revealed the calculating heart of the debauched representative.

It came to me that detectives and politicians were somewhat similar. We dealt in passion while pretending to be objective, if not without sin.

"I don't know a name. Whoever it was called the office. She told the switchboard operator that she was my girl-friend. That got her to my aide. She told her that she knew about a detective investigating me when I was in New York. Our system captured the number. I could send it to you from my office."

I liked him, even when he was trying to find my identity.

"Sure," I said. "Send it to handy@handy9987.tv3."

"What's that?" he asked while writing down the e-mail.

"My electronic address," I said, and smiled. "Tell me, Congressman, why did you go to that motel when you knew there was a detective on you?"

He looked down and then up. He shook his head and gave me the weakest smile.

"You said her name was Mimi Lord?" he asked.

I wrote down the number on a small piece of paper from a notepad I carried. Tearing out the leaf, I handed it to him.

"She'll take care of you," I said, and then I stood.

"What about those pictures?"

"What about 'em?"

"What will you do with them?"

"Erase them from my tablet and forget them after that."

"How can I be sure?" he asked, reminding me of a very old popular song.

"There's no reason for me to hurt you, Congressman. If I wanted to do that I'd either give these to Stoneman or dou-ble the price on you."

"You said you were a Democrat," he suggested. "Maybe you don't like my politics."

"Ever since Reagan busted the unions, both sides of Congress have become lackeys to the rich. They all get

40

made, paid, and laid out of the picked pockets of men like me."

Acres frowned a bit. Maybe he felt insulted, maybe not. At any rate he nodded at me and I returned the gesture.

I left Gucci's Diner feeling better than I had in quite some time.

6.

I WAS BACK in the office at a few minutes past three. My good mood had subsided in equal proportion to the memory of solitary confinement and the ramifications of Beatrice Summers's letter.

A letter.

Who sent letters anymore? The unlined paper was tinged pink and the ink was peacock blue. The writing was even and without blobs or cross-outs. There were no misspellings, and the written lines were straight and parallel to the top and bottom of the machine-cut sheet.

All these details said something. There was intention behind that letter. One or more rough drafts were written down somewhere else and then copied onto the good stationery with a sheet of bold lines beneath it to make the lines even; *onward, Christian soldiers.*

The NYPD database system, which I had access to because of Patrolman Henri Tourneau, had no Adamo Cortez working anywhere in the department. The Private Investigator's Database, which I paid eighteen hundred dollars a year for, told me that for the past nine years Beatrice Summers had lived in Odumville Township, outside of Saint Paul.

I wondered what the former Nathali imagined when she thought of God or what the deity might have envisioned when considering his sinful, repentant acolyte.

For my part, whenever I closed my eyes I was in that lightless cell again. It smelled of piss and sweat. Fluttering insects flew through the darkness. Men groaned and complained beyond the sweating metal door of my detention.

A silver bell sounded.

Opening my eyes, I was looking out the second-floor window onto Montague Street again. It was November, but the cold hadn't set in yet. The sun was shining brightly. A woman stopped across the street and, looking up, saw me.

The silver bell sounded again and I roused myself, turning away from the glare of the happenstance pedestrian. I ambled into the receptionist's room, which my daughter occupied every day after school.

The front door to the office was locked, of course. I only ever felt secure behind locked doors.

The electronic eye above the hall-side doorsill transmitted an image to the small monitor panel on the wall. It was a slender young white woman, dressed in blues and whites. Her dress was only vaguely businesslike. She was carrying a brown leather briefcase and pulling a carry-on gray fabric travel bag.

Looking up at the lens, she had the beauty of youth... and the sorrow too.

"Who is it?" I said into the speaker system.

"Willa Portman. Is this the detective Joe Oliver?"

I pulled the door open and she gasped as if something shocking had happened.

"We had a four o'clock, right?" I said.

"Y-yes. I'm a few minutes early."

"I have a friend who always tells me that whenever he gets there he's right on time."

She smiled and, pulling the wheeled travel bag, walked into the office.

"Right this way," I said, gesturing toward my private door.

"Where's Aja?" my prospective client asked.

"She's a high school student, should be in any minute."

Willa gave me a worried look but then went through the door to my office.

My workplace is a fairly small room with a high white plaster ceiling and one huge floor-to-ceiling window. The walls are brick and the floor dark wood. My desk is an ash table with no drawers. I don't keep supplies or records in my office; Aja's much larger room is the repository for files and office materials.

"Have a seat," I said to the nervous girl.

She considered the request a moment, then sat on one of the ash chairs set out for visitors.

"It's an unusual office," she said, her head moving from side to side.

"Why are you so jumpy?"

"Um. I don't know, I mean, I guess being here means that I'm really going to do this. You know when you just think about doing something it still isn't quite real."

"I know what you mean," I said with more feeling than I intended.

Willa, I believe, heard the honesty in my tone, and this seemed to relax her.

"My name is Willa Portman."

"You said that already."

"I'm an intern doing research work for Stuart Braun."

"Stuart Braun. Now, that's a big deal."

"Yeah," she said through a sneer. "He is a big deal, a very important lawyer for those people no one else cares about."

Stuart Braun was the radical lawyer-celeb who was representing A Free Man, a black militant journalist who had been arrested for the killing of two police officers three years earlier. Born Leonard Compton, Man was found seriously wounded a few blocks from the shoot-out, in the Far West Village. The gun he had on him was the one used in killing the officers. The bullets had passed clean through his body, so the guns that shot him could not be identified.

Man refused to implicate anyone else who might have been with him that night and denied having anything to do with any murders. He was facing the death penalty, which New York State provides for cop killers. He showed no remorse and, in general, refused to cooperate with the police or prosecutors.

Before Braun got involved it seemed pretty clear that New York was going to have its first execution in a very long time.

The Braun Machine, as it was known, took the case to a new level. An appeal was granted after Braun showed that much of the evidence against his client had been circumstantial and his publicly assigned lawyers were incompetent. Newspapers suggested that a self-defense plea was in the making. Protests proclaiming "Free Man" were being held from coast to coast.

I wasn't a fan. When it came to cops as victims I was just another brick in the Blue Wall. Few civilians understood how hard it is to be a policeman when almost everybody is afraid of you and suspicious too. The mayor, the city council, and half the civilian population were willing to believe the worst of us when we put our lives on the line 24/7.

Us.

I still considered myself a cop. In my days on the force I'd been sucker-punched, stabbed, spit on, shot at, and singled out by a thousand videophones. Every time I'd make an arrest the community seemed to come out against me. They had no idea how much we cared about them, their lives.

"So are you a lawyer, Ms. Portman?"

"I passed the bar this past June," she said. "But I'm working for Braun because he does the kind of work I want to do."

"And what does Stuart Braun want from me?" I asked.

"Nothing."

"Then why are you here?"

"I'm here because Mr. Man is innocent and Stuart Braun is about to sell him down the stream," the young woman replied.

"River," I said.

"What?"

"The saying is 'sell him down the river.' "

"Oh." Willa looked at me with both desperation and anger in her eyes.

"I thought Braun had committed himself to saving Man," I said.

"He had," she said, "at first. He gathered all kinds of evidence against the cops that Manny shot—"

"He's admitted to the murders?"

"N-no," Willa Portman stuttered. "I mean, yes, but not the way you're saying. They were trying to kill him. They were stalking him. They'd already murdered three of his blood brothers and paralyzed the other one. They were after him and he just protected himself."

She'd been looking around while making these claims but ended the sentence by looking into my eyes.

"So," I prompted, "Braun was gathering evidence..."

"He had days and times, ballistics reports, and testimony from reliable witnesses who could be vetted."

"Sounds like a case."

"It was. It is. But then, two weeks ago, Stuart, I don't know...he turned cold. There really isn't any other way to say it. We were supposed to go see a church lady named Johanna Mudd. Ms. Mudd had agreed to testify that Officer Valence received payments from Deacon Mordechai to provide access to young homeless people for the purpose of forced prostitution."

"Run out of a church?"

"The Last Rite of Christ Baptist Church ran a charity that was supposed to help runaway and orphaned girls and boys. Mordechai and some of his friends had the access. Valence, Officer Pratt, and others ran the business."

"So that's the defense?" I asked. "That Man and his crew were fighting a prostitution ring?"

"Not just that," she said. "Not just that. Manny says that the cops were involved in all kinds of criminal activities. There was stolen merchandise, drugs, and murders.

People were being killed if they tried to stand up to them."

"But then one morning the Honorable Mr. Braun went cold, you say."

"I asked him when we were going to leave to see Ms. Mudd, and he said that we weren't. I asked why, and he told me that everything A Free Man had told us was a lie; that he was the one who had killed his blood brothers because they were going to turn in Valence and Pratt."

Eugene "Yollo" Valence and Anton Pratt were the cops Man had been convicted of killing. They were decorated uniforms who often worked as bodyguards for the mayor and visiting dignitaries.

"Maybe Braun's telling the truth," I suggested. I knew too many innocent cops who had been blamed for crimes they didn't commit. I was one of them.

"Ms. Mudd has disappeared," Willa said. "I went to talk to her a few days later, after failing to get her on the phone. Her son Rondrew told me that she was missing. He said that she went to meet Stuart and never returned."

I sighed. It was an unexpected exhalation. This I knew was due to the fact that the prospective client had caught my interest.

She clasped her hands and looked down at the hardwood floor.

"Hi." Aja was standing at the door. She was smiling, her short hair standing up at various angles like a field of spiky wild grasses. Her blue jeans might as well have been painted on, and her blouse didn't come anywhere near the waistline.

I wanted to ask if this was within the boundaries of the

school dress code, but then Willa looked up, tears streaming from her eyes.

"Oh, baby," my daughter exclaimed. She rushed to the
lawyer's side, kneeled down, and hugged her.

Between my sudden breath and Aja's concern I knew that
I'd spend at least a day or two investigating Portman's case.

"Come on with me." Aja was helping the sad young
woman rise from the chair. After lift-off they made their
way to the washroom annexed to the outer office.

In their absence I tried to see a connection between
Beatrice's letter and the case of A Free Man. I knew that
there was no direct link, but the similarities might be a
way for me to solve a case close enough to my own so
that I might feel some sense of closure without returning to
Rikers.

If Man was innocent and I freed him, then it would be,
in some way, like freeing myself.

I was looking out the window again.

"I'm sorry, Mr. Oliver," Willa Portman said to my back.

"You want me to take notes, Daddy?"

"I want you to go down to the drugstore," I said, "and
pick me up a pack of those little notebooks I use."

"But I could take notes here."

"Go on." I stood up to underscore my directive.

The words between familiars often mean a lot less than
tones and looks. Aja saw that I needed her gone from the
office and she obeyed.

Through the open door I could see A.D. collecting her
bag and going out the front. I waited maybe ten seconds
and then sat down again facing the dewy-eyed girl.

"You see how much trouble there is in this," I said.

"Is that why you asked Aja to leave?"

"She's my daughter and you're twelve miles of bad road."

Willa winced.

"If even one thing you told me is true," I said, "then there's bad news and murder to go all the way round."

"But Manny's innocent," she cried.

"I thought he was married."

"Huh?"

"The way you talk about him. It sounds like you're his girlfriend."

"No."

"Really?"

The way she looked up at me almost made me grin. The magnetism between young lovers (even when they're old) is the gravity of the soul; undeniable, unquestionable, and, sooner or later, unwanted.

"Only once," she said. "When Stuart had another case to attend to and I was recording Manny's deposition. I—I respect Marin. She's the mother of their child, but because they aren't legally married they won't even let her visit except behind a Plexiglas barrier.... He needed somebody."

"Johanna Mudd has really disappeared?"

"Yes."

"And Braun has pulled back on the case?"

"He shredded the files," she claimed. "He said that they were all lies."

"So the evidence is gone?"

She reached over, putting her hand on the roller bag.

"When I got the job working for Mr. Braun, my college adviser, Sharon Mittleman, told me that I should always make copies in case something went missing. Mr. Braun didn't want the files stored electronically. He said that hackers could get into any memory device. So I'd come in at night to use the copy machine."

"How much do you have?" I asked, my respect for the prospective client rising with each word.

"Thirty-three hundred and seventeen two-sided sheets."

"Six thousand pages?"

"Closer to seven."

Seven thousand pages. Suddenly I was scared. Any evidence is a detective's friend, but I imagined reading through the pages while some shadow crept up behind me with a loaded pistol in its all-too-solid hand.

"You know I can't do work pro bono like Braun," I said, flailing around for an exit strategy.

She put the briefcase on the table and opened it, revealing stacks and stacks of paper-slip-bound fifty-dollar bills.

"Almost nineteen thousand dollars,." she said. "It's half of an inheritance I got from my grandmother. I know we can't go to the police and also we can't have any connection between us. I've been taking money out of the account a thousand dollars at a time. I want you to prove Manny innocent and get him released from prison."

"What if he wants to go back to Marin?" I asked.

"If you love someone you set them free," she said with all the force of the pop song.

Looking at the pretty young woman with the sad, sad face I thought about the last twenty-four hours and how much I had changed. Between Congressman Acres and Beatrice Summers I was on the verge of becoming someone, something new.

On the verge but not quite across the line.

"Hold on to that money for another day," I said.

"Why?"

"I'm going to look over these papers and make up my mind then."

"Everything I'm saying is true."

"That may be, but still, I have to convince myself."

"But you're my only hope, Manny's only hope."

"Why do you even think you can trust me?" I asked, the divine words leaping from my lips like Athena from Zeus's brow.

"Jacob Storell."

7.

JACOB WAS THE son of Thomas and Margherita Storell. The father owned and ran a small hardware store on the Lower East Side and the mother was the director of a private women's club called Dryads. Tom sold hammers and nails while Rita and her friends prayed to the spirits of trees.

The wife called me after reading the top line of my ad in the Yellow Pages—**KING DETECTIVE SERVICE**—because of the word *service*. She felt that there was duty and dignity in the use of such a word.

That was eight years ago. The divorce was dragging, and Monica's lawyer had threatened to have my new accounts attached if I didn't pay her initial fee.

I needed a job, any job.

Tom Storell told me that his son had been arrested for robbery. He'd gone into a stationery store also in the East Village and emptied the cash register while the clerk was with a customer somewhere in a back aisle. The police were called and happened to be only seconds away. They arrested Jacob before he had made it to the corner.

"He needs a lawyer," I advised, "not a detective."

"The police have a videotape," Tom said with hopeless conviction.

"But we are sure that he would never do such a thing," Margherita added. "He's so good-hearted that ever since he was a child the other children would get him into trouble. Go see him. Look at the evidence. It would be a service."

So, for a down payment of eighty dollars on four hundred, I went to the precinct in the East Village and asked to see my client.

"You the one they got for misconduct, right?" the desk sergeant asked.

"Falsely accused," I replied.

The fifty-something cop was beefy but pale. There were errant hairs on his otherwise clean-shaven jowls, and his eyes had almost given up on color altogether. I was standing three feet away from him but imagined a rank scent and took half a step back.

"Interrogation room nine," the sergeant told me. I never got his name. He handed me a clear plastic badge with a red card in it. The card identified me as V9.

Walking down the corridor toward the interrogation room area, I was struck by sudden claustrophobia. The walls seemed to want to move in on me. The floor felt uneven, and the imagined smell of the unnamed sergeant was pungent in my nostrils.

I stumbled and righted myself with my left hand against the encroaching wall.

"Whoa, brother," a man said, putting a hand under my left arm. "You okay?"

He was Asian, probably Chinese, wearing a patrolman's uniform and black-rimmed round-lensed glasses. His eyes were friendly and he didn't smell at all.

"Thanks," I said. "I guess the days kinda add up."

"And count down," he added. "Aren't you Joe Oliver?"

"Yeah."

"Man, they fucked you. If I had been the detective on that investigation, nobody would have ever seen a tape. I mean, you didn't hit her or nuthin'."

Back then this was new fodder for my discontent. Of course a brother in blue would "lose" evidence like that. And the police were always the first eyes on the scene.

"Thanks," I said, standing up straight. "What's your name?"

"Archie, Archie Zhao."

"Interrogation room nine up ahead, Archie?"

"Just around the corner."

The IRs were no more than broom closets in that precinct. When I opened the self-locking door, the solitary occupant flinched in his chair and put his hands up as far as the restraints would allow.

He was a short, pudgy young man in jeans and a long-sleeved plaid shirt. He'd been beaten pretty badly by the look of his face. The left eye was completely closed and his lower lip had been busted up. There was a lump the size of a golf ball on his right cheekbone.

"I'll confess if you want me to," he said.

That was all he needed to say. I had been him not long before. There were moments when I would have said anything to stop the fear of what might happen next.

"Your mother sent me, Jacob."

"She did?" One eye opened wide while the other strained for sight.

"You okay?"

"They hit me. They hit me hard."

"Did you steal that money?"

"Are you going to take me home?"

From the looks of him I would have said he was mid-twenties, but he spoke like and had the manner of a child.

"Not right this minute, but if you answer my questions truthfully, I'll do my best to prove you innocent."

That's when he started crying. He put his head in his chained hands and blubbered. I took the seat across from his side of the detainment table and waited. After a while the crying became fearful and louder. He started yelling and trying to pull himself free from the cuffs that were attached by a chain, threaded through a hole in the table, to a steel eye anchored in the concrete floor.

I remained silent, allowing him to vent. I knew the feeling.

After a while he calmed down and sat up, after a fashion.

"I'm sorry," he murmured.

"No blame," I said. "Here you get arrested for something you didn't do and then they beat you for tellin' the truth."

Jacob looked at me with his Quasimodo eye.

I asked, "Why did you take the money out of the cash register?"

"Sheila told me I could."

"Who is Sheila?"

"A friend I met."

"Met where?"

"In the park on Bowery. She said her father had a store and that he'd give us some money for dinner. She was very hungry."

The whole thing took about three hours. I got Officer Zhao to let me see the security tape from the scene. It was obvious that someone off camera was telling Jacob what to do; probably Sheila. And it was likely that she had another friend who lured the counter clerk into a conversation in a back aisle.

The arresting officer's report said that there was no money found on the suspect. He was only three doors down and the money had already been taken from him.

The detective in charge of the interrogation was Buddy McEnery, a contemporary of mine who took shortcuts every chance he could.

I had a rep too. I liked the ladies and I was a stickler for details. Almost all of my arrests ended up in convictions.

I convinced Buddy to access other security cameras in the area to try to get an image of Jacob leaving.

"I'm sure you'll get a shot of a girl and a guy or maybe two girls who fooled the kid."

"He still did the taking," Buddy, a swarthy Irishman, said.

"Have you talked to him?"

"Sure," he said, "with this." He held up his left fist.

I refrained from hitting him and said, "I'm sure his high school records will say that he's a special needs student."

"A retard?"

"Let me take him home, Bud, before you and the department get sued."

McEnery wore a gray suit that had gained its silvery

sheen with age. He stared at me, distaste outlining his lips, and finally said, "You're not one of us anymore, are you?"

"Jacob's a good kid," I said to Willa, "but I don't think of him as a trustworthy reference."

"Jackie was a stock boy in my father's hardware store," she said. "He was kind of like my friend. He told me about you, and his mother said that you were able to get him out of jail in just a few hours. When I asked her about using you, she told me that you were committed to service and truth."

I don't believe in the supernatural, but some people I've met seem to see things that are hidden from me. I don't know if it's intelligence or a mode of perception beyond my understanding, but there are those whom I trust beyond the borders of simple logic; Margherita Storell, though I had met her only once, was one of these people.

"So you'll go over the papers tonight?" the untried lawyer asked.

"Give me two hundred and fifty from the cash and I'll read it. Maybe I'll have some advice about it, maybe not."

"Maybe you'll take the case if you think there's some merit?"

I waited four heartbeats before saying, "Maybe."

Willa departed, and for a while I was alone and at peace the way a soldier during World War I was at peace in the trenches waiting for the next attack, the final flu, or maybe mustard gas seeping over the edge of a trench that might be his grave.

I was thinking about Acres and Summers and now Man too.

To get my mind off these troubles I logged on to my IP, hoping for good news or at least a worthwhile ad.

The seventeenth e-mail in the list was from bacres1119 @repbacres.com. The only message was a phone number.

8.

AFTER WORK I took Aja-Denise to a new French bistro on Montague called Le Sauvage. I had boeuf bourguignon and she coq au vin. The red wine was good and I only let her have a sip.

"Are you gonna take Willa's case?" she asked after I refused her a second taste.

"How much did she tell you about it?"

"That guy A Free Man is innocent and she thinks you can prove it."

"You can't mention that to anyone," I said.

"I won't. I'm just talking to you."

A man two tables away was giving us side glances now and then.

"There's another thing," I said.

"What?"

"Do you use the computer I gave you?"

"Yeah. Why?"

"Do you ever take it home?"

"It's a laptop, but it weighs twelve pounds. I wouldn't take that thing anywhere."

"So you never took it home."

"Uh-uh," she uttered, but there was a look of hesitation in her eye.

"What?"

"The files are on the cloud. I usually download the work to my computer once a week to catch up on things I might not have finished. Is there anything wrong with that?"

I love my daughter. If I had to spend the rest of my life in a moldy coffin buried under ten feet of concrete with only polka music to listen to, I would have done that for her.

"Is something wrong, Daddy?"

"No, honey. It's kinda late. I'll give you a ride home."

"Okay. Are you going to take the Man case?" she asked as we stood.

"Please don't ever mention that name again. Not to your mother. Not to anyone."

"Okay." She looked at me pleadingly to underscore the promise.

I was parked right off Montague, but before we got very far someone called to us.

"Excuse me," he said. He approached us from the front of Le Sauvage.

I wondered if I had forgotten something.

It was the man who had been giving us glances: a white guy standing at about five nine, wearing a green-and-yellow sports jacket with black shirt and trousers.

"Excuse me," he said again as he reached us.

His shoes looked as if they had been woven from straw.

"You don't have to go with him," he said to my daughter.

61

"Huh?" was her reply.

I didn't know whether to give him an uppercut or a kiss on the lips.

"You got it wrong, man," I said. "This is my daughter."

He blinked and then took a closer look. The resemblance is there if you look past the optimism and the pain.

"Oh. I'm so sorry. Excuse me. I thought . . ."

"Look," I added. "I appreciate you looking out for a young woman, but there's no trouble here."

"You thought he was my boyfriend?" my innocent daughter proclaimed incredulously.

"I lost my youngest to the street," he said, addressing me.

"Next time you should take a cell phone picture and call the cops," I suggested. "Safer all the way around."

The ride out to Plumb Beach was fun. Aja loved listening to Sidney Bechet because "his horn sounded like somebody talking."

I told her the story about how Bechet got involved in a duel with another musician in Paris because the guy had told him he played the wrong notes.

"Really?" she said. "Did he shoot the other guy?"

"They were better jazzmen than they were marksmen. Some bystander got shot. I think it was a woman."

"Like me if I talk about your cases," she said.

"Probably not, but maybe."

Monica's husband came to the door of their three-story whitestone. He was expecting my daughter to come alone.

"Joe," he said.

"Coleman."

"What are you doing here?"

"Daddy has to talk to Mom," Aja said with authority in her tone.

"About what?" Coleman Tesserat addressed the question to me.

"Joe?" Monica called from the second-floor landing.

"Hey, Monica," I said. "I have to talk to you about something."

"Call me tomorrow."

"Can't," I said. "It's LAD."

I managed not to smile at the frown that twisted into Coleman's lips. He wanted Aja to call him Daddy and resented the fact that his wife and I had a secret abbreviation system to communicate with.

My ex-wife harrumphed and then said, "Let me put something on. I'll meet you in the kitchen."

"I'll keep you company till she comes," my daughter said.

"You will go to bed," Coleman said.

He was a light-skinned Negro with handsome features. My height, he was ten years younger than my ex. Coleman was an investment banker and pretty well-off; the kind of man who liked owning things, or at least controlling them. I appreciated this quirk in his personality because it alienated my daughter.

The evil look she gave him was cute on a sheltered seventeen-year-old, but one day Coleman and Monica would experience the hatred seething underneath.

"Okay," Aja said. Then she kissed me on the cheek and whispered, "Good night."

I went through the first-floor sitting room to a smaller dining area and into the L-shaped kitchen. I sat at the small table where the family of three ate breakfast and sometimes dinner.

I was thinking of the best way to broach the serious talk that she and I needed to have. LAD meant *life and death* in our code system. Hearing that, she knew I meant business.

Maybe fifteen minutes later, Monica came in wearing a teal sweat suit. Coleman followed. He was clad in jeans and a black T-shirt.

"Well?" he asked. "What is it?"

"Tell him to leave," I said to my ex.

"You don't order me in my house," Coleman said.

"Please, CC," Monica said in almost a whisper.

He wanted to fight. I did too. Instead he turned away, walked through the rooms to the stairs, and stomped his way to bed like Rumpelstiltskin after a hard day making gold on his Wall Street spinning wheel.

When we were both sure that he was gone she said, "What is it?"

"You mess with me all the time, M.," I replied. "Send me threatening letters, have lawyers send me threatening letters, and every once in a while you try and get at me through A.D. That's cool. I take it in stride. I don't come to you and ask why didn't you do something to help me, your daughter's father, when they were trying to bury me under the prison."

"You know why," she said like Moses on high.

"And so you do this?" I asked, running my finger along the deep scar down the right side of my face.

"I didn't cut you."

"But you could have stopped it from happening. You could have gotten up off our monies and made my bail."

"I had to worry about our daughter, her future."

"Yeah," I somewhat agreed. "And the best way to protect her is to make sure I keep paying for what she needs to live."

"Coleman provides."

"But it helps to have that extra check. I mean, even his six figures would be stretched trying to fit the bill at Columbia."

"What do you want, Joe?"

"I'd like it if you didn't try and get me shot."

The look on her face was that of an innocent listening to the ravings of an idiot.

"When you called Bob Acres," I continued, "you didn't know what the circumstances were."

The dismissal in her gaze faded.

Monica had been a beautiful young woman. She had deep brown skin and features that spoke of western Africa. She was loving and sexy, smart and loyal. I had betrayed her, there was no excuse for that—but it was enough that she let me languish at Rikers.

"You warning a man I'm investigating could end up getting me killed. What if I decided to investigate Coleman? What kinda dirt you think I could dig up on him?"

I knew at least part of the answer to that question. I was pretty sure she did too.

"I—I never heard of a Bob Acres," she said lamely. "Is that that congressman?"

"He sent me the number of the person who warned his aide. Your cell phone number."

"Coleman has nothing to do with this."

"Take me to court, report me to the authorities when I'm six days late on a support payment, tell my daughter exactly what I did to make you so mad," I listed, "but fuck with my work again and I will make you regret it. I will torpedo this perfect life you got so bad that you won't even be able to come up for air. Do you understand that?"

I didn't wait for an answer. I just stood up and retraced my steps to their front door, and walked out to the street.

There was a chill in the air. I liked it.

9.

ONE FLIGHT UP from my second-floor office is the apartment where I live. It too has an eighteen-foot ceiling and two magnificent windows that look out on the gentrifying thoroughfare. I have ceiling-to-floor deep red curtains cut from a light fabric derived, somehow, from bamboo. I open them at night because the lights are on at the front of the room and no one can see in.

My entire apartment is one big room and a water closet. I have a footed, deep-basin iron bathtub, a king-size bed on a three-foot-high dais, and a mahogany desk that's more than a hundred years old.

Leaving the rest of the room dark, I turned on the desk lamp and opened the suitcase full of records that Willa Portman brought.

Either Willa or her boss was very organized. A blue folder set atop the great pile of paper was an index that pretty much laid out the defense for A Free Man, née Leonard Compton. It contained his personal history, his political involvements, his work and military experience, and the events leading up to the night that Officers Valence and Pratt were killed.

Laid upon the table of contents page of the blue folder was a three-by-five photograph of a smiling middle-aged black woman. The smile revealed a golden upper front tooth, and the eyes told of intelligence and certainty. Etched in red along the bottom of the photograph was the name: JOHANNA MUDD. Willa Portman, I was sure, had placed that picture there because the disappearance of Ms. Mudd was the reason for the investigation.

When he was still Leonard Compton, Man served as a master sergeant in the rangers. He'd received high scores as a marksman and had won many medals, at least hinting at his bravery and nationalism. When he left the armed forces he went to City College and then became a high school teacher in Upper Manhattan, where he worked hard to keep his charges, boys and girls, out of trouble.

Leonard wrote articles for a small uptown paper called the *People's Clarion*. He started out writing about his military experience, but as time passed he began to detail crimes done to young people in and around the black neighborhoods of New York City.

At some point along the way he joined, or maybe started, a group called the Blood Brothers of Broadway. This group consisted of five men and two women.

Tanya Lark had been one of Man's success stories. She was a gangbanging killer who scared everybody she met until he showed her that anger and violence could be redirected to help the community.

Greg Lowman was a security guard for Trickster Enterprises, a toy company that had diversified (according to Braun's sources) into various technological concerns. Lowman was a black member of the NRA and a solid believer in every American's right to defend him- or herself.

Christopher "Kit" Carson had done six stints in jail, mostly for burglary. One of these was due to an arrest that Pratt had made.

Son Mali was an Africanist who believed that one day a revolution would tear the United States apart. His day job was that of a master plumber.

Lamont Charles was the slickest member of the Blood Brothers of Broadway. He was a suspected con man who had never been charged, a Lothario of almost mythic proportions, and a poker player so devastating that he was allowed in only certain professional games from Atlantic City to Las Vegas.

Lana Ruiz was a Dominican who had cut the throat of her pimp in his sleep but somehow managed to get a judge to call it self-defense. Her picture was that of a beautiful dark-skinned woman who seemed defiant even while smiling for the photograph.

The BBB was not a fortunate lot. Lowman, Carson, and Mali had all been murdered in the eighteen months preceding Man's shoot-out with Pratt and Valence. Lamont Charles had been shot but he survived; a triplegic living in a nursing home on Coney Island.

Lana Ruiz had been convicted of armed assault and attempted murder, while Tanya Lark had dropped off the map completely.

That was a whole lot of mayhem even for a militant political group, even for a Saturday night in summertime in Brownsville, New York.

There was a long list of witnesses who had claimed that the dead cops were involved in criminal activities and two witnesses who at first claimed that the cops opened fire on Man (they gave nearly identical testimony), only to recant within three days of each other.

Even though Braun hadn't mentioned it in his arguments, I couldn't see why the former Leonard Compton would decide to take on the cops in a one-on-two shoot-out. He was a marksman and they trained professionals. Why not set himself up on some roof and take them out when they were on a job?

And why drop a case just because the client might have been guilty? It was the lawyer's job to work with the law, not worry about right and wrong.

I must have read four hundred pages when I noticed that it was closing in on 5:00 a.m. I should have gone to bed, but all that evidence gave me a thought: If Adamo Cortez wasn't actually the name of an NYPD cop, then maybe it was an official alias or a confidential informant.

It was at that moment I knew I was going to take both cases: my frame and A Free Man's murder conviction.

I was born to be an investigator. For me it was like putting together a three-dimensional, naturalistic puzzle that in the end would be an exact representation of the real world.

From the deep bottom drawer of my ancient desk I took out two reams of paper, both pastel colored—one blue and the other pink. That way my outline of the two investigations could be stacked together while following two different strands. I had, in my failed career, used as many as five colors to keep my place.

I'd been paid two hundred fifty dollars to work an eight-hour day seeing if the two investigations made sense. I had a clear pathway because nobody knew what I was up to.

For the first step I took a white sheet from the top drawer and penned across the top COMMON ELEMENTS.

The first question shared by both cases was whether or not I needed a partner in the process.

I considered Gladstone Palmer. He was my friend; there was no doubt about that. He went into Rikers and made sure that I was safe in solitary. When I was working a seventy-hour week at two security jobs he lent me the money to start the detective service, then sent me my first few clients. And Glad knew how the department worked. He was connected to every precinct, every captain, and most foot soldiers of the NYPD. His input would be invaluable and... if he was able to clear my name, he might also clear a pathway to his own advancement.

But Glad's strengths were also deficits. He *did* know all the important players on, and off, the force and so might be beholden to people I'd have to hurt. Add to that the fact that I was trying to clear a cop killer of the crimes he was accused of while admitting that he pulled the trigger... that would be of no help to my friend.

Patrolman First Class Henri Tourneau was another choice. The young Haitian-born cop's father asked me to help him prepare for getting on the force. I guided Henri through every step, including training himself in computers so that he'd have a skill that most prospective cops lacked. Once he was in I counseled him on how to deal with everything from his captain to the rank and file. I told him what rules could be bent or broken and those that were sacrosanct.

One thing he was never to do was admit that I was anything other than a friend of his father's.

Henri allowed me to roam through the general databases, but using him as a partner in these investigations was above and beyond for the young and recently married policeman.

No other cop fit the bill, and so I let my thoughts range wider. There were half a dozen PIs I knew from work I'd done over the years. But I wasn't close enough to any of them to feel they could be trusted with issues so serious.

The sun was beginning to peek over the bank building across the street when I thought, reluctantly, of Melquarth Frost. Melquarth, or Mel as he was better known, was a vicious criminal.

Mel had done many things wrong in his life. He'd robbed banks, murdered rivals, tortured marks, set bombs, and belonged to a few dangerous heist crews that had executed some of the most daring robberies of the twenty-first century so far.

I came across the lifelong criminal when the FBI tasked a few city cops to shore up some gaps in a net they set for the Byron gang. Ted and Francis Byron were truly architects of crime. They had planned and carried out at least eight bank burglaries where they were able to blast out an inner wall through to cash-gorged vaults.

On these jobs they always took along a man like Mel in case there was a need to fight.

The job was done at a little after three on a Wednesday morning at a midtown bank on West Fifty-Sixth. I was guarding a subway grate on Sixty-Third that the feds said might be used as an exit. It was just me because they didn't think it likely that anyone would get that far and the brass was charging them twenty-five hundred dollars a head for boots on the ground.

I listened to the takedown over a secure line that all the participants had. The explosion had come at 3:09. Soon after that, six of the seven bank robbers were captured without a round being fired.

There was a lot of chatter over the seventh perp. I stayed at my post because that was the job and I always did my job—unless there was a woman somewhere in the way.

Thirty-two minutes after the takedown the grate to the subway lifted slightly. I watched from shadow, timing my intervention.

I could have called for backup, but by then the suspect would have escaped. I could have shot him in the leg or foot, or killed him for that matter, but that's just not the kind of man I am. So instead I waited until one hand shot up out of the ground, snapped a cuff on it, and quickly attached the other link to the heavy metal grating. Then I put the muzzle of my service revolver to the man's head and said, "Let me see that other paw and it better be empty."

I received the Medal of Exceptional Merit for the arrest, bestowed upon me by the chief himself. The FBI had me go to their headquarters, where the local director shook my hand.

All that honor went away when Melquarth was put on trial. The other six bank robbers were tried together, but because Mel was captured alone and quite far from the scene, his lawyer, Eugenia Potok, was able to separate him from the rest.

Before I testified, the prosecutor "interviewed" me, suggesting that maybe I heard the accused admit to being involved with the crime. The other men refused to bear witness against one another and so had Mel.

I could not, in good conscience, say anything but what I knew on the stand. I had determined early on in my career that as a cop I would always adhere to the letter and the spirit of the law. Law for me was scripture.

Melquarth beat the charges, and I was transferred to night duty on Staten Island for the next three years.

Time passed. I was framed, incarcerated, and thrown out on my ear—so it's easy to understand how I might have forgotten all about Melquarth. And then, only two years ago, I was sitting in my office, looking out the window, and thinking about solitary confinement.

"Mr. Oliver," Tara Grandisle, Aja's predecessor, said over the intercom.

"Yes, Tara."

"A Mr. Johnson to see you."

"Who?"

"He says he wants to discuss a case with you."

As far as I knew, this Mr. Johnson was just another prospective client. I had no idea that he was the man who earned me three years on a Staten Island boat.

"Send him in," I said, pocketing my snub-nosed .32 just for insurance.

When Melquarth Frost walked through the door I nearly pulled my weapon.

My visitor smiled and held his arms out, revealing open palms.

I hit the intercom and said, "We need some pumpernickel for the pastrami."

"Okay," Tara said. That was our code for her to clear out.

"Mr. Oliver," Mel said.

"Melquarth Frost."

"You can call me Mel; all my friends do."

"I'm not your friend."

"That might be," he said. "But I'm yours. Can I sit down?"

I thought about the request a beat longer than was civil and then said, "Sure."

He was wearing a medium gray suit that was loose enough for freedom of movement but tailored in such a way to look businesslike.

"What can I do for you?"

"Just did three on a nickel in Joliet," he said, as if this was somehow an answer to my question. "My second conviction and my last."

The man was the opposite of his suit. He was lean and dangerous-looking, with olive skin, short brown hair, and dark eyes that women must have adored. His hands were heavily muscled.

"You bought a suicide pill or something?" I asked.

"Guy shot me in the back when we were through with a bank job," Mel said. "Shot me right there in the bank for sixteen percent divided by five." He shook his head in disgust.

"And he's out here somewhere?"

"No." Melquarth Frost just twisted his lips and I felt a twinge of fear. "He hooked up with a girlfriend'a mine after the job."

"So maybe it wasn't just the one-fifth of sixteen percent."

Mel smiled and then grinned. "He was supposed to meet her at the Carving Table in North Chicago one night and someone shot him in the eye."

"All that public knowledge?"

Instead of answering me he went on. "Cops saved my life and then did this pissant job of framing me. They shoved money from the bank in my pocket, but my lawyer proved it wasn't me put it there.

"I had an illegal firearm on me. If they had let it alone I'd'a gotten twelve years. But they had to deal it down if the cops didn't want to be caught doin' what they do."

Another thing I noticed about my visitor was the way he sat. His legs were spread wide. He pulled over an empty chair and laid his left wrist on top of the backrest. His right hand lay on his knee. It was as if he was at home, enjoying life more than a billionaire.

He gazed at the space above my head, thinking about a hard life with a sense of élan and maybe even a little whimsy.

"So?" I said before he tried to move in.

"I got five years, and from the first day they had me in solitary confinement."

I must have winced, because a smile flitted across the career criminal's lips. He nodded slightly.

"It almost broke me," he continued. "Almost did. I remember shouting for days. Then I cried. And finally one morning—I guess it was morning because that's when I woke up. On that morning I found the peace to think about my life. I went over the whole thing from grade school to solitary, and you know what I figured?"

"Not in the least."

"That in all that time you were the only one treated me fair."

"What the fuck? I arrested you for bank robbery."

"You coulda shot me. You coulda hit me in the head with a lead pipe. You sure as shit coulda testified that I had somehow mentioned the bank job. I know your bosses were mad when you didn't lie."

Mel leaned forward, now with both hands on his thighs.

"So you came here from Illinois to thank me?" I asked.

"I already told you," he said. "I'm not goin' back to prison. I came out here to ply my old trade and to tell you that if you ever need a good turn I owe you a few."

That was a very important nexus for me. It was rare for anyone to see in me what I saw in the mirror. Melquarth might have been a villain, but he was a villain with my number in his pocket.

I wasn't about to share that intelligence with him.

"What kind of trade?" I asked.

"Watchmaker."

"Really?"

"When I was fourteen they wanted to put me in juvie for assault and battery. The judge gave me a choice of enrolling in an after-school program or being locked up. I chose watchmaking with a little Jew named Harry Slatkin who did watch repair on Cherry Lane. He taught me a lot. Later on I applied that knowledge to bomb making, but in my spare time I studied watches."

"You know," I said, "that even though I'm no longer a cop I'm still on the other side of the line from you."

He laid a small white business card on the desk and said, "I hear you play chess."

"Yes, I do."

"Chessboard is a neutral place. I go to Washington Square Park in Greenwich Village most Mondays, Wednesdays, and Saturdays. I play there. Number's on the card. If you ever wanna match wits across that line, just gimme some warning and I'll have the board set up."

He rose from his chair with ease. He nodded instead of holding out a hand. I nodded back and he left.

I looked up the name Melquarth on the Internet soon after he left. He'd been a patron god to Hannibal before the general attacked Europe. He was also associated with Ba'al, considered by Western religion to be a manifestation of Satan.

Over the next two years since then, we've played about a dozen games. After the third, which he won, we got a drink together. After the fifth, which he also won, we had a meal.

10.

IT WASN'T YET 7:00 a.m. when I climbed the concrete stairs to the raised pedestrian walkway across the Brooklyn Bridge.

There was a chill in the morning air, but I had my windbreaker on, a sweater beneath that. Pedestrian traffic was still pretty light at that time of day and the breezes can get a little stiff. The combination of solitude and cold somehow imparted the feeling of freedom; so much so that I was on the brink of laughter. I knew these emotions indicated an instability of mind, but I didn't care. A man can live his whole life following the rules set down by happenstance and the cash-coated bait of security-cosseted morality; an entire lifetime and in the end he wouldn't have done one thing to be proud of.

It was a forty-nine-minute walk from Montague Street to Manhattan. Once in the rich man's borough I went past city hall all the way to the West Side, where I turned left on Hudson.

Three blocks down, there was a diner called Dinah's across the street from Stonemason's Rest Home.

*　　*　　*

"Mr. Oliver," Dinah Hawkins said in greeting when I sat down at the counter. "I haven't seen you in three months."

"I usually go straight over, D. But today I wanted to stretch my legs and think."

"You didn't walk here all the way from Brooklyn, did you?"

"Yes, ma'am."

"It's not good for your health to overdo, Mr. Oliver."

Dinah was a good-size woman who worked twelve hours a day, seven days a week. Well past sixty, she had biceps bigger than mine, and I was sure that she could work alongside most longshoremen with no great strain.

"It's the only exercise I get," I lied.

"You're looking good enough without it." Her Irish-green eyes sparkled, and I knew that she was what her father would have called a hellion when she was younger.

"Got any interesting cases?" she asked, putting a mug of black coffee at my station.

I discussed my job with certain people who had nothing to do with law enforcement. But when it came to my new cases I couldn't be quiet enough.

"I had this public figure liked to do threesomes with T-girls," I said.

"What's that mean? Tiger girl?"

"I think the street term is *chicks with dicks*."

The bell to the door behind me sounded. In the mirror I saw a young man wearing a suit designed for an older, and probably more successful, banker. The young man—he was somewhere in his mid-twenties—looked at us for a few moments, then walked over to stand at the cash register.

"Oh!" Dinah had rosy cheeks and a mouth that could become a perfect circle. "There was one of those lived in the apartment across the hall from me and Dan. Miss Figueroa we used to call her. She was the cleanest creature I ever knew. Dan was the one had to tell me she was a he. I swear I couldn't tell at all."

"How is Dan?" I asked.

Dinah beamed at me. "Thank you for askin', Mr. Oliver. Him and me take a walk every evening along the Hudson. He tells me the same stories over and over and I love him more every time he does."

"Excuse me," the young/old white banker-boy said.

"He always remembers you," Dinah continued, ignoring the young man. "He says, 'How's that nice colored boy helped Arnold?' I know he shouldn't say it that way, but he can't remember to learn."

"Excuse me," said the banker.

"What do you want?" Dinah snapped.

"Two coffees with milk and sugar to go."

"For the takeaway window you make a left out the door and then left again." She looked at me, raising her eyebrows.

"But I'm late," he said. "Just do this now and I'll use the window after."

"You'll use the window now. There's a big sign and I don't like doin' the takeaway."

"That's not a very people-oriented business practice," he judged.

"Neither is knockin' you upside the head, but I will do just that if you don't move yer privileged ass."

A flash of anger passed over the young man's face. He glanced at me and I shook my head—ever so slightly. I'm pretty big and almost as strong as Dinah, so he took the hint and left, muttering wordless complaints.

"You didn't have to bother yourself, Mr. Oliver," Dinah said when he was gone. "I can take care of myself."

"I wasn't worried about you, girl. I just didn't want to have to be a witness after you broke his nose and he called the police." This was true.

Dinah laughed and we took a breath to find the thread of our conversation again.

"Have you seen my grandmother lately, D.?"

"She comes over for a smoke most afternoons unless it's rainin' or too cold. We go out back while Moira serves the late crowd."

"How does she seem?"

"Wise as a prophet and crafty as a fox. She wishes that your uncle would come by."

"He's always working," I said.

Uncle Rudolph was in Attica, imprisoned there for an insurance scam so complex that the prosecutors were never able to pin down the exact amount he'd embezzled.

"Oh well," Dinah opined. "At least Brenda has you."

"May I help you?" a good-figured blonde asked. She was standing behind the reception counter of the upscale retirement residence. I was liking her style.

In her forties and proud, she wore a green-and-pink-speckled silk blouse to accent a tight black skirt.

Some women just don't get old.

"Joe Oliver," I said. "I'm here to see my grandmother."

"Does she work for one of the patients?" Blondie asked, as easy as if she were talking about the weather.

"No." I was losing the edge of my attraction.

"Um..." She was really confused. "Does she work for the facility?"

"She's a resident," I said. "Brenda Naples. Room twenty-seven oh nine."

For a moment the receptionist, whose name tag read THALIA, doubted me. But then she worked a little magic on the iPad registry.

"She *is* here," Thalia said.

"Has been since before you," I said, "and will be long after you have moved back to New Jersey."

"I'm very sorry, Mr. Oliver."

"Me too," I concurred. "But maybe not for the same reason."

"Baby," my grandmother said. I had knocked on the open door and then entered her room.

She stood up from a chair that was set at a height halfway between a regular seat and a barstool. Her dress was bright yellow and her skin the blackness of a night sky.

I kissed her lips because that's what we'd always done.

"Sit on the bed, darlin'," she said, waving toward the single-mattress cot that was the main purpose for her room.

She fell back into her carpeted wood chair, then momentarily raised her shoulders to prove how happy she was to see me.

"How've you been, Grandma?"

"Fine," she said with a sneer. "That white man Roger Ferris keep askin' me to go hear some music at Lincoln Center. I tell him every time that I will not go out on a date with a white man. I mean, if it was a double date and he had a white girlfriend and I had a black boy, then that would be okay."

"What did he say to that?"

"That we didn't have to kiss good night." There was the hint of a smile in her scowl.

"What's that got to do with it?"

"He says that if there's no kiss, then it wasn't a real date. And that if I knew before we went that there wasn't gonna be no lip action, then I wouldn't have to think we were on a date."

"That's a pretty good argument, if you ask my opinion," I said.

"No one askin' you."

"Roger Ferris. Isn't he that guy who owns most of the silver in the ground in the world?"

"I wouldn't know. The only ground people up in here have is in the cemetery, waitin' for the little we got left on our bones."

"How's our other friends?" I asked.

"Stop it, King. You and I both know that you not here at no eight thirty in the mornin' to make small talk."

I do love my grandmother. The milestone of ninety years was well behind her, but she read the *Daily News* every morning and did all my sewing. She was a shade under five feet tall and hadn't brought the scale up past a hundred pounds in years, but she was a power to reckon with.

Stonemason's was one of the most exclusive retirement/nursing homes in the world, but something about my grandfather's career as a fireman got him and her put in a benefits clause that I had never seen.

Brenda Naples still walked, smoked, and talked back. It's an even bet that she'll outlive me.

"What is it, King?" she asked.

I told her about the letter from Beatrice Summers and the danger of me following down that evidence.

She concentrated with her eyes and ears, and maybe even by scent.

"You got to do it, baby," she said when I was through. "All a man got is his sense of what's right and what's not. If you know you been done wrong and you know how to make it right, then you don't have no other choice." Her dialect veered back toward its Mississippi roots when she was being serious.

"I've always known," I argued.

"But no one else ever gave you hope or a name," Grandma countered. "And before you had more important work to do."

"Detective work?"

"No, fool." She snorted. "Aja-Denise. You had to see her become a young woman before you could take care of yourself. That's just mother wit."

I didn't say anything because she had said it all.

"You wanna come have breakfast with me in the commissary?" she asked.

"Sure."

11.

ROGER FERRIS JOINED me and my grandmother for breakfast. He was a year or two younger than she, and six feet even at that great age. He was lanky and crowned with a mane of silver hair, a reminder, no doubt, of his nearly limitless wealth.

Grandma Brenda seemed to enjoy his company. I guess the breakfast table was exempt from date status.

Roger was a gun enthusiast and a pacifist too.

"Any person who learns a deadly art," he told me over chicken sausage and egg-white herbal omelets, "whether it be competitive boxing or sharpshooting, must be held to a higher standard. I mean, a man with a semiautomatic can kill a dozen people faster than he can utter their names. That's a crime against God."

"That's why it's so hard being a cop," I said with a nod and a sip of decaffeinated coffee.

"How do you mean?" the man worth eight hundred seventy-nine billion dollars asked.

"There you are," I said, "out on the street with your piece

and people who *might* be armed. They're afraid of you, mad at you, wantin' revenge for something one of your other brothers in blue might have done. But still you got to keep your *pistola* holstered because you have the power *and* the responsibility."

Roger smiled at me and nodded. I could see that guns for him were a symbol for the power of his wealth, and for that brief moment he saw us, even if not exactly as equals, somehow as the same.

"Your grandmother is a wonderful woman," Roger said to me at the elevator door. He had wanted to walk me there, and my grandmother seemed to approve.

"Has been for a very long time."

"She says that you had to quit being a cop because you got into some kind of trouble."

"Trouble ambushed me with my pants down and my nose open." I didn't know why I was so candid with Ferris at that time. Now I understand that he radiated a kind of confidence and the feeling that he could be trusted.

"Brenda said as much," he said, nodding. "She's amazing. Very intuitive and completely free of guile or greed."

"She says that you want to take her to a concert."

"She told me, not unless I can get a better tan."

"She wants to go, Mr. Ferris. You keep up the pressure and she will, sooner or later."

Ferris smiled and gave me a clear view of his pale blue eyes. They were sad eyes. I imagined that soon he and my grandmother would be sitting side by side at some fancy concert.

"When you went to the can, your grandmother told me that you might have some trouble coming up."

"You know grandmothers," I said. "Sometimes they get overprotective."

"Well," the billionaire replied, placing a hand on my shoulder. "If she's right, you just give me a call. You'll find that there's not much in this world that scares me"

He handed me a business card and gave me a nod.

Late November still had its warm days that year. I stood out on the street composing five e-mails on my smart-phone. I'm a little obsessive about electronic communication. I reread each communiqué at least three times and then put each one through a spell-check. After finishing I went to the C train, riding it downtown back to Brooklyn Heights.

I dabbled around on the Internet for a while looking for keywords that included *Adamo Cortez, arrest, police officer,* and *testimony.*

It was 10:07 when I finally dialed the number.

"Hello," a man said.

"Mr. Summers?" I asked.

"Yes."

"This is Joe Oliver. I believe that you know about me."

"Hold on."

The phone's receiver clattered and then came the sounds of children expressing happiness and complaints. I heard her voice before she got to the phone. It sounded nothing like the woman I remembered begging me to pull her hair.

"Hello?"

"Mrs. Summers? It's Joe Oliver."

"Yes. I was expecting your call."

Somewhere on the other end of the line a door slammed and the noises of midwestern early-morning domesticity ceased.

"To begin with," I said, "I want you to know that I appreciate your letter and what it means. I know you didn't have to reach out."

"Thank you, but you're wrong there, Mr. Oliver. Since I came back to the church I have thought about all the bad things I've done. Some of them there's no coming back from, but . . . but in your case speaking the truth is the least I can do. When would you like me to come to New York?"

"Let's talk about that a little later," I said. "First I want to ask you some questions."

"Okay," she said on a sigh.

"You said in the letter that you had been arrested and then coerced into pressing charges against me by a man named Adamo Cortez."

"Yes."

"This man said that he was a policeman?"

"He *was* a policeman," she corrected, "a detective."

"And he was the one who arrested you?"

"No. I was picked up with my, with my, um, boyfriend at that time, Chester Murray. They brought me to the station house on One Thirty-Fifth."

"The thirty-second precinct?"

"I don't know," she said. "But it was on One Thirty-Fifth. I remember that it smelled like disinfectant."

"They all do at some time or other."

"I guess they must," she said, trying to let my poor attempt at levity in. "I don't remember the names of the officers that arrested me. Chester was driving, but I had leased the car. There was twenty pounds of cocaine in the trunk. They took me to this room and wouldn't let me talk to Chester or call a lawyer or anything. They didn't even let me go to the toilet..."

Beatrice went silent there for a minute or more. I knew what she was thinking. If a cop wants to turn an arrest into an agent, he puts a scare into him, or in this case, her. Hunger, humiliation, and hurt are the tools. Not all worked on every perp. You had to create a specific cocktail for the personality. For Beatrice it was fear of isolation, maybe a little withdrawal, and a bladder so full that she had to relieve herself without benefit of the facilities.

"I was there for at least a full day before Detective Cortez came to see me." She was once again defeated by the illegal methods. This reminded me of Rikers and the burn on my face when I was slashed by the jagged edge of a number ten tomato can lid.

After another long pause she continued. "He said that they could hold me for two days more without pressing charges and by then Chester would have turned on me."

"You think he would have?" I asked. I don't know why.

"Yeah. Chester once gave evidence on his cousin just so they wouldn't put another mark on his record. He wouldn't have even gone to jail, but he turned Jerry in anyway."

"What did Adamo look like?"

"Short for a man. Black hair with a pretty thick mustache. His skin was brown like a brown egg if it was shellacked."

"Did he have an accent?"

"I—I don't remember."

"What did he say?"

"That I'd get a year in prison for every pound in the

trunk." A sob escaped her reserve. "That I'd never have children or even a chance at a decent life."

"And," I deduced, "I was the price to get you out of it."

"Yes."

"Did he tell you exactly what he wanted you to do?"

"Yes."

"What to do in the living room, what you should tell me
to do, everything?"

"Yes." That time the word hurt.

"And did you really go so far as to press charges?" I asked,
wondering why I wasn't angry.

"He had me transferred to another station. There he gave
me some papers to sign."

"What then?"

"He took me to a house in Queens and kept me there
for a week. I was in restraints most of the time. He—he
raped me."

"And then he let you go?"

I could almost hear her nodding. "Yes."

Beatrice and I shared the next spate of silence. I could
hear her breathing—over a thousand miles away.

"Do you remember anything else?"

"No."

"Are you planning to press charges against Detective
Cortez?"

"I hadn't even thought about that. Isn't it—isn't it too
late?"

"Yeah. But you could fuck up his retirement pretty good."

"I know you're upset, Mr. Oliver, but could you not use
that kind of language, please?"

"Sorry."

"Why do you want to know if I want to press charges?"

"The guy you were arrested with was named Chester Murray?" I asked instead of answering.

"Yes."

"Did you see him again?"

"Never."

"Was he your pimp?"

"That was another time, Mr. Oliver. When do you want me to come to New York?"

"What makes you think I want you to come out here?"

"To testify. To prove that you didn't do what they said you did."

"I don't think I need you for that, Mrs. Summers. You gave me a name and a trail. That's enough."

"Really?"

"Yeah."

"So that's it?"

"Unless you remember something else."

"The thing you asked about Detective Cortez."

"What thing?"

"He had an accent. It was a very New York kind of talking. You know what I mean?"

"I certainly do. Thank your husband for me, Beatrice," I said, and then I hung up.

12.

I WAS DEEP into the cases and not even a day had passed.

I cleared off the desktop in my apartment and on a pink sheet of paper I wrote—*Someone in the department was definitely involved in the false accusations against me. At the 32nd a man named Adamo Cortez, posing as a detective, coerced Nathali Malcolm into pressing charges against me for rape. Correct spellings and her testimony are attached below.*

After taping Beatrice's letter at the bottom of the page I placed the pink sheet in the center of the green blotter on the empty desk. This simple act sent a thrill through my scalp and shoulders. Finally it had begun.

Leaving the excitement on the third floor, I took the trap-door rope ladder from my apartment down into the office below. I usually take the hallway stairs between floors, but that morning felt secret, outlaw.

There was a pulley system to roll the hemp rungs back up and a long pole kept in a far corner to close the trap. I sat at the window in my private office and stared down at the working-class pedestrians being shown up and disdained by the street.

I didn't say or do anything but ponder for the next couple of hours. I hadn't had much sleep because my mind could not shut down completely. The lack of sleep and deep disposition of mind caused a descent into a fugue-like state. There was no me but just the details of future blue and pink pages. There was an eggshell with a mustache and a ranger with a pistol in his hand. There was a dark hole that seemed to hold intelligence, and a girl-child all grown up.

The phone pulled me out of the temporary retreat.

"Hello," I answered, maybe a little dreamily.

"Joe?"

I was still in that faraway place. The voice was familiar but nameless.

I groaned and the vibration brought knowledge.

"Hey, Henri. Yeah, it's me. I must'a dozed off. What time is it?"

"Three thirty. What kinda shit you into, man?"

"How's your father?" I asked while trying to remember the e-mail I sent that morning.

"Adamo Cortez," my caller insisted.

"What?" I said, and then, "Oh...yeah."

"Yeah. I called in and said that there was a guy saying that he was a CI for a Detective Adamo Cortez. They said they never heard that name; it wasn't in their files. But a few hours later on, two suits from One Police Plaza came down to the street to see me. The street, Joe."

"What they want?" I asked, the void receding behind me.

"They wanted to know everything. Everything. Where I met him. What he said. Was it near a video camera?"

"What you say?" I asked, almost fully back to normal.

"I just made shit up. Said I was doin' a foot patrol in Central Park, which I was, and this guy comes up and tells me that I should tell my superior that Bato Hernandez has to make a drop. He said to say that he needed to speak to Adamo Cortez, that Cortez knew how to make contact."

"What they say?"

"They wanted a complete description. What the guy wore, how old he was, and everything else. They even asked if anybody saw us."

"They wanted an eyewitness alibi?"

"Yeah."

"Were you ready?"

"You're the one told me that I always had to be ready with a lie, Joe. That I should have one all worked out in my head because you never know."

"I must have told a hundred cops that, Henri, but you're one of only two that took me up on it. I'm sorry, kid, I didn't think you'd actually call in like that."

"I tried the database," the Haitian cop replied. "He just wasn't there. Not as a cop, a CI, or even some suspect. Nowhere. But I thought that if somebody called it in, then they might look in some secret database that the uniforms don't know about."

"With a question on your lips and a lie in your pocket," I said in admiration. "You know, there was something I never taught you, kid."

"What was that, Joe?"

"That sometimes you can be too smart."

"So what are you into, man?"

"Is this a safe line?" I asked, way too late.

"Pay phone in the lower level of Grand Central. I'm surprised these suckers still work."

"Don't worry about what I'm doin', Henri. It won't do either of us any good. But tell me the names of the suits."

"Inspector Dennis Natches and Captain Omar Laurel."

"An inspector," I said. "Damn. Did they give anything up?"

"Not really. They threatened me with a review. Said that I should have detained the suspect. But I said that he wasn't a suspect, that all he did was to say to ask a question, and anyway, I thought he was crazy." He spoke as if he were arguing with the brass, showing that he was a good cop, a good liar.

"Nothing else?"

"That's what Laurel asked," Henri replied. "When he did I asked, 'Like what?' And he asked did the guy give any other names? I told him that French was my first language but that I had excellent English except for all the foreign names. 'At one point,' I said, 'he asked me to try "Guys-which" or "toucan"—something like that.' "

I grinned at my desk, thinking that the kid would be a great detective one day.

"And did he come up with a fit?" I asked.

"He said, 'Cumberland'?"

"Too smart by half," I said. "Listen, man, forget you talked to me. Drop the whole thing."

"You not gonna tell me what it's about?"

"Your father once told me that the day after you were born he bought a pistol. He said that he'd never needed one before, but when he saw you he knew that he had to be ready to die for his son."

"That's my dad. Good luck, Joe. Call if you need me."

One e-mail answered and four to go.

My second e-mail was sent through a remote router that stripped off any electronic connections to me. I identified myself as Tom Boll, an investigator working for parties interested in the disappearance of Johanna Mudd. I knew that Braun had set a meeting with Mudd and that when he didn't show up she disappeared. My sources (whatever those might have been) had informed me that he, Braun, was investigating the conviction of the cop killer A Free Man. I went on to say that I needed information about his case in order to see if his enemies were also against Ms. Mudd.

That was a long shot, but I thought I might at least have electronic communication with the lawyer-celeb, gathering a few crumbs in the process.

At 4:14 p.m. Aja-Denise walked in. I was sitting at the reception desk considering the tips of my left hand's fingers. My teenage daughter wore a red dress that was barely acquainted with her upper thighs and white vinyl platform shoes that elevated her to near my height. The green straps of a backpack dug into her bare shoulders.

"What?" she asked me.

"Are you wearing *anything* under that slip?"

"Daddy!"

I held up a lecturing finger and said, "Just think if you walked in here and all I had on was a T-shirt and a pair of those skin-tight satin trunks that those men were wearing at Sunset Beach. Because, girl, that would be overdressed compared to what you got on right now."

The thing about me and A.D. is that we know what to say to each other. She shifted a little uncomfortably and placed her arms in such a way as to cover some of her flesh.

"Everybody dresses like this."

"Answer my question."

"I guess I wouldn't want that," she agreed. "But if I go all the way home I won't be able to work for you today."

"What you got in the backpack?"

"A trench coat."

"Put it on."

She opened her mouth to protest but I opened my eyes wide and she took off the incongruous drab green backpack instead.

The trench coat was light tan and short hemmed. She put it on, fastening all the buttons and tying the sash around her waist. The coat wasn't much longer than the red slip and it fit her like a dress suit. But at least there was something left to the imagination.

"You know we're gonna have that talk someday soon," I said.

"I know." She gave me that wry expression inherited from her mother.

I love that child. During my most difficult years it was only her and Gladstone who never let me down.

The buzzer to the door sounded and A.D. went to answer.

It was the in-person reply to the third e-mail I dispatched.

"Hey," Aja said with real welcome in her voice. She backed away from the entrance, exposing Willa Portman wearing a simple and mostly shapeless black-and-orange dress and a pink sweater, and carrying that same briefcase.

"Hi-i," she said to all and sundry.

"Miss Portman."

"Mr. Oliver. I hope I'm not interrupting."

"No. Aja and I were just discussing the office dress code. She told me that I cannot wear a wifebeater to work."

Willa smiled and I gestured for her to enter my office.

"Want me to come take notes?" A.D. asked.

"No," I said before closing the door.

"I see you got it," I said to my unlikely client when we were seated.

"Nineteen thousand two hundred and fifty dollars and a pretty nifty briefcase too."

"Pretty nifty," I parroted. "Where you from?"

"A small town in Ohio called Martins Ferry."

"The poet James Wright is from there."

"Who?"

"Never mind. I read a lot of those files you left. It's certainly suspicious, and I can't see why a lawyer of Braun's caliber would back down. So I'll put the money in a safe place and use it until the case is solved, Man is dead, or I decide that he's culpable."

"Thank you."

"Are you still working at Braun's office?"

"I plan to quit tomorrow."

"I don't think that's such a good idea."

"Why not?"

Before I could answer there came the haunting notes of "Clair de Lune" by Debussy. Instantly I hit a button on the intercom that would mute any sound and turn on a red light on Aja's desk. Then I took a burner phone from the top drawer, and as I picked up the phone I put a finger to my lips for my client.

I pressed a button on the side of the burner for the reply to the second e-mail of the day.

"Mr. Braun?" I said.

"Mr. Boll."

"I was hoping that you'd call. I'm really stumped with this case."

"Who are you?"

"A private detective working with a concerned group over the disappearance of Ms. Mudd. No one has heard from or seen her in over a week and we're very concerned about her welfare. She has diabetes and her grandchildren depend on her for childcare."

"There's nothing wrong with Ms. Mudd," Braun said in his most reassuring, most dissembling lawyer's tone. "No one knows her whereabouts because no one needs to know."

"I don't understand you, sir."

"It's not for you to understand. Just take my word when I tell you that Johanna Mudd *was* in danger, but now she's someplace safe."

"Even her daughter and son don't know how to reach her?"

"It's better for everyone that they don't."

"I can't say that to my clients."

"Her son and daughter?"

"No. An interested third party."

"This is a very delicate situation, Mr. Boll. You must give me your clients' names so that I can assure them myself. And so that I can impress on them just how important secrecy is."

I took the appropriate six beats to pretend to be considering this action.

"I can't just hand over my clients' names," I said. "But I will meet with them and tell them there's more to the case than I at first thought. I'll tell them that you're willing to meet..."

"I need to meet with you too, Mr. Boll. We have to talk."

"About what?"

Willa was staring at me with a fearful look on her face.

"The phone is not a place to share secrets. Do you know Liberté Café on Hudson?"

"Yes, I do."

"Meet me there at seven thirty tonight. I believe I can convince you of the need to keep this quiet."

"I can't make it till nine thirty," I said. "Got a few important e-mails to catch up on."

"Okay," he said quickly, too quickly. "Nine thirty. I'll see you then. How will I know you?"

"I'll have a red pansy in my lapel," I said before disconnecting the call.

When I returned the phone to the drawer Willa asked, "That was Mr. Braun?"

"It was."

"You told him about what I said?"

"I sent him an e-mail informing him that I was Detective

101

Tom Boll, private, and that I was working for certain concerned parties who wanted me to find Johanna Mudd. He knows that I know about the Free Man case, but that much is in the papers."

"Did you say about him dropping the case?"

"No."

She sighed.

"But he may suspect that I'm getting information from inside his office. So the best thing you can do is stay on the job. If anything comes up I need to know, I'll give you another number you can call me on."

The young lawyer gazed at me, realizing, for the first time I believed, how deep in shit she was.

She nodded and even forced a smile.

"I guess this is what I asked you for," she said.

"You want we should drop it?"

She searched my eyes for the answer. After a good long time she said, "No. I never really knew how much a man can be a victim of the law until I met Manny. He's a killer but he's no criminal. I can't turn my back on that."

I gave Willa the number of another burner I owned and then showed her to the door.

I stood there staring at nothing after she'd gone.

"Did Mom do something to you?" Aja asked from behind me.

"Yes," I said to the door.

"Did it have to do with me?"

I turned to look at my trench-coated blood. "She looked at my files."

"How do you know that?"

"I can tell when people look at certain files," I lied. "Files you never opened before."

"That's not really so bad, is it?" Aja asked.

"No. But from now on don't take work out of the office, okay?"

She nodded and that was enough.

13.

AJA WAS GONE by 6:30. I dressed and was ready for the night by 7:00.

The last talk I had with my daughter had put the trouble with Monica to bed, but I forgot, as most men are wont to do, that what happens to me is not necessarily up to me.

Upon exiting the door onto Montague Street I heard a man shout, "Oliver!"

The street was crowded with shoppers beginning to think about dinner and Christmas and who felt that they should be outside before the bite of winter sent them home for the season.

A group of young men and women, mostly black, were fooling around near the curb. From around the twenty-something revelers came Coleman Tesserat, Monica's boy-toy husband. He was dressed for jogging with the hood down. The sweat suit was yellow with dark blue or black piping.

I had a short-nosed .45 revolver in my windbreaker

pocket, but that hardly seemed necessary. Later that night things might be different.

"Coleman," I said.

A sky-blue-haired black girl watched us. She heard the threat, as I had, in Coleman's voice.

"What did you say to Monica?" he demanded.

"Why you wanna ask me that and you already know?"

Coleman got to within twenty-four inches of me. He was a black belt in some Eastern exercise system and thought that taught him how to defend himself.

"I asked you a question," he said with all the confidence of the dead.

I said, "You already know."

The blue-haired girl touched a young man's shoulder.

"I'm not afraid of you," Coleman was saying.

"If that was true," I said, still looking at the girl, "you wouldn't be in my face."

"I could kick your ass right here," Coleman warned.

"In front of witnesses?" I said innocently. "And me with my hands at my side."

"Stay out of my business," he said, understanding that he'd made a tactical error confronting me like that.

"Did your wife tell you why I said I'd look into you?"

"It doesn't matter."

"She called a man I was investigating. If he was of another nature I might be dead. She was fucking with me for no reason. I just pushed back. And the next time you come at me, be ready to kill, because I won't stop coming till it's over."

I walked away with all kinds of nonsense racing through my body and mind.

Teenage hormones sang in my heart and sinews because

I wanted to beat Monica's new husband to pulp. Under that feeling was the revelation that my preoccupation with the opposite sex had returned. I knew this when I saw Blue-hair looking at me.

I was ready.

There's an illegal private club on Avenue D down near Houston. It takes up the three-level subbasement of a huge public housing project.

You push the button for apartment 1A and the buzzer lets you in. You come to the door and say a name. If they like the name, you go through the door and down some stairs, coming to another door. This opens to a very large room that is quiet and usually half-filled with men and women who need privacy on the level of a secret society. There are comfortable chairs and tables, walls lined with bookshelves, and servers wearing either tuxedos or miniskirts.

The residents of that building never complain because the owners of the nameless club have at least three security people watching the entrance at all times. There's no mugging, drug dealing, or prostitution above the basement—ever.

I had not been to the club before, but I knew of it.

"Looking for Mel?" asked a lovely blond black young woman standing behind the cast-iron podium at the bottom of the stairs. She wore a little black dress, black hose, and a microchain silver necklace that had a red stone as its jewel.

"Yes, I am."

She took me through a doorway behind the podium,

down a slender hallway, to another flight of stairs that led to another large room with fewer occupants.

"At the opposite wall," she said.

I saw Melquarth Frost waving at me from the place the hostess indicated. I couldn't help feeling that I was actually about to make a deal with the devil.

He stood up when I approached the table. I got the impression that this was a show of great deference. We shook hands. His powerful paw felt like a winter glove filled with concrete.

"Mr. Frost."

"King—I got your text. Did they let you in like I said?"

"They sure did."

We sat and appreciated each other a moment. He wore a lemon-colored suit that was loose but hung well. The shirt was lapis replete with errant silver and golden threads weaving through. I wore a felt-lined brown trench coat, black trousers, and black leather shoes with rubber soles.

I had thirteen years on the force, six of those as a detective, and Frost was the most dangerous criminal I had ever come across. Our few meetings had convinced me that he felt in my debt, though we had never discussed this obligation after his first visit to my office.

We might have been about to start speaking, when a midheight, slump-shouldered man wearing a white jacket and black pants walked up to the small round table.

"Mel," the man said in a voice that was hard and clear.

"Ork."

"Who's your friend?"

"Nobody for you to worry about."

"A guy up at the bar told me that he looks like a cop he used to know."

"Go back to him," Mel said, "and say that he should mind his own business."

Mel and Ork peered at each other maybe a quarter of a minute. The latter's nostrils flared, then he walked away.

"Friendly place," I commented.

"Crooks are a skittish lot," Mel countered.

"I thought you gave all that up."

"I just like the atmosphere. Sometimes you get the need to talk to people who have the right language behind their eyes."

I nodded.

"What can I do for you, King?"

"Tell me why you came to my office that day," I said simply.

"I told you already."

"Maybe pad it with some details."

"Why?"

"Because I might want to ask you for something and you're named after Satan."

Melquarth Frost grinned.

"I saw a red bird in Prospect Park two days before you busted me," he said.

"A red bird."

"Pure scarlet," he assented with a vigorous nod. "At first it was just a flash up in the trees, in between the leaves. But then it landed on a branch maybe forty feet away. It was the most beautiful thing I'd ever seen. I found myself hoping that it would get closer so I could get a better look. I was sitting on a park bench getting my head together for the job. The thing took wing and landed on the lawn in front'a me. It was big, almost the size of a crow, and there was a single black feather on the crown of its head."

There was what I can only call a beatific look on the ex–heist man's face.

"And?" I said.

"He looked at me and I knew that that meant something. Here some completely wild animal comes right up to you and looks you in the eye. That means something."

He had me.

"What?" I asked.

"I wasn't sure about the exact message, but a bird means freedom and the color red means pay attention. And I thought that a bird like that, a bird that stood out like a flare in the night, was something like me.

"And then, when the prosecutor asked you to say something about me that would throw me under the bus, you refused. You were the better man when I was running and again when I was helpless.

"Don't get me wrong. I could have done my time. I wasn't afraid, but you weren't either. You were like that red bird in the tree and then you came down. That was the sign—as clear as the nose on Ork's ugly face.

"I was committed to one more job and, like I told you, my partner shot me in the back. That right there was the final straw—the business was finished with me."

I was convinced that Mel was crazy. But his psychopath's vision of the world seemed cohesive and certain; something I could trust to be what it was.

"I'm involved in a couple of cases," I said after an appreciative pause. "I'm gonna need some help and I thought maybe I could hire you. I got a small budget and could hire a man. It's not heist money, but you're not a heist man anymore."

"You got it."

"Don't you wanna hear what it is?"

"Sure. You got to tell me, but, Mr. Oliver, if that red bird asked me to follow him I would have said yes too."

"How much will you charge?"

"A dollar now and a dollar when it's through."

I took a dollar bill from my wallet and handed it to him.

"You want to take a walk with me?" I asked Melquarth Frost.

He put the dollar in his breast pocket and stood.

I followed him up the stairs and out into a fate filled with madmen and red birds, nameless cops and women who fooled you again and again.

14.

WALKING ACROSS FROM the East Village to the West was a pivotal, even a transitional journey in my life.

My father was a criminal and therefore I had become a cop. I was framed and threatened and so stopped being official and did the work as a private dick. Every step I had taken was an equal and opposite reaction to my father—you might say that it had nothing to do with free will at all.

But me walking down those chilly autumn streets with a man so evil that no crime deterred him meant that I had taken the first steps on a different path, a path that was mine and mine alone.

"I know there's no way for me to make up for what I was," Mel was saying as we made our way north on Hudson. The dark brick of the old buildings imparted their gloom onto his lecture and our destination. "I mean, I did it all and it doesn't mean anything. Maybe if I felt it, I would want to make amends..."

He kept talking, but I wasn't listening too closely. I knew somewhere that this was new for him too, that he wasn't the kind of guy who told you anything unless it was either absolutely necessary or a lie. Melquarth, maybe for the first time, was thinking out loud, while I remembered my cell in solitary and how my enemies had broken me, made me cower like a dog.

"There it is," I said after six long blocks.

The Liberté Café was on the east side of Hudson, having big windows and outside tables that only a few people used. It was mainly an overpriced pastry shop that made complex coffees and little sandwiches that pretended to be French.

"Can I help you?" a young caramel-colored woman asked. She had big freckles flanking her broad nose and a space between her front teeth.

"How about that table there?" I suggested.

"Sure. I'll get Juan to bring your menus."

I could see that Mel would have preferred a table tucked away behind the counter, but I knew that such seating would make us look suspicious.

Juan was a smallish bronze-skinned man with a debonair mustache and eyes that had somewhere else to be.

"I'll have the prosciutto on a baguette and a green tea latte," I told the young man when he asked the floor for my order.

"Coffee, black, with some bread," Mel said.

When Juan went away Mel asked, "So what do you want with this guy?" referring to Stuart Braun.

"Have you ever met him?"

"No, but I knew a dude in Q that Braun got out from under a murder one charge."

"Braun was in California?"

"No. But the guy had killed somebody in New York and then another man in Sacramento. California extradited and convicted him after Braun did his magic out here."

"I don't want to say why I'm looking into him quite yet," I said.

"It's your dollar."

I was beginning to like my satanic sidekick.

"So what's your story, Mel? I mean the real deal."

He looked at me. His eyes were truly dead, but regardless of that there was gratitude in his stare.

"Prison psychiatrist says that I have borderline personality disorder with intermittent psychotic breaks that both relieve the pressure of unconscious guilt and make me dangerous."

"That sounds crazy."

"Don't it? I asked the woman, if I was that far gone why was I in prison and not in some mental facility?"

"What did she say?" I asked, looking up to see a trio of unlikely customers walk through the glass door. The big men all wore jeans, cotton sports jackets, and patterned shirts of various styles.

"That modern law in the United States was based on economic class and what the popular opinion classified as evil," Mel said, answering my question. "She said in the modern world a man who beats his own head against the wall is crazy but the guy slams somebody else's head is criminal."

"Three guys walked in," I said.

"I see 'em in the mirror."

They were talking to the sweet-skinned freckled girl.

"The fat one in the light jacket is a guy named Porker," Mel added. "I don't think he knows me. I was supposed to kill him this one time, but his girlfriend decided that she felt sorry for his wife and gave me my fifty percent kill fee."

The men were looking around. Finally they decided on the partially concealed table that Mel coveted.

When they were settled, shy-eyed Juan went over to take their orders.

"So your story is a prison psych putting a textbook diagnosis on your actions?" I asked, telling Mel that we were just going to watch and wait.

"No. I was just giving you the official answer. You know that's how most people know everybody else. They read it in a newspaper ad or maybe a letter from home."

"So what's the real answer?"

"My mother was a Catholic girl. From the age of three she went with her mother to church every Wednesday and Sunday. When she was nine she pledged her life to Jesus Christ and each and every word in a single book.

"Then one night, when she thought she was alone in the cathedral, a man dragged her into the confession box and raped her. She was barely a teenager and right there in the church too. That shit warped her brain.

"Her mother and father ordered her to get an abortion, but she told them that that would be against God. They kicked her out the house and she lived in a Catholic dormitory, where she gave birth, named me after the demon, and never, ever showed me any love.

"I was a duty like Job's trial for her. She housed me and fed me and told me every day that I was the son of evil."

I looked into Mel's dead eyes, thinking that my life might not have been as bad as I thought.

"You know Porker's real name?" I asked.

"I forget, but I know where to get it."

After that we dallied over our drinks and food. Mel had a vast range of knowledge that had nothing to do with crime. He knew quite a bit about evolution. He told me that his greatest wish, when he was a child, was to change into something different; like wolves had become dogs or dinosaurs birds.

When my watch said 10:37 the three thugs paid their bill, got up, and left. They hadn't seen a man with a red flower in his lapel. Stuart Braun wasn't there either.

"I guess we can go too," I said maybe half an hour after Porker and his crew were gone.

Outside the restaurant Mel said, "I killed the mother-fucker."

The old me would have been on the alert for a confession, but I had already crossed over that line in the East Village.

"Who?"

"My father. I asked around until I heard about a guy from my mother's old neighborhood who had gone down for rape a few times. I met him in a bar and, after a whole lotta rye, he told me about a thirteen-year-old girl he raped in a confession box. He said that was the sweetest nut he ever had.

"A little later on I made some excuse to get mad and hit

115

him in the teeth. I wiped some'a the blood up with a hand-kerchief and left him on the street.

"The DNA lab identified him as my father and I met up with him again. He'd been so drunk that he didn't remember gettin' knocked out. I took him to this abandoned house in the Bronx and put all kinds of pain to his ass. When he was dead I poured seventeen gallons of sulfuric acid into a big ole bathtub and that motherfucker was gone from the world. It was like he never even existed."

"Because he raped your mother?" I had to ask.

"Because he made me and made me what I am and didn't even know it. And on top of that he wouldn't have given a damn even if I told him."

15.

I TOOK A yellow taxi home.

Montague Street was empty. Coleman Tesserat might have been hiding in some doorway with a gun in his hand. Maybe the exposure of his crimes on Wall Street would have salted him away for twenty years—I didn't know. I *did* know that I wasn't afraid to die, that since deciding to go up against the men who took my life away, I had no fear.

"King-baby," she said.

Turning my head to the left I saw Effy Stoller. Five three with fifteen pounds over what her physician would have called perfect weight, she had big lips and skin darker than mine. Her high, high heels might as well have been bare feet, she was so poised, and her hair had been done into the shape of a seashell that would exist in some far-flung future when humanity had devolved itself into geologic memory.

"I know I'm a little late," I said as she walked up to me. "I thought you'd be gone."

She kissed me full on the lips and said, "I knew you'd get here. If you e-mailed me it had to be something hard."

Effy had been a prostitute in the old days when I had a beat. She'd was run by a pimp named Toof who came from somewhere in the Midwest. He worked her hard and beat her regularly. But she never complained or turned him in.

Then late one Wednesday night when I was on the street in Midtown, an older woman hobbled up to me and said that she'd heard a shot from a building I knew well.

On the top floor a door at the far end of the hall was ajar. There had been as many eyes on me as there were roaches in the wall, but nobody came out to tell me anything—it wasn't that kind of building.

Inside the apartment, Toof was on the floor in his ivory-colored gabardine zoot suit; the left side of his skull and most of its contents were on the wall. Effy sat nine feet away at a dinette table in the tiny kitchen. She was drinking the good cognac from the bottleneck, something I was certain Toof would have never allowed her to do.

The gun was on the table. It was a huge six-shooter, .41 caliber. I picked up the piece and sat across from her.

"When I woke up this morning I knew he had to die," she told the tabletop.

"Why's that?" I asked.

"He got a new girl. Pretty thing."

"And you were jealous?"

"The first time I seen 'im hit her somethin' changed. It was like I had died and the gatekeeper was showin' me my life. He give me a chance to go back and fix it. All I had to do was get a good night's sleep to figure how."

Toof had done all kinds of bad things, and Effy had always been, more or less, easy to work with. If I busted her she took the arrest with style. She deserved better and he'd gotten exactly what was coming to him.

Toof had a back door to his tenement apartment. I helped Effy to her feet and told her where she could go for the night. Then I put the .41 at the back of my pants and called in the homicide dicks, as was my duty.

Effy was my fifth e-mail of the morning. I knew I'd be needing some comfort when it came to sleep.

She undressed and bathed me, gave me an oil massage all down my spine to the middle of the gluteus maximus. When that was through she turned me over. Her breasts and stomach glistened from the oil.

"You not hard, King-baby; don't you like me no more?"

"I thought maybe we could try and talk for a while," I said.

"What you need to talk about?"

"You know how one time you told me that you woke up in the morning and knew what you had to do?" We had not discussed that night before.

"Yeah," she said with a slight nod and a steady gaze.

"I woke up a few days ago."

She lay down beside me and put her hand to my chest. We stayed like that for long minutes.

"I stopped trickin' six years ago," she said.

"Then why are you here?"

"I knew what you was feelin' after they lied on you. I knew. And when you called me I came because that's what a woman does when a man save her life. He don't have to love her or care about her or nothin'. But if he save her life, then she gots to take care on him. And even though I'm a professional and fully legit masseuse now—if you call, I come over."

"I guess this is the last time I'll call," I said.

"We could still get drinks or sumpin'," she offered. "Now, turn ovah."

The new massage was softer and ranged wider. She did my earlobes and between the toes, the webbing between my fingers and the big tendons of my feet. All the while she was saying something, but I couldn't quite make it out.

"Daddy?"

I hadn't been in a sleep that deep for a very long time. Not since before my days in solitary had I slept well at all. A few hours here and there was the most I could hope for. But that day, with A.D. shaking my shoulder, I awoke from slumber that had been completely given over to rest.

"Yeah, baby?"

"Have you been asleep all day?"

"What time is it?"

"A little after four."

I sat up, keeping the blanket wrapped around me.

Aja was wearing a light brown dress that came down to almost the knee, and though it revealed her figure it didn't cling.

Looking at this mature attire I realized that she was even more alluring and looked old enough to do something about it. I chuckled to myself, realizing that I couldn't keep my chick in the egg.

"What you lookin' at, Daddy?"

"Fate."

"Are you okay?"

I thought about her question and finally said, "Sit down."

She perched at the edge of the bed and cocked her head the way she had as a child.

"What?" she asked.

"I wanted to say that watching you grow into a woman is really the best thing I've ever done."

"I talked to Mama," she said.

"Oh?"

"She told me what she did. She tried to say that it wasn't all that bad, but I said that she couldn't have no idea what might happen if she outed you like that. I think she understood."

"Go on downstairs," I said then. "Let me get dressed."

16.

EVEN WITH WAKING up that late in the day, the afternoon was almost normal. Aja made phone calls and filled out checks for me to sign after she was gone. I looked down on Montague Street, thinking about Effy pretending that she was a hooker in order to give me what I needed and Mel flying out of hell in the guise of a scarlet bird to be my guardian angel.

I intended to use Willa's money to pay for a full investigation into Stuart Braun's case on A Free Man. But first I had to make a little headway on the frame certain elements in the NYPD had hung around my neck.

"Angles and Dangles," a woman with a deep and raspy voice answered on the fourth ring. It was six thirty and Aja was packing up to go.

"Let me talk to Marty Moreland," I said.

"Who?"

"My friend Marty said he'd be at the bar and I could call ... at six sharp."

"To begin with," the woman said, peeved, "it's six thirty. And even if whoever you said was here, you got to call the pay phone you want to talk to a customer."

She hung up and I smiled.

"What's so funny?"

Aja was standing there looking at me from the doorway.

"I like my job," I said.

"You working on that thing for Miss Portman?"

"I surely am."

"You scared Coleman the other night."

"Oh really?"

"Him and Mama been talkin' about it every night after they think I'm sleep. She's wondering what he did that you could catch him on."

"What does he say?"

"I can't really hear what he says. He whispers mostly and she shouts. But you know what, Daddy?"

"What's that?"

"I think you should find out what he did and turn him in."

I looked closely at my daughter, at the dark place in the light of my life. She turned her head in a pose of absolute seriousness and came in to take one of the ash clients' chairs.

She wanted me to know that she wasn't kidding.

Something about the gravity of her gaze lightened my mood by half.

"I can't do that, baby."

"Why not? You know Mama get all mad about you and that woman, but she was seein' Coleman when you were still married. I saw a letter from him to her that was written a year before they put you in jail."

"She had good reason," I said, admitting my own sins without naming them.

"But it was him who told her to leave you in jail."

"How do you know that?"

"One time when she said that she felt sorry for the time you were in jail, he said that they had talked about that when it happened and she made the right decision to cut the cord."

That almost got me. I might have done something if I didn't know that Monica needed no help abandoning me.

"Are you spying on your mother, A.D.?"

"She did it to my computer. She go through my stuff all the time."

"Well...I don't want you to do that anymore," I said, managing to put some weight into the words. "And I would never send a man to prison. Not unless it was my job."

"But what if he deserves it?"

"Doesn't matter."

"Why?"

"Because I been there. I know what it's like and I'm just not that evil."

She sniffed and looked at me, learning as she did so what her father valued and what she might be.

"I'm goin' to Melanie's house tonight," she said after a long lag in the conversation.

"Studyin'?"

"Just to get away from that house."

"Your mother knows?"

"She mad too. She mad at you and now at Coleman. All she ever wanted was a life like they live on the TV. And all she ever got was the front page of the *Post*."

It was something I said from time to time. I laughed and she snickered. We got up at the same moment to hug each other good-bye.

Angles and Dangles was a dilapidated bar about eight blocks from the old navy yard. There were a few small neon signs in the dirt-caked windows provided by defunct beer companies. Inside, nautical knickknacks like life preservers and big oak ship wheels hung, leaned, and sat on shelves here and there.

Some of the men who drank at the bar and the few tables along the walls might have been seamen at one time or another; the rest had been dockworkers. The woman behind the bar, Cress Mahoney, was the heavy voice that had hung up on me. She was faded but still lovely at almost fifty. Her graying hair had been brown. Her blue eyes had a spark to them.

Everybody was white in there and they all noted my skin color.

"You still make that grog with lemon juice and water?" I asked Cress when I bellied up to the bar.

"Do I know you?" she asked with a sandpaper larynx.

"I only ever ordered from Pop Miller before today."

"You knew Pop?" She was doubtful.

"Knew? Is he dead?"

The question hurt Cress. She loved the old guy.

I liked him myself and hadn't heard of his passing. The only reason I called the bar was to make sure that it was still there after so many years.

"Heart attack fishin' out on his rowboat," she said. "They didn't find him for three days. He'd floated half the way to Delaware."

"He left you the bar," I stated.

"What do you know?"

"That 'Cress Mahoney is the finest woman on the Eastern Seaboard. She could gut a fish or spear a shark better than most'a yer so-called seamen.'" I approximated his accent well enough to convince her of my half-truth.

"What's your name?"

"My father named me Thor after a comic book he read one time."

She'd never heard of me but still smiled at my imagined christening.

"And what do you want here?"

"Grog."

I knew her lover, Athwart "Pop" Miller, and more about her history than I was willing to say.

I had turned Pop into my CI when I found out about a regular marijuana delivery that he ran down at the docks. I didn't interfere but instead made him identify and then report on Little Exeter Barret. Pop didn't like Exeter because he dealt in heroin. I had a deep interest in the ferret-faced runt because he could lead me to the biggest bust in New York City history.

I only ever came to the bar after hours, so Cress was unlikely to know my face or anything about me.

"I don't recognize you," she said.

"Pop an' me used to play Go after he closed," I said. "He told me that his clientele wouldn't like a man of my shade playing Chinese checkers at his bar."

"Atty tried to teach me," she remembered aloud, "but I just didn't get it."

"They say Go is harder than chess. Pop said he picked it up on a tour of Southeast Asia in the merchant marines."

"And why you think I own the place now?" she asked. "He's got three kids and two ex-wives."

"But only one lusty wench," I quoted, "that he wanted to be marooned with in the South Pacific."

The tension went out of Cress then. I could see in the mirror behind her that her clients were losing interest in me. America was changing at a snail's pace in a high wind, but until that gastropod mollusk reached its destination I had a .45 in my pocket and eyes on all four corners at once.

Cress served the sweet rum drink and I savored it.

I was reading an iPad version of the story of Joan of Arc, looking up now and then to see the denizens of an old way of life bring their world back for a night.

There was an old-fashioned jukebox that hadn't had its contents swapped out for thirty years . . . Brandy was a fine girl and she'd have made a good wife but his woman was the sea.

Maybe two hours later a man said, "Hey, mister." He'd installed himself on the barstool to the right before I looked up.

"Yeah?"

"Do I know you?" His skin was wizened and burned brown from oceangoing sunlight. The eyes might have had a color other than brown, but he squinted.

I smiled and turned Joan off.

"Why do you ask?" I replied.

"Never seen you here before, but you look familiar."

"You'd remember if you knew me."

"You that bad?"

"I'm just a sucker for real grog is all, my friend."

"Now we're friends?" he asked. Sitting up straight he was still a small man.

Two hours and all I knew was that Joan was a pivotal event in the culmination of the Hundred Years' War. She had saved France and been betrayed by the king she'd crowned. They said she was a virgin, but I reserved judgment.

I'd already decided that Angles and Dangles was a bust when the runt sailor had drunk enough to try to pick a fight. Two hours wasted with sixty seconds of value tacked on to the end.

I raised my hand to get Cress's attention, intending to pay my bill and leave. But then the door opened and Little Exeter walked in.

"Yes, Mr. Thor?" Cress asked while I watched the little rat wade through the crowd to a far table.

I looked at Pop's barmaid lover and said, "Give my friend a triple of whatever he's drinkin'."

"Johnny, are you beggin' drinks again?"

"Hell, no," my newest best friend proclaimed. "Make that rye, Cressy."

"We were talkin' sea stories," I lied. "He's a good guy. You can bring me another grog too."

It was almost two in the morning when three unsteady patrons staggered out of Angles and Dangles.

I'd left the bar just short of an hour earlier and set myself in the shadows of a doorway across the street.

Little Exeter was among the staggery crew. They parted company half a block away.

I followed my quarry for three blocks, sticking to the opposite side of the street, keeping my distance.

The streets were dark and lifeless except for rats running around the edges and a window light here and there. One heavily bearded homeless man pushed his overflowing shopping cart down the middle of the street proudly; one of the last humans in the world who had survived the holocaust of humanity.

Little Exeter was reeling, teetering, and stumbling, but now and then he'd stop and perform a near-perfect dance step that revealed a completely different man from the one I'd stalked a decade before.

I didn't care.

When I was sure there was no one around I moved quickly, coming up and knocking him senseless with a fist bolstered by a roll of nickels.

Dragging him into a little alley, I let him fall on his back and then squatted down so he could see my face, illuminated by an automatic prowler light put there to scare potential burglars.

"Who you?" he said.

I took out my pistol and pointed it at the center of his forehead.

"I do sumpin' to you?" he demanded.

"I need a name, Mr. Barret."

"Huh?" He didn't know whether to be drunk or afraid.

"Who in the police did you answer to fourteen years ago when you were running aitch outta the docks?"

His little eyes became big and he blinked like some kind of rain forest creature looking for a way out.

"Um, um, um...Cumberland," he said. "Hugo Cumberland."

That was the first time since Rikers that it came upon me in full force.

It was dark and dank, bug infested and rank from the odor of maggots in that alley. And I was, once again, a murderer-in-waiting, now with a gun in my hand and a man I yearned to kill prostrate before me.

It's not that I wanted to pull the trigger; it was just that I was going to pull it and he was going to die. There was a powerful revelation in that burgeoning reality.

I think Little Exeter must have seen his death in my eyes and so the fear drained away, leaving only the seriousness of the last moments of a wasted life.

That look on Exeter's face reminded me of Aja somehow. This brought to mind her asking for Coleman to be scuttled, for me to destroy him and her mother. If it hadn't been for her, Exeter would have died in that filthy passageway.

I stood up quickly and ran.

When I got to my car, five blocks away, the pistol was still in my hand.

"Hello?" she said sleepily. "Is that you, King-baby?"

"Yeah," I said after a short pause to catch my breath.

"What you doin'?"

"Sittin' in a car down near the old navy yard."

"What you doin' there?"

"When I was in Rikers they broke me. Broke me like a china plate."

Effy knew when to be quiet.

"They tore me down," I confessed. "I thought I was tough, but everything I knew and believed in just slipped away."

My face was going through all kinds of gymnastics to avoid crying.

"What you doin' in that car, Joe?"

"I was looking for a name. There's someone down here I thought might have it."

"Did he tell you?"

"He did."

"Did you kill him?"

There was something so intimate about the question that for a brief span of seconds I didn't feel alone. And because of that epiphany I realized that I felt alone almost all the time—when talking to people, walking down crowded avenues, even when I was talking with Aja.

I was alone because no one else seemed to know what was in my heart. Only Mel to a certain degree and now Effy, whom I had had all kinds of kinky sex with. None of that mattered because in order to truly be with somebody you have to be in their mind.

"Did you, Joe?" she asked again.

"No," I said, "I didn't."

"Did you do anything to him?"

"I knocked him down."

"Did he deserve that?"

"About a hundred times over."

"He's still alive?" Effy asked.

"He is."

"You a good man, King Joe," she said. "In any country,

language, religion, or wild place—you a good man. You knew me when I didn't know myself."

"Thanks," I said, then I disconnected the call.

I put the pistol in the trunk and drove home at a snail's pace; that same snail that was bringing humankind to a new understanding of the same old shit.

17.

WHEN AJA WAS a baby I'd watch her sleep, sometimes for an hour or more. Her face changed expressions with whatever dream she was having or with anything shifting in the room or inside her. She made errant noises and reached out now and again.

Sleeping, it seemed to me, was an act of innocence. That's why I stayed awake after almost murdering Exeter Barret. I knew that peaceful slumber was for babies, whereas only nightmares awaited a man like me.

Little X had provided corroboration of the intelligence Henri gleaned from his superiors. Not only was there a man in my downfall named Cumberland, but he dealt with heroin and his first name was Hugo.

If the name was an alias it was well chosen. It sounded like a real name, but then again it had a fancy quality that might be a shield.

I used Henri Tourneau's passwords to get into the police

and informant files of the NYPD. There was no Hugo Cumberland anywhere.

Google told me that there was a man of that name who
had died more than twenty years before. He was a carpenter
who had four children, one wife, and a house in Nyack. At
the time of his death he had lived sixty-one years and his
youngest child, a son who was twenty-three at the time of
Hugo's death, was named Adam.

Adamo Cortez and Hugo Cumberland. Albeit thin, it
was the only shred I had to hold on to at 4:19 in the
morning.

There were no CIs or cops with Adam's name, but there
was the record of an incident, fifteen years earlier; a shoot-
out in East Harlem, a falling-out among dope dealers, and
a man named Adam Cumberland was grazed on his left biceps. The investigating officers believed that Cumberland
was an innocent bystander.

He filled out a witness report but disappeared before the
inquest. If he was a police plant there was no record of him
in the system.

It wouldn't have been a lot of information even if I was
still a police detective. I could go to the hospital or to the
false address he put down in his statement. But all of that
was over twenty years ago.

I stared at the screen and scrawled down the names. The
last initial for both false names was C. Maybe it was the
original Hugo Cumberland's son.

My cell phone sounded after maybe an hour of searching
for the scion of the dead carpenter.

"Hello?"

"Joe?"

"Hey, Effy. It's five thirty. Don't you sleep?"

"Don't you?"

"Tell me something."

"What?"

"Do you have a boyfriend?" I asked this to stop thinking about the tumble of names in my head.

"I thought you were never gonna ask me questions like that."

"I wasn't," I said, "when I thought you were a working girl."

"I still took your money."

"At the old rate."

"Are you okay?" she asked.

"Yeah. Don't I sound it?"

"I was up worryin' about you," she explained. "You have never called me askin' for friendship before now."

"Thank you, honey, but I'm fine. I lost it there for a minute and I needed someone who understood to hear me out. So you can go to sleep now and I will call you for coffee one day soon."

"Joe?"

"What?"

"Nuthin'," she said.

Sitting there in the early hours before the sunrise I was grateful for Effy's call. There was nowhere to go with Adam or Hugo right then, so I decided to pay attention to some other aspect of my humiliation and demolition.

I had turned off the burner phone Stuart Braun knew. I did this just in case he had resources that could locate an active number.

There were two people who knew the number and two messages.

The first was from Braun.

"Mr. Boll," he said. "I went to the Liberté Café and you never showed. This is a very serious situation and I really need to speak to you and your clients. If you were to go public with your suspicions, many people would suffer."

Especially you, I thought.

"Please call me and let me know when we can meet," Braun said. Before disconnecting the call he paused a long minute, hoping I'd been listening and was just about to pick up.

The second message was from the devil.

"Hey, King," Melquarth Frost said. "Just thought I'd call and tell you that I'm closing in on the name you asked me to get. I'll tell you when I have something."

I like detective novels. The dick is either smarter, braver, or just luckier than his nemeses. He, or even she, works pretty much alone, sticking out his jaw whenever there's a blow coming. If he gets arrested that's okay. If some pretty young thing needs sex, it's probably not the right time for him, or her, just then.

The literary PI usually takes on one case at a time and he stays on the trail until it is solved, whether or not justice is done.

Sometimes I liked to pretend that I was a detective out of a book.

With this thought in mind I went back over the things I knew, details that might open an unexpected door. What might Tecumseh Fox think about Willa Portman? If I were Watson peering over Sherlock's shoulder, what odd detail might he be considering?

Outside the window it was still dark, but the workers were on the street tramping off to jobs that would never earn enough to pay their bills.

And as I watched, the name Chester Murray floated to the surface.

Henri Tourneau's access code revealed Chester's long record with the NYPD. He'd been arrested for theft, pimping, assault, and even rape. He was on-again, off-again as a CI with various officers I didn't know. I copied down the names in case they came up later.

The interesting thing about Chester's file was that the arrest record ended about three weeks before my bust. Since then he'd been a witness in a variety of drug and prostitution cases.

He was a black man, what my daughter's teachers would call African American, six three, and my age. He'd gone to public school until the age of fifteen and he was considered a predator by most of the detectives who had investigated or worked with him.

There was an open file on him about a woman, Henrietta Miller, who had gone missing nearly twenty years before.

If I wanted his address or number I'd have to come up with higher clearance than Henri had.

That was no problem.

I went upstairs to my apartment and spent another hour or so making notes on pink and blue sheets of paper. These

137

I sorted into a leather folder that I put into a shoulder bag along with a silver flask of sour mash whiskey and a loaded .45 with an extra box of shells.

At 6:45 I boarded the first car of an uptown A train. It was already crowded with people from all classes commuting into Manhattan. Next to me sat a young black woman reading *Journey to the East* by Hesse. She was rapt in the language of the long-dead Nobel laureate.

In her early twenties, she was dressed for office work but not sleekly like a manager or VP. I figured she was a college student working as a receptionist or data entry clerk. Her profile was what I could only call friendly, so I said, "I tried *The Glass Bead Game* but couldn't get through it."

She looked up at me as if expecting to see someone else. "What?"

"*Magister Ludi,*" I said.

"You read Hesse?"

"*Journey to the East* and an early one called *Knulp.*" I could see the question in her eyes so I added, "There was an accident this one time and I couldn't read for months. I never really read very much before that, but once I could do it again it was like I couldn't stop for the next five years. I still read but just not so much as before."

"How did you end up reading somebody like Hesse?"

"Worked my way sideways from the existentialists."

The look on her face was trying to deny my claims but unable to find a reason why.

"What?" I asked. "Don't I look like I can read?"

"I don't know," she said, an authenticity in her tone.

"You're dressed like a janitor except for that leather bag. I guess you could be a professor."

"Retired cop."

"I expect cops to read Tom Clancy or something."

"What got you reading Hesse?"

"I'm majoring in comp lit at Hunter. Our senior year we have to write, like, a thesis."

I stuck out a hand and said, "Joe Oliver."

"Kenya. Kenya Norman," she said, reaching out too. "Are you trying to pick me up, Mr. Oliver?"

"No," I said. And that was mostly true.

18.

I GOT A phone number before getting off at Port Authority. Kenya Norman, the young scholar, was headed for Brinkman/Stern, an investment company in the Sixties that specialized in new technologies.

"I figure I won't be distracted from my work if I'm not interested in what my day job is," she told me.

"Whoever you are," I concurred, "you have to love what you do or you end up hating yourself."

She gave me an odd look and I felt for a moment that I was looking into a mirror.

Taking my cue from Henri Tourneau, I went to a pay phone on the third floor of the interstate-run travel hub.

The phone rang only twice before he answered, "Braun."

"Mr. Braun, Tom Boll here."

"Where were you?"

"There was another case I had to take care of. I'm sorry if I put you out."

"Where are you?"

"On the street. I like to use pay phones when I can. Feels anonymous. Know what I mean?"

"We need to meet."

"Not really."

"No? I thought you were looking into Johanna Mudd's disappearance."

"I told my clients about you and they decided to take what they had to the police."

"That's a mistake..."

He said more but I hung up in the middle of his protest. I wanted him a little nervous.

"Ecstasies," a young woman said.

"Mimi, please."

"And who may I say is calling?"

"Joe."

"Just Joe?"

"That's not what my mother would say, but you can tell Mimi that it's Joe and he needs some ruby slippers."

"It's not even eight in the morning," the lovely voice argued.

"If you look up the code words you'll see that it doesn't matter what time it is."

Even her harrumph was fetching. I wondered what the operator looked like.

Minutes passed and then: "Joe?"

"Hey, Mimi."

"You in trouble?"

"No more than usual."

"Then why am I awake?"

"Did a guy call you with a reference from me?"

"Federal man," she averred. "Is that what this is about?"

"No. I need to get a line on a man you might have some business with. A Chester Murray."

"That piece'a-shit traitor? I'll give you his information if you promise to kill him."

"I can assure you that I'll do worse than that."

"You still AOL?"

"I am."

"A dinosaur. I'll get somebody to send you what you need."

I bought three maple-glazed doughnuts and a Styrofoam cup of black coffee from a cart on the first floor. Then I made another call.

"Watching the watchers watch the watched," he said.

I grinned. "Hey, Mel."

"You're up early."

"I heard a worm turn and went out lookin'. You got anything?"

"Not quite yet, but I will soon enough."

I hadn't had a cigarette since solitary. I went to a little kiosk right outside the bus station and bought a pack of filterless Camels. I coughed a little on the first drag but after that it was a fine memory.

I smoked the cigarette halfway down and then crushed it under the toe of my right shoe.

My real phone beeped and I saw the e-mail that Mimi Lord promised.

"Excuse me," a woman said.

She was probably thirty but looked like she was closing

in on sixty. She wasn't white or black, but that's the closest I could come to defining her race. Her hands were very dirty and the violet-and-black dress she wore looked like it might unravel at any moment.

"Yes?"

"You got a cigarette?"

I handed her the nearly virgin pack.

I found him at the address Mimi's e-mail provided, in a storefront on a stretch of Flatbush that had not yet been kissed by the gentrification bug. The entire space was no more than a few hundred square feet and the only furniture was a desk and four chairs.

Chester was sitting behind the desk with a size-fourteen-shod foot resting upon it. Two other men, one white and one not, were seated in chairs that flanked him. They were all smoking and drinking from small paper cups.

There was a good deal of laughter among them.

I'd driven past the big-windowed storefront private club and parked the car in a garage six blocks away. My shoulder bag was in the trunk, under the spare, but the .45 was in my pocket—I was carrying a pretty mean pocketknife too.

"Can I help you?" a man's voice asked from behind me.

I was standing across the street and four doorways down from Chester's hole in the wall.

Turning, I saw a small man with grayish skin looking up from about half a foot below my height. His sports jacket was shapeless enough to be a sweater and the waistline of his pants rode a little higher than where his navel should have been. Maybe seventy, he had a full thatch of gray hair and old-fashioned spectacles glazing auburn eyes.

The sign on the display window of the store behind him read, NILES AQUARIUMS AND FISHES. I didn't know if Niles was a name or some poetic reference to an ancient river filled with fish.

I looked down into the man's eyes and said, "Tom Boll. I was, uh, well, I was, um, thinking if I should come in and ask for a, you know, a job."

This declaration surprised the old man.

"I like fish," I said. "I mean I like to watch 'em. I like to eat 'em too, but I know you people don't sell that kinda fish."

"I'm not hiring any staff right now," he said.

"I know that. I mean, if you was, there'd probably be a sign in the window or somethin', right? But I was wonderin' if maybe you had some kinda work that you always meant to be doin' but never get around to it. You know, somethin' heavy or dirty. I don't mind gettin' my hands dirty. And I could really use a few dollars."

The old man gauged me. I was just talking to blend in while watching Chester and his cohorts drink and guffaw. What I expected was that the fish merchant would send me away, but if asked later, he'd remember some poorly educated, nearly homeless man looking for work.

"I have a storeroom in the back," he said. "Junk's been piling up in there the past thirty-seven years."

It was the perfect job for a mendicant like I was pretending to be.

The store wasn't much larger than Chester's place, but it was crowded with aisles of shelving that supported at least fifty tanks for fish. There were no saltwater tanks or exotic, big, or expensive fish. His aquariums were filled with schools of tiny catfish, zebras, tetras with bright orange spotting, big-bellied hatchetfish, and enough goldfish to populate a small pond.

Past the store proper was a little office where the old man, Mr. Arthur Bono, had a desk sitting under a corkboard decorated with dozens of pictures of good-looking young men—all dressed quite nicely. I figured that he cut these out of fashion magazines like *GQ* and *Esquire*.

From the office there was a door to a storage room that was stacked almost to the ceiling with debris of all kinds. There were broken-down cardboard boxes, broken tanks, empty cylinders of fish food, big plastic garbage bags filled with pizza boxes, dozens of empty wine bottles, and other transitory food containers.

The smell in there was pungent, but I didn't mind.

"You gotta pair of work gloves?" I asked the elderly shop owner.

He was a little guy, but his hands were larger than mine.

I went to work binding and then carrying the refuse through a back door, down an alley that ran along the side of his store, and out to the curb.

The next four hours were occupied with the removal of at least two tons of rubbish.

At the curb I could easily watch Chester and his men. They mostly smoked and drank. There was a pizza delivery that occurred when I was binding trash in the storage room. And then there was a larger drop.

A fair-size U-Haul truck drove up and two Hispanic-looking young men started unloading smallish boxes with the help of Chester's minions.

I had done a fairly poor job of stacking the trash and so used that opportunity to straighten out the mess.

There were maybe thirty boxes moved by the men into Chester's make-believe office. They stacked them quickly and haphazardly; men in a hurry. The truck drove off and Chester and his men went back to sitting and laughing, drinking and making smoke.

I'd been working on the trash pile for forty-five minutes or so when one of the men, the white one, came across the street. He was walking toward me.

I considered shooting him.

It was one thing to have the urge to kill Little Exeter. After all, he might have been part of the scheme to destroy my life. But this guy walking across Flatbush, with his hands hanging empty at his sides, was no threat and I had no reason to harbor him any ill will.

I had been thrown back into the creature formed by my imprisonment. I was a rabid dog with hardly a scrap of civility to hide the shame.

The man passed near me, nodded a friendly greeting, and went on to a black Ford parked a few doors down. He drove the car to the storefront and then, with the help of Chester and the other man, loaded the boxes into the trunk and backseat of the automobile.

Nobody could ever say that criminals were at the top of their class in public school.

"Mr. Boll," Arthur Bono said to my back.

"Yes, sir." I turned away from my prey.

"Here you go." He handed me three crisp new twenties.

"Damn," I said. "I only figured to get about half this."

"You made a deep dent in the room," he told me. "And

paying off the books costs a lot less. I'm going home now. You know, I don't feel right being out at night."

"Uh-huh." I wanted to see what Chester et al. were up to behind me, but it made sense to maintain my subterfuge.

"You should buy you some new clothes," Arthur advised. "You know clothes make the man. If you come back to-morrow morning you could finish the job and maybe make enough to buy a new shirt or even a jacket."

I thought of the young men pinned to the corkboard in his office. He was trying to compliment me.

"I'll be here at nine," I lied.

The old man smiled, shook my hand, and turned away.

Chester was standing on the curb watching as his hench-men drove off in the dark Ford. He kept an eye on them until they had driven out of sight and then went back into his empty space.

I was right behind him.

19.

HIS LEFT FOOT crossed the threshold, and mine did too. He felt my presence, but before he could respond I hit him in the back of the head with my .45. He went down on one knee and I hit him again—hard.

While he floundered on the green-and-black linoleum I did a cursory body search, coming up with a small-caliber pistol. Then I pulled the ceiling-to-floor curtains across the picture window and flipped the wall switch for the overhead fluorescent lighting.

Chester was holding the back of his head with one hand while trying to push himself up with the other. He was moving his lower jaw around as though he'd been hit there.

"Stay down," I told him.

He stopped moving, and looked up to see me straddling one of the metal folding chairs. The .45 was in my hand, pointed at his forehead.

He was up on one elbow and confused, but when he shrugged, maybe a preparation to rise, I pulled back the hammer on the gun.

The fear factor of a cocking hammer is the real advantage of a six-shooter.

He stopped moving, but his eyes were hard at work.

He was long, strong, and considering his chances of turning the tables from a prone position.

"You do and I'll shoot you in the knee," I said, "still ask my questions, then walk out the back door, leaving you a cripple for life."

"What you want, man?"

"You ran a woman named Nathali Malcolm some years back."

His face twisted, trying to show without telltale words that he didn't know what I was talking about.

"Oh?" I mocked. "Did I say that I will shoot the other knee if I'm not happy with your answers?"

"What you mean, ran?"

"If you tryin' to wait until somebody comes to the door," I said, "I will shoot you in the face and take my chances with the rest."

"That was a long time ago," he complained.

"I'm askin' right now. I'm not gonna do it again."

"I haven't seen Tatty since she got busted years ago."

"You were both arrested, but they let you off," I said. "You had twenty pounds of cocaine in the trunk'a your car and they didn't even book you."

"Who are you?" Chester Murray asked.

"Who was the last cop you talked to after they arrested you?"

"That was over ten years ago, brother. How you expect me to remember the last cop or the first?"

I stood up, my lips twisting in the anticipation of pain.

I was way out of balance in that curtained room. I should have taken the fishmonger's offer and spent another day watching Chester and his men. I should have planned out the interrogation, but I was playing it fast and loose because sooner or later, I knew, the men who had framed me would catch on to my ad hoc investigation.

Chester pulled his head back, sensing my desperation.

"Cortez," he ejaculated. "Detective Cortez. I didn't get no first name."

"What he look like?"

"I don't know, man. That was a long time past, and back then I was high day and night. I think he was Puerto Rican. Short, you know? I don't know."

Something in my eyes was scaring the gangster. It scared me too.

"What was the deal he gave you?" I asked slowly.

"He didn't want—he didn't want me to make any noise about Tatty. He said that she had information he needed and he didn't want no lawyers or nuthin' askin' about her."

"Is she your woman? Because you know that cop didn't give me no choice. If I'd'a gone up against him he would'a put me down. It was her or me and—and—and he said he just wanted information. I figured me bein' quiet would help us both."

I was silent for quite a while then. Chester and I were looking at each other, but I was sure that we were both seeing things outside that storefront.

"What's in the boxes your men drove off with?"

"You don't know?"

"Don't make me ask again, fool."

"G-g-guns. It's guns."

*   *   *

Walking the six blocks to the parking garage, and then driving back to my place on Montague, I was going over and over recent events. From the college girl to A Free Man. From the old man across the street to Chester.

I was standing right at the edge of a line that had to be crossed sooner or later.

So far Chester was still alive. I was too.

"Hi, Daddy," A.D. said when I walked through the office door.

"Honey. How you doin'?"

"Fine. You like my dress?" she asked in a bratty tone.

Standing up, she did a half turn. The dress was a dull orange color and the hem was down to her calf. It complimented her figure without broadcasting it. I knew that it cost $87.99 off the rack.

"Your mother let you wear that?"

"You remember this?" Surprise took over the spoiled look on her face.

"I was with her when she bought it. I'm surprised she still has it."

"Mama don't throw out nuthin'. I took it outta her back row in the closet."

In some ways I'd be married to Monica for the rest of my life. At least we did this one thing right.

"Any calls?"

"A man came and said that he would be waitin' for you at the wine bar."

"What man?"

"White guy with funny eyes," Aja said. "He said his name was Mel."

Before going down the street to Laniard's Wine Bar I went into my office and put away three shots of whiskey. I wanted a cigarette and lamented giving the pack away.

Wearing a dark cranberry jacket and walnut-brown trousers, he was sitting at a high stool at the window, looking out onto Montague. When he saw me he waved and maybe gave a wisp of a smile; mirth on the face of a demon. I was glad I'd had the whiskey.

I passed the maître d', a tall man in a black suit and tie. He gestured for me to wait, but I pointed at Melquarth, who, in turn, put up a welcoming hand.

I climbed up on the stool next to him.

"You look like you been workin'," he said.

"Got paid sixty bucks."

"Every penny counts."

"Why are we meeting here, Mel?"

"I didn't think you'd be too happy with me sitting in the office with your daughter."

He was right about that.

"Can I get you something?" a young woman asked.

My nostrils flared when I saw the young Asian woman clad in a coral-colored minidress. For ten years I'd held down the passion in me. But that was over. The dog was out.

"No, thank you," I said.

"I'll have another Barolo," Mel told her.

"Yes, sir."

"So?" I asked when the waitress was gone.

"I'll finish my drink and then we'll take a ride down to the Verrazano Bridge. We're going to Staten Island."

He might as well have added, "Across the river Styx."

Day turned to night in the time it took us to get Mel's vintage Ford Galaxie 500 and drive to Pleasant Plains, Staten Island. We didn't talk much; didn't turn on the radio or play CDs. Wherever we were going it was serious business.

On the south side of the small town, there stood an abandoned church. I say abandoned, but what I mean is deconsecrated. It was surrounded by an eighteen-foot stone wall. The only entrée was through a remote-control iron gate. The rectangular brick structure loomed at a height of at least two and a half stories. Twelve slender stained-glass windows ran from the ground to the eaves of the steeply slanted, dark-green-tiled roof. On one end was a silo-like cylindrical steeple, also made of brick; it rose ten feet above the rest of the structure. There was a satellite dish at the very center of the extreme-angled lower roof.

Mel drove us to the middle of the circular driveway in front of the once holy refuge.

"This is where you live?" I asked as he unlocked the double-door entrance.

When we crossed the threshold, lights snapped on in quick succession. It wasn't a huge building as far as churches go, but the high ceiling, empty space where there were once pews, and then the raised altar made me feel rather small.

"I stay here sometimes," Mel said, answering the question that I had forgotten with the light.

"Where do you sleep?"

"In the station house."

"The what?"

"This way."

Behind the altar was a small door that led to a cramped spiral stairway going down.

As in the church, the moment we entered the stairs, a series of lights came on. Thirty-seven steps led to a door barely wider than a coffin's lid. Through this door we entered a desolate room swathed in dim light abutted by a wall-size window behind which sat a bloodied man wearing only a T-shirt and boxers. His wrists were chained to a stone wall and his ankles to the floor.

The man was both pitiful and forlorn, but that's not what caught my attention. I knew the guy. He was the one Mel called Porker. One of the men Stuart Braun sent to ambush me at the West Village coffee house.

"Can he see us?" I asked.

"No."

"You been interrogating him?"

"Softened him a little bit. I was waiting for you to come up with better questions."

Mel went into a small alcove next to the left side of the window-wall. From there he pulled out a pair of folding chairs. He set these up in front of the interrogation cell window as if it were a really big-screen plasma TV.

The room we were in was dark and dusty, but Porker's room was all light stone and bright light.

"Yep," Mel said as we looked at his private production. "This is a station house of the Underground Railroad."

"Say what?"

"There were people on Staten Island who wanted to free as many slaves as they could. Over in Elliotville and under this building they did just that."

For maybe ten seconds I was distracted from the prisoner.

"I bought this building for a refuge and maybe some other business," Mel continued. "But then I discovered what had been going on back before the Civil War. I kinda like it. People should break the law if it doesn't suit them."

"Can he hear us?" I asked, motioning at Porker.

"Soundproof."

"What's his real name?"

"Simon Creighton. He was born in Jersey City. Breaks legs. Beats his girlfriends, but they love him anyway."

"What have you gotten out of him?"

"I just been beatin' him. You know... setting up the lexicon for when you got here."

"You just beat him?" I said, looking at the leg breaker's bruised, battered, and bloodied face through the slightly green-tinted glass wall.

"Anything one man does that another man understands can be defined as language," Melquarth quoted. "I read that once in an article on philology. I was looking up poisons but found that instead."

Mel went back to the little alcove from which he retrieved the chairs and came out with a very long black trench coat, a pair of thick black gloves, and a pure white mask that was reminiscent of Greek marble statuary of the gods. The white face was beautiful and manly, dispassionate and beyond pedestrian human expression.

"I put on this shit," he told me, "and it scares poor Simon almost to death."

"You got one for me?"

"Don't need it."

"Why?"

"There's earphones in the mask and an omnidirectional mike too. You just listen to what Porker got to say and tell me if I should be asking something else."

Mel first donned the trench coat, which came down over his shoes. After that he put on the mask and then the gloves. He turned that motionless and beautiful white face to me, nodded, and then went to a door on the right side of the window. That door led to another. Mel closed the first and then I saw him enter the white stone cage.

He stood motionless for at least three minutes staring at Simon Creighton.

At first the obese prisoner stared back. He was afraid, definitely, but also trying to put up a brave front. Thirty seconds into the stare down he began to tremble.

"What the fuck do you want, man?!"

Mel remained stock-still.

"Just tell me what you want . . . please."

There came a snort in the room that didn't seem to originate with either man.

"What the fuck do you need?" Simon pleaded. "Do I know you? Did I do somethin' to you?"

Mel moved his head ever so slightly, and Simon tried his best to skitter away. His chains actually rattled.

I was getting scared myself.

Another minute went by. Then Mel took a step. When

he moved you couldn't see the foot motion, so in a way he seemed to be floating.

"Please don't!" Creighton started screaming, and even though we were way under a stone building, and sound-proofed to boot, I was half-certain that somebody would hear.

Mel descended on the chained man, punching, gouging, and kicking Simon with vitriol.

The beating went on for maybe ninety seconds before I said, "Mel."

He continued and so I said, "Mel, stop it, man. I want him conscious and able to talk. I want him alive."

Three more blows and Mel stood up from the bleeding, blubbering man. He turned to what must have been a mir-rored interior, and I could see three spots of blood on the otherwise immaculate mask.

"Ask him why he was at the Liberté Café the other night."

"What were you doing at the Liberté Café?" It was Mel's voice but somewhat altered, and it didn't come from him but rather speakers in the walls of both cell and anteroom.

Simon started shivering. "Me and Fido and Vince was there to catch a man with a red flower in his buttonhole, but he never came."

"Who sent you?"

"A guy named Marmot, William James Marmot."

"What were you going to do with the man when you got him?"

"I don't know."

Mel kicked Simon in his left cheekbone, slamming his head against the white stone wall behind. The impact left a pocked red imprint on the granite surface.

Simon actually shrieked.

"We was supposed to grab him and question him about who he was workin' for," he said. And because he didn't want to get kicked again, he added, "Marmot's a private security analyst who works with this guy named Antrobus, Augustine Antrobus. Marmot didn't know, but Vince knew that him and Antrobus was a team."

"What does this Antrobus do?"

"He has a security business too, but he's a loner, like. He does work through private contractors. Just a couple'a women in his office. Vince once did a gig for him."

"What were you supposed to do after you got your answers?" Mel asked.

"Do what?" Simon said with feigned innocence.

"Yeah," Mel agreed. "Do what to the dude with the red flower in his buttonhole."

Simon started crying, not so much like a man or a woman but more like a child bereft at both his misdemeanor and its punishment.

"That's all I need, Mel," I said. "Come on back out here."

Simon Creighton sobbed while Mel and I sat in the folding chairs. He removed the mask and placed it on his lap. It sat there tilting back, looking up at me as if in judgment.

"You know the people he said?" Mel asked.

"No. But I should be able to find out easy enough."

"I could just kill this one," Mel remarked after a few beats of silence.

The madman created by Rikers was still there in my head. The greatest crime I'd committed so far was in the four seconds it took to consider Mel's offer.

"Did he see you when you grabbed him?" I asked as a kind of charade.

"Nah. I put knockout gas in his car. When he opened the door it was released," the watchmaker bragged. "He was out before he could get the key in the ignition."

"Then he doesn't know anything about us."

"He knows what we asked him. He could tell somebody that."

"Probably won't," I said with faux sagacity. "But even if he does, they don't know who I am. Maybe if they know someone has identified them they'll get rash and make some mistake."

"Might be right," Mel agreed. "You know, this is the second time I was primed to kill this motherfucker. I don't like the tease."

Taking a deep breath, he went to his all-purpose alcove and came out with a slender white leather briefcase. He got down on his knees, set the case on the chair, and opened it. He took out a hypodermic needle and syringe that had already been prepped.

Looking up at me with a smile he said, "Always be prepared."

Again in his mask Mel approached Simon. The prisoner cried and begged, twisted and turned, kicked and even tried to bite Mel, in order to avoid that injection.

I drove one of Mel's cars—a 1973 dark-brown GTO. He took the wheel of Simon's car—a Cadillac from the nineties. Simon was unconscious in the back seat of the Brougham.

We crossed over into New Jersey.

I followed them across the Korean War Veterans Parkway, past New Brunswick, and down U.S. 1. Three miles toward Trenton there was a turnoff.

It was a rest stop designed for car problems and tired truckers. The rest stop was empty. By the time I got there Mel was standing next to the Caddy.

"He'll wake up in the morning fucked outta his mind," Mel assured me on the ride back to Brooklyn. "He'll be thankful to be alive and wondering where the fuck he was. He'll be so scared that it might even be worth it not killin' him."

"You're crazy, aren't you, Mel?"

"Yeah. I guess I am. I don't wanna be. It's not like I can get to it, you know what I mean? I love life. I'm good at shit. It's just . . . I don't know."

20.

I GOT INTO my apartment sometime after 3:00 a.m., lay down on the raised bed, and stared out into the darkness of the room. I could tell by the quality of my consciousness that I wouldn't sleep that night.

I stayed there in the bed so that at least my body could be at repose. I tried not to think about the cases or the things I had done that day.

I finally settled on remembering the retired merchant marine Athwart Miller and how we'd play Go in his bar after it was closed at night. I could have picked up whatever information I needed in a few minutes, but he always had hot grog ready and the board set out at the far end of the bar.

I never even came close to winning. He was far superior to me, but I was the only person he knew who'd come to the bar and play him.

I once asked why he'd even waste his time playing someone so inferior to his skill.

He said, "I play you because you're here and every time

we sit down you're a little better. The best you can ask for is an opponent that improves. It's like looking into a mirror with your eyes closed."

I woke up surprised that I had fallen asleep. Before letting the day get away with me I said a silent thanks for the gifts of the dead.

Among the thousands of pages of notes that Willa Portman provided was a file on Lamont Charles: gambler, con man, and the only survivor of the Blood Brothers of Broadway not in prison or missing.

The photographs of Charles showed a handsome man with almost copper-colored skin and straightened hair. He had a killer smile and eyes that somehow came up out of the photograph.

He was a resident of the Aramaya Rest Home on Neptune Avenue in the heart of Coney Island. It was a three-story brick building not two blocks from the ocean.

The reception area's walls were lined with chairs and sofas on which reclined at least two dozen old men and women who had outlived their usefulness but still clung to the memories and hope of life.

Mostly but not all white, they stared, read newspapers, talked to themselves or others. Sprawled out, leaning on canes, and trapped in wheelchairs, they napped, dozed, cried, and muttered. The room smelled strongly of urine, dead skin, alcohol, and disinfectant.

I walked down the aisle of tortured souls, a modern-day Dante wandering through a half-hearted beach re-sort in hell. The inmates reached and called out to me.

They watched as I went by, wishing, I believed, that they had the strength to walk away from their private damnation.

"Can I help you?" asked a blue-haired lady in nurse-like white. She was somewhere in her sixties, which made her the second-youngest person in the room.

"Lamont Charles," I said.

The short, well-preserved white woman's face brightened and she gave a smile usually reserved for grandchildren and fond memories of the dead.

"Mr. Charles," she said as if the words were a mantra designed to open the gates of heaven.

"Yes. Can he have visitors?"

"I don't know why he doesn't have more. If we had a dozen like him I think we might get something accomplished."

I had no idea what she meant but asked, "Can I see him?"

The small elevators at Aramaya were in constant use so I took the stairs to the third floor and followed the receptionist's directions to the recreation room.

It was a large area with a succession of windowed doors leading out onto a deck that looked over the ocean.

This room was a maze of sofas, chairs, wheelchairs, and game tables. There were at least forty residents in the same sad shape as their brethren downstairs. I looked around for a somewhat younger man, three-quarters paralyzed.

"Can I help you?"

The question was asked by a twenty-something black

man with bulging muscles and an orderly's teal garb. He had the use of all his limbs.

"Lamont Charles."

He was the only person out on the deck. It was a mild day, maybe fifty-five degrees, with a toothless breeze wafting through. Lamont was sitting in an electric wheelchair, holding a mirror in front of his face with his one good hand. He'd put down the mirror, pick up a comb, run this through his hair, and then retrieve the mirror to examine his work so far.

"Mr. Charles?" I asked.

Still looking at himself, he said, "Yes?"

"My name is Oliver, Joe Oliver."

I moved between him and the view of the ocean.

After a moment he looked up and said, "Cop?"

"Used to be. A long time ago. Now I'm private."

He put down the mirror and smiled like he used to in the old days before being shot down.

"You like it out here?" he asked. You could hear North Carolina in his voice.

"A little chilly."

"That's why I got me two blankets. You know the smell'a that place back there is bound to be bad for you. So I come out here every day to clean out my lungs. I don't care how cold it gets, a red-blooded man needs fresh air."

A seagull swooped down and landed on the railing maybe a dozen feet from us. It gave us its sidelong glance, hoping for crumbs or maybe a discarded fish.

"Why you here, Mr. Oliver?"

"I've been asked to look into the conviction of A Free

Man. There are those who believe he was set up to be killed and then, when that failed, framed."

"You got ID?"

I held up my PI's license in its leather folder.

"Hand it here," Lamont said.

He took the ID and held it like he had the mirror. Then he sniffed and handed it back.

"Manny's on death row, brother. What you think anybody could do 'bout that?"

"Maybe prove that Valence and Pratt were dirty and that they not only tried to kill Man, but they also killed, and in your case wounded, most of the rest of the Blood Brothers of Broadway."

Charles's right eye started fluttering. His smile turned, momentarily, into a sneer.

"Hurts like a mothahfuckah, you know, man?" he said.

"What does?"

"This pain in my back. They prescribed oxycodone, but I only take it on the weekends. I only take it then 'cause everybody deserves a li'l peace sometimes."

I didn't know what to say. I felt bad for lamenting a few months in solitary confinement compared to what Lamont and all the other residents of Aramaya were experiencing.

"Who hired you?" Lamont asked.

"I can't say."

"Manny know you on the job?"

"Not yet."

The smile came back to the gambler's lips.

"You know once the state sentences a man to death you got to have DNA evidence or Jesus himself got to climb up out the ground."

"DNA won't help here," I said.

"And J.C. busy," Lamont agreed.

He looked past me over the water and I leaned back to perch on the weatherworn wood rail.

"What happened to you, Mr. Charles?"

That was the right question. He wasn't going to worry about anybody but the man in his mirror.

"They shot me in the back," he said. "Shot me five times and ran. They didn't know how lucky I was, must'a thought I cheated at cards."

"Gamblers shot you?"

"Fuck no. A gambler would give me a head shot. Any gambler know me knows my luck. Shit. I win when I wanna be losin'."

"Was it Valence and Pratt?"

"Or somebody they worked with," Lamont said. "They killed all the rest'a my friends, Lana's in prison, and Tanya's missin'—prob'ly dead. I say a prayer to Manny every night for gettin' us some justice. You know them cops was bad, from drugs to hos. And you better believe they didn't give a damn."

"What did they do?"

"Sold drugs to kids and kids to child molesters. Then they blackmailed the child molesters. They took over private business like gamblin' and killed anybody aksed why. Manny was a war hero and schoolteacher. How a mothah-fuckah like that gonna turn his head an' forget?"

"Sometimes people like that work with people like those cops," I suggested.

I was trying to get Lamont angry, out of his game. But he just grinned.

"You think he decided to make a clubhouse for the triple B and invite kids to play snooker and do their homework because he wanna turn 'em out? That's a white man's game, man. When seven brothers and sisters get together to help po' kids that's just what they doin'. An' you was a cop so you know it's true."

I had my doubts, but what stumped me was Lamont seemed to be telling the truth.

"If you people were so poor and so innocent, then how do you pay for this rest home?" I put to him. "This shit cost maybe a thousand dollars a week."

"Thirteen hundred sixty-fi'e dollars," he corrected.

"You win that at bingo?"

"I'm a gambler but I'm no fool, Mr. Oliver. I had me lifetime-care health insurance since my brother Andrew died in my house from lung cancer. Took him seventeen months to pass on. Me and him and his wife, Yvette, lived in my one room. Make this place look like Disneyland."

"If you and the other Blood Brothers weren't competing with the cops, then why they come down on you like that?"

"Why any American go to war?" he said. "We was fuckin' with they business. We talked to the girls and boys they prostituted and organized marches in front of stores they protected. Manny hired a lawyer to sue the city. He thought that that would keep us safe from reprisals." Lamont grunted a laugh. "Mr. Man was a optimist . . . no, no, he was a *idealist*. He believed in what he was doin' and he got you to believe it too."

"Who was the lawyer?" I asked.

"Rose Hooper."

"Manhattan practice?"

"Used to be. Bein' a lawyer I suppose that she now sits court in hell."

"Murdered?"

"Mugging, they say." He looked up at me. "What do you say?"

Being a cop, I didn't want to believe Lamont. He was the kind of guy I rousted and arrested, questioned, and, if the need arose, threatened. But I had lots of experience with seasoned liars. He didn't seem to be one of them.

"Mr. Charles?" a woman said.

She was in her thirties but carried herself in a younger pose. She wore a green dress and a frilly white sweater. Her black shoes had respectable heels and her makeup had been applied with care. There were little gold flashes at the corners of her eyes.

New York white, she had no discomfort standing alone on a deck with two black men.

"Miss Gorman," Lamont said. "Meet Mr. Joe Oliver. He used to be a cop."

Also being New York white, she wasn't necessarily fond of people in my profession.

"What do you want with Mr. Charles?"

"I..."

"He came here to aks if me and Manny weren't fingered, Loretta."

"Are you investigating Lamont's case?" she asked me.

"Not directly," I admitted. "I'm trying to see if Mr. Man's conviction might be an injustice."

I was used to the disbelief in her gaze.

"Me and Miss Gorman are goin' out for hot dogs, Mr. Oliver. We do that at least once a week."

"You guys friends?"

"I used to volunteer here before I got a job at Mercy Hospital," she said. "We started our hot dog lunches then."

It was no surprise that a young woman would be smitten with Lamont. Women didn't necessarily need good men to excite them. What they needed, and most men needed too, was somebody who understood their desires and their fears—not necessarily in that order.

"Well," I said, pushing up from the splintery railing, "I guess I'll let you guys get to it."

I'd reached the door when Lamont called out, "Oliver."

I turned to see him scribbling something down on a little tray that the wheelchair offered.

When I got back to him and his date, he said, "I believe you."

"Oh?"

"Lotsa cops and lawyers and other thugs have been up here talkin' to me about Manny. They wanna know if he did anything wrong that they could pin on him. You know, like if he shoplifted a can of stewed tomatoes once, that proves he's a murderer. I haven't told them word one. But you ask the right questions and even if you don't like me you still got natural respect."

This compliment reminded me of Mel.

"Here." He held up the slip of paper. On this he had printed an address and a phone number.

"Miranda Goya. She the one girl we saved who I know where she at. You don't have to call her. I'll do that. But you could go there anytime tomorrow afternoon or after that. Manny put his life on the line to save that girl. She will stand up for him."

I considered the address for a few seconds, felt my brow furrow, and wondered whether I had convinced Lamont of my intentions or he was setting me up.

"Naw, man," the gambler said. "Even if I thought you was dirty I'd just say I didn't know nuthin'. I ain't about to put my one good hand in cuffs over some ex-cop I don't know."

"You read minds, Mr. Charles?"

"Better. I read men."

21.

I DROVE HOME, parked the car in the small underground lot that Kristoff Hale has for his tenants, and then once again walked across the Brooklyn Bridge.

That was midday and so there was a good deal of foot traffic. The path is divided—on one side pedestrians ruled and on the other bicycles whizzed past. There isn't enough room for both and even if there was, tourists don't really understand. They're often standing in the bike path, posing for pictures or taking in the sights. And then there are those privileged individuals who feel that they have just as much right to be in the bicycle lanes as the bikes do.

I stick to the side of the path marked for pedestrians, refusing to move out of the way of couples and groups who don't get or respect the rules. I like the rules; following them proves to me that I'm a civilized man.

I turned left on Broadway and hoofed it down into the heart of the Financial District, what they call Wall Street. I came upon a huge steel, glass, and blue marble building owned by Citizens Bank of Eastern Europe, whoever they might be.

It was a bustling building populated by a broad swath of cultures sporting everything from twig-littered dreadlocks to pinstripe blue silk. There were eleven banks of elevators. Number nine was dedicated to Suliman Investments between floors forty-four and fifty-eight.

"May I help you?" a tall black guard in a brass-colored uniform asked me.

Behind him stood two other guards, one white and the other descended from Asia. I wondered if they sent out guards the same color of people they might have to refuse entrée.

"Joe Oliver for Jocelyn Bryor," I announced.

"Do you have an appointment?"

He was a young man who it seemed was prone to jump to conclusions. He had already decided that I would be turned away and asked the question to cut to that eventuality.

"Joe Oliver for Jocelyn Bryor," I repeated.

"I asked you a question," the hall guard—his name tag read FORTHMAN—said.

"I didn't come here to answer your questions, son. I came here to see Ms. Bryor. It's your job to call her assistant and announce me."

"I'm not your son."

"But you are their bitch." I was ready for a fight. Those residents of Aramaya had made me mad at God and all his, or her, creation.

"What?" Forthman said in a threatening tone.

The Asian sentry, an older man, read Forthman's shoulders and hurried toward us.

"What's the problem here?" he asked. He had a slight English accent. At least this surprised me.

"I asked him if he had an appointment," the young black man blamed.

"I'm here to see Jocelyn Bryor," I said to the new player.

"But he don't have no appointment."

The Asian man looked at me, into my eyes, and asked, "What is your name, sir?"

"Joe Oliver. Some people call me King."

"Wait here, sir," the older sentinel asserted gently.

"But, Chin—," Forthman managed to say.

"I'll take care of this, Robert" was Chin's reply.

Chin went to a standup desk anchored to the wall and pulled a phone from behind the plain facade.

Robert Forthman was staring daggers at me so I made a gesture with both hands, welcoming him to make manifest his anger.

He clenched his fists and I smiled. He took a step forward and the white guard moved up behind Forthman and uttered something. Forthman hesitated and the white man said something else. With a violent turn, the tall black uniform did a complete one-eighty and walked down the aisle of elevators to and through a doorway on the opposite end.

"Ms. Bryor will see you," Chin said before Forthman was gone.

The white guard gestured for me and I went to stand next to a lift door.

He pushed a button and said, "That kid's a light heavyweight."

"That all? I thought he might'a had a gun."

The elevator door opened and I went through.

The white guy leaned in after me, held a card in front of a sensor plate, and pressed the button for floor fifty-seven.

The car floated up at a respectable speed. I wondered about my reception. Gladstone told me about Bryor quitting the force and moving to the private sector. I had reason to hate that woman. This was why I was willing to pick a fight with a boxer.

The doors to the onyx-and-gold elevator car opened onto what looked like a foyer to some grand East Hampton mansion.

A beautiful black girl in a very tasteful dress greeted me.

"Mr. Oliver?" she asked.

"Yes."

She was tall and thin, probably athletic. Her dress was the pink of the inside of a deep-sea clamshell. The necklace she wore was beaded with light-blue sapphires and her shoes were the pale and red-brown of the fur that some forest creatures produce.

"Miss Bryor will see you now."

"And your name is?"

The question caught her off guard but the smile didn't falter.

"Excuse me," she said. "My name is Norris, Lydia Norris."

"Lead on, Ms. Norris."

She took me down long wide halls that were carpeted and quiet. There were office doors that were mostly closed and very little foot traffic.

At the end of a cream-carpeted passage was a double doorway. Lydia pushed open the eight-foot-high, four-foot-wide doors and stood aside, gesturing for me to enter.

The office was wide and deep, with a curved window for the wall overlooking Ellis Island and the Statue of Liberty. The carpet was dark brown and the oval desk was chiseled from a stone much like white slate.

There was a dark blue sofa with no back to the left. Jocelyn was sitting there wearing an emerald ensemble that might have been either a full-length dress or a pants suit—though it was most reminiscent of the new gliding suits that modern daredevils used to fly from precipitous mountainsides.

She stood from the sofa to greet me. Like many a woman cop, she was pretty short. Her facial features were boxy, but even still she had the unexpected beauty of Isabella Rossellini.

"Joe," she said with a guilty smile.

"Jocelyn."

"Come sit with me."

I approached her and we shook hands. We were ex-cops, so hugging was pretty much out of the question.

"It's good to see you," she said when we were seated.

"I'm actually surprised that you let me up here."

"Why would you say that?"

"The way you handled my investigation I figured you had me for some kinda masher deserved to be thrown under the jail."

Her squarish, delicate face expressed pain. She looked away at her stone desk and then out into the sky.

"I am very sorry for what I did to you, Joe," she said, bringing those wandering, lustrous brown eyes back to me. "The only reason I never called was because I didn't think I deserved asking your forgiveness."

"Uh..." I was at a loss for words to say the least, stupefied by the claim and its apparent honesty.

I had hated this woman for showing my wife the video of me and Nathali/Beatrice. I came here to confront her for participating in my frame. I was willing to fight the guy downstairs because I couldn't, or at least wouldn't, strike her.

"What?" she asked. "You thought I had something to do with what they did to you?"

"You—you showed that video to my wife," I said. "She left me in Rikers when we had money for bail."

Jocelyn was near my age, and I was slowly being convinced of her beauty. It was like the dawn of a morning after the death of a beloved king. Everything was beautiful but salted with the sorrow of his passing.

"I'm sorry for that too," she said. "I believed that you'd raped that woman at the time. But even if it was true, there was no reason to show Monica that tape. Everything I did concerning your case was wrong."

"Did you set me up?"

Jocelyn gave no assent. She just gazed at me like a land-bound midwestern farmer seeing the sea for the first time.

"You've thought that for the last ten years?" she asked.

"And more."

"I heard they had you in solitary for three months."

I brushed two fingertips across my scar.

"To keep from gettin' any more like this," I said.

"When they told me where you were I was actually happy," she admitted. "A man, a policeman using his authority to rape a woman the way everyone said you did; that man deserved to suffer."

"Who said?"

"That woman who blamed you, my superior, Prosecutor Hines," Jocelyn listed. "There was that video and papers waiting for you at the station.

"And then one day I heard that you'd been released. That the charges had been dropped and you were off the force.

"I went to the files and everything was gone. No tape, no statement, not even the report of your arrest. I tried to find Nathali Malcolm, but there was no record of her either.

"I went to every person I knew connected with the arrest, but no one told me anything. My old supervisor said to forget about it. She said that you had been fired with no pension and even the union was hands-off.

"That's when I knew that you'd been set up. There was something you were into that made you a danger. They used me to go after you because they knew how I felt about cops and sexual misconduct. They knew I'd go after you with all my ability.

"I quit the force ten months later. When the precinct captain asked me why, I told him that I just couldn't take the shit anymore."

I believed her. I knew what she said was true. They had given my friend Gladstone the assignment. They had set up Beatrice so she couldn't say no.

"Prosecutor Hines must have known something," I said. "He might have pressed charges based on a lie, but when they asked him to drop the case...he must have known something."

"Ben died seven years ago," she said. "He'd moved back down to North Carolina and had a stroke."

"And you were too ashamed to call me and tell me what they'd done?" I accused.

"No. No, Joe. I was sure that you knew who did it and why. I thought you kept quiet either because they paid you off or that they'd kill you if you said anything else."

"Kill me?"

"I figured they put you in jail to let them finish you in there," she agreed. "If you died there, nobody would ask questions. After all, you abused that woman hiding behind your shield. I thought you had made some kind of deal with whoever framed you and they let you slide with a dismissal."

Her words sat me back on the backless couch. I put my left fist down on the leather cushion to keep from falling sideways.

"So you really think they were going to kill me and then they changed their minds?"

"That's the only way it made sense," she reasoned. "I mean, they had you, but obviously they didn't want you in court. One reason I never came to you about it was that I thought that you had been made part of the deal, whatever that was. If I got involved they might have come after me."

I leaned forward, putting my elbows on my knees. They were trying to kill me at first but then changed their minds. This rendition of my experience actually made sense. With a decent lawyer I had a good shot at getting the charges dismissed.

"Why are you here, Joe?" Jocelyn asked.

"I came to blame you for framing me," I said. "That and to get the names of the people you worked with."

"Why now? I mean, it's over, right?"

"My daughter's all grown up. Nobody needs me now."

"So you're just gonna get yourself killed?"

I hadn't put it in those words, but she was right. Whoever set me up like that wouldn't hesitate at murder.

"Have you ever heard of Adamo Cortez or Hugo Cumberland?" I asked the corporate security analyst.

There were three jets in the sky over New Jersey, circling Newark Airport. Next to them was Jocelyn Bryor's beautiful face wondering about my question.

"What is this, Joe?" she asked.

"I need to find out who set me up."

"Sounds like you already know."

"Not so it makes any sense."

We sat a minute more.

"My girls are eight and thirteen," she said.

"I'm not asking you to do anything, to testify to anything. I just need to find out who did this to me. I got to know."

Jocelyn took a deep breath and then said, "It was a man calling himself Adamo Cortez who brought Nathali Malcolm to me. He said that she'd been forced to have sex by you and was afraid for her life. He showed me the video.

"Five months later I was down at headquarters to meet with a psychiatrist over my increasing lack of interest in the job. I saw Cortez and approached him. He put me off and left. When I asked the woman he was talking to about where he went, she said he left the building but that his name wasn't Cortez; it was Hugo Cumberland—a private specialist sometimes used by the department."

"What kind of specialist?" I asked.

"Are you here to yoke me, Joe?"

"No. What kind of specialist?"

"She didn't say and I didn't ask."

The air between me and Jocelyn was thick and soundless.

She didn't want to be talking to me but still felt a sense of duty. I didn't want to know what I'd learned, but I couldn't wipe it away.

"The woman didn't tell you anything else?" I asked.

"No. But Adamo wasn't at her office. He was sitting with a captain named Holder. I asked Holder's assistant for Cumberland's number, but she said that Cumberland was just a name he used and that his real name was Paul Convert."

"Why she tell you that?"

"Girls can be chatty, Joe. And most of the time we don't take men's secrets so seriously."

"He was a short guy with a mustache?" I asked. "Looked Puerto Rican?"

"That's him."

Walking north half a block on Broadway, I turned right on Exchange Place and had just crossed New Street on the way to Broad when two official-looking SUVs cut me off—back and front.

Four doors slid open and men in dark uniforms disgorged from the vehicles.

I considered going for my pistol, but when two more men jumped out, I gave up on that mode of self-defense. Instead I stood still with my hands a few inches from my sides. The men tackled me like I was a football dummy, took my gun, and clapped on restraints, hand and foot.

I saw a couple of shocked pedestrians before a black bag was put over my head.

The next thing I knew I was in the back of one of the SUVs. It was moving and I was not.

22.

THE DRIVE WAS a bit more than an hour, I figured. We went through the Battery Tunnel and into Brooklyn—I was pretty sure about that. We drove long enough to make it somewhere out in Queens but not much farther. Whoever had grabbed me wanted to stay in the city.

That alone told me a lot.

When the car parked I was getting ready to yell as soon as the door slid open. They might kill me, but I'd leave a marker that maybe Mel or Gladstone would find.

But my captors had thought of that. Someone shoved a rag filled with sweet-smelling chloroform over my nose and mouth.

I had to breathe.

Coming to on a basement floor, I was aware of being cold; chilled to the bone, as my father used to say. The air was dank, filled with fungal spores, bringing to mind the heavy atmosphere of graveyards and dungeons. My hands were cuffed behind me, but my legs were unfettered. I made it to my feet, trying to keep down the deep-seated anxieties of a man terrified by dark containment.

There was a low-watt bulb imparting its tame glow from the low ceiling. A pretty long and steep stairway led up through a hole-like corridor to an upper door. I put one foot on the bottom stair and a deep gong sounded.

I took no more steps and within seconds the door above opened.

"Stay off the stairs," a man silhouetted by light called down.

"Why am I here?"

His reply was to slam the door shut.

There was a stool and a worktable in the cramped cellar. No exit except for the steep stairway. There were no tools to be seen, no weapons or objects that could be turned into weapons. The men who accosted me were young and well trained. I certainly couldn't hope to defeat even one of them with both hands shackled behind my back.

I walked around for maybe an hour, looking to see if there was anything I could turn to my advantage; there wasn't.

And so I decided to sit on the stool and lean back against the edge of the worktable—awaiting my fate.

Waiting is the detective's stock-in-trade. We wait for the right hour, a certain phone call, or something different from what has gone before. It's not a profession that's a natural fit for my nature, but the great thing about human beings is that they can and do adapt.

The natural boon of spending most of my time quiescent and inactive opened the trapdoor of deep thought. I fell right into it.

Sitting on that stool I decided that my captors were after me over the frame and not A Free Man. Not that it made much difference. In both cases I was the pariah and they the judgment if not actually the law.

Something slammed down and I realized that I had fallen asleep on the stool. Two men stood in front of me in the flimsy light. One of them had an automatic pointed in my general direction. The other man, I figured, had put down the tray loud enough to wake me up.

The armed man, dressed all in black, was tall and masked. His disguise was like a ski mask but it was designed expressly for the purpose of concealing his identity. The second guy wore a simple brown suit, no mask, and exhibited no weapon. He was on the short side, with skin darker than most white men.

"Stand up and turn around," the unmasked man commanded. "I'm going to unlock the cuffs while you eat."

I did as he said and he as he promised.

There were three fried eggs, four strips of bacon, a glass of grapefruit juice, and a cup of coffee on the brown resin tray.

My stomach was upset from the chloroform, but I ate and drank, as I had learned to do in prison. You never knew when the next meal was coming.

"You are the cause of great concern," the man without the mask or gun said. The words were sophisticated, but the accent was deep Brooklyn. "People all over New York are asking why you don't leave well enough alone."

"Who are you?" I replied.

"My name is Adamo Cortez. I think you had your friend the Haitian cop ask about me."

"Your name came up," I said in a relaxed, informal tone, "and I decided to see what you know . . . Detective."

"Where'd my name come up?"

"In a dream."

The liar didn't like my lie.

"Stand up and turn around," he said, a little less friendly than before.

"I still got a piece'a bacon on my plate."

"Lean over and eat it like a dog."

On one hand I wanted to hit him, but on the other I didn't want to be shot. So I stood and turned and allowed the chains to be snapped back into place.

When I was seated again, the masked man with the automatic went back up the stairs and closed the door.

When the gunsel was gone, my true captor leaned up against the table next to me.

"You've been talking to people," he said. "Making noise, brandishing guns. You went to see Jocelyn Bryor and Little Exeter Barret. You're asking questions about me. I don't like that."

"I haven't asked a thing about you . . . Mr. Paul Convert."

The fairly genteel look on my inquisitor's face evaporated. His brows furrowed as if maybe he was the heavy in some silent film from the Golden Age. He stared at me, stood away from the table, maybe considered hitting, stabbing, or shooting me, and then went up the stairs.

I shouldn't have used the name I'd learned. I should have asked forgiveness and buried my anger in other cases—A Free Man, for instance. But there comes a time when a man has to stand up and be heard, a time when their threats do not outweigh his freedom.

*   *   *

The time for waiting was over. Now that I knew the players, I also knew the play. They were going to kill me, and soon.

I'm a pretty supple guy. Once a week for six years I took yoga classes at a studio on Montague until the rent pushed out the young lesbian couple who taught there. They moved only about a mile away, but I didn't have the time for that commute.

Still, my hips and knees were pretty limber, and with real concentration I was able to get the big toe of my left foot over the chain between my wrists. The right foot was easier, and my hands, though not free, were at least in a position to do one thing or another.

I shattered the stool, making one of the legs a good club. Then I searched around the cellar one more time, looking for either an exit or a better weapon. I found neither.

Then I examined the stairs.

Only the first three steps seemed wired for the alarm. This gave me a slight edge. I took the round seat of the stool and the leg turned club in hand and leaped up to the fourth step, teetered a bit, and then found the inner balance the yoga instructors always talked about. I climbed the rest of the way, stood as far to the side as I could, and then carefully let the seat roll down. It did as I wished, and when it hit the last three steps, the gong went off.

I pressed back against the wall, the door flung open, and a foot crossed the threshold. I hit his ankle for all I was worth. He tumbled forward, and I hit him across the nose with a swing that Babe Ruth would have been proud of. He tumbled down the stairs and I raced after.

I was able to retrieve his automatic and aim just as another mercenary appeared at the top of the stair.

I shot only twice. I didn't know then that these were the only two men left to guard me.

I could see the sole of my second victim's shoe from where I crouched. The man I'd battered into unconsciousness was still breathing. I searched him for more weapons but found none. After maybe thirty seconds, I began to make my way back up.

The man was dead. One shot had made a hole just above the right eye. There were a few items of value left on his clay: the key to my cuffs, a telephone number scrawled on a neatly folded sheet of paper, and a cell phone that looked like it had just been cut from its plastic wrapper.

In his wallet was an identity card for Security Managers Inc., a worldwide prison, prisoner transport, and mercenary provider. His name had been Tom Eliot.

On the third floor of the suburban Queens house I found a briefcase chock-full of fifty-dollar bills. Payment for my demise, no doubt.

I handcuffed the unconscious soldier to the worktable in the basement, then used his keys to drive one of the SUVs out of the driveway.

23.

IT DIDN'T TAKE long to become a fugitive, just a few days of pretty good police work.

"Hello?" Aja-Denise said on the seventh ring. "Who's this?"

"It's me."

"Hi, Daddy." There was a smile in her words.

I was driving across the Fifty-Ninth Street Bridge.

"Honey, I got to talk fast so listen close."

"Okay." She got serious.

I told her the general outline of my situation in no more than four sentences.

"What you need me to do?" she asked.

"Tell your mother and her fool of a husband that you all need to be out of town in the hour. Tell her that it's cops' rules."

"Cops' rules," she repeated.

"That's right."

"How can I talk to you if I have to?"

"I will text the next number I get to Tesserat's phone using that code we made up."

"Okay," she said, and we both disconnected.

"Hullo," he answered, a dreamy note to his voice, sounding almost like a real watchmaker-repairman from another era.

"Somebody connected to the cops grabbed me with pay soldiers. I think they were planning to kill me."

"You all right?"

"Free and not wounded. I got one'a their cars and phones."

"Ditch 'em both and get over to me."

"First I got to settle," I said. "But I'll be there by tonight."

I parked the SUV at an underground garage in Midtown. I exited, trying my best not to be recorded on their security cams. After that I climbed down into the hole in the ground.

At the best of times I don't like subways. All those people, and many of them, I knew from thirteen years on the force, were armed. Buskers, pickpockets, madmen and -women, and then all the potential victims, whom no police force on earth could protect.

My breathing in the crowded southbound car was erratic, and I could feel my heart beating. That cellar had been my grave for some hours, but it was just now that the terror was settling in.

Six times I decided to leave the country. Canada and then maybe Mongolia or Lithuania, Cuba or Chad. Jackie Robinson's son made a new life for himself in Tanzania. Six times I steadied myself and thought of how I could dig my way out of a grave with no name on it.

The worst part of that leg of the journey was that I didn't have a book on me. I needed to read something. It didn't matter what.

A woman across the aisle got off at Thirty-Fourth Street leaving a throwaway newspaper on the seat next to her. I literally leapt out of my seat and grabbed the rag before anyone else could. Then I went to the chrome pole set between the center doors of the car and read all about Chinee Love, a black-skinned, yellow-haired New Age singer whose band played pots and pans behind her performance-art songs.

I climbed out of that hell at the West Fourth Street station and walked nine blocks to Name-it Storage facility. Their records knew me as Nigel Beard. I had a pretty big space on the thirteenth level.

It was a crowded room, twenty by twenty-five feet. There were boxes of books, papers, weapons, and other, more particular, tools of my trade.

But before I did anything else I sat down in the stuffed chair that I kept dead center of the secret workspace.

There was electricity, so I had light. There were a thousand books, so I didn't have to read.

Over the next hour or so my breathing normalized and my heart gave up its drumroll. I was innocent of any crime. Those men had kidnapped me. I had every right to defend myself.

And then there were the simple pleasures of life: a comfortable chair and air to breathe, no chains or chimeric criminals who would kill you just for wanting to reveal the truth.

*   *   *

After calming down I used bottled water, bar soap, and a disposable razor to shave my head.

Against the south wall of the storage room stood a rosewood armoire that was eight feet high and six wide. From this I took a makeup case I bought while taking a class called Hollywood Makeup Techniques.

I studied that particular facet of cosmetics for one reason—to be able to don convincing fake facial hair when I needed anonymity. I realized over the years that a mustache made my face look different. Something about my nose, the distance between my eyes, and the shape of my skull.

After attaching the natural-hair lip wig and sideburns to hide my telltale scar, I waxed my bald pate and then studied myself in a hand mirror, as Lamont Charles had done.

I was pretty well satisfied with the results.

There was a dull ochre trench coat hanging from the closet pole of my wardrobe. It was stuffed with wadded material so that when I put it on I looked forty to fifty pounds heavier.

I then spent a good while looking at myself in the full-length mirror that lined the inner left-side door of the armoire. While checking out my disguise, I was considering a next move.

The disguise was solid. Scar, size, face, and hair all altered enough. On any other job I would have stopped there. But this was a situation where I couldn't afford a mistake. My visage was still too cop-like.

So I reached into the armoire and took out a pair of horn-rimmed glasses with clear, thick, nonprescription lenses. The transformation was now complete. Rather than a Cro-Magnon cop I was a Neanderthal nerd.

One thing I had learned in high school was that in sports you always had to move in a direction that your opponent did not expect. From Ping-Pong to prizefighting, the man with the unexpected moves was the player most likely to win.

Police work is a kind of intellectual sport, like Go or chess. And sometimes you have to make a move to fool yourself, a move that will keep you from putting yourself in the enemy's line of fire.

That's why I decided to pay a visit to Augustine Antrobus.

Antrobus Limited was listed on Fifth Avenue in the upper Sixties. It was a tall and slender building plated with shiny brown stone with slit-like windows that made an odd pattern like a modern painting composed of matchsticks.

"May I help you?" a guard asked. He was standing behind a chest-high station made from see-through yellow plastic.

"Antrobus Limited."

The security man looked ten years younger than he was, and appeared to be forty. His blue eyes took in my bulky coat, shiny pate, and geeky glasses. Though unrecognizable, I did look odd.

"Name?" he said after this brief moment of hesitation.

"Nigel Beard." The ID in my wallet said the same.

There was a computer in front of the guard; I could see it through the yellow plastic.

"I don't see a Beard here," he said after a moment or two.

"Call them and see."

Security didn't like the command, but he picked up the phone and hit some numbers.

"I have a Beard down here says he wants to come up." A few words passed, and he held the phone down and said, "The girls in his office don't have any record of you either."

"Tell them that it's about William James Marmot. Something I think they'll want to be apprised of."

Again that natural hesitation and then a few more words through the wire.

He put the phone down and looked me in the glasses.

"Floor twenty-two."

"Thank you kindly," I said, experimenting with my new, disposable personality.

It wasn't a crowded building. Only a young woman in a black skirt and white blouse and I waited for the elevator. The doors of car 8 opened, and I gestured for her to go first. She was multiracial, with a broad, friendly nose and brunette hair that strained toward red.

I hit the 22 button and she the number 2.

She must have noted me looking and said, "They lock the stairwells because they're afraid of terrorists coming in through the exit doors. Otherwise I'd be walking."

"When I was a kid," I said, "I thought that if I worried about every way I could possibly die, then none of them would happen and I'd live forever."

The doors opened, and she gave me a big gap-toothed grin, then walked out.

For the next twenty floors I turned my thoughts to Stuart Braun, A Free Man, and a fat man whom I almost decided to let die. There was a definite parallel between me in that Queens basement and the Staten Island Underground Railroad station where I passively participated in the torture of Simon Creighton. There was almost a karmic balance there.

The doors to the elevator slid away like the curtains to a very small stage, and I was on.

A short and slender man in a violet suit was there to meet me. The guard downstairs hadn't said anything about a man working in the office, so I decided that this guy was security. Olive-skinned white, he had eyes that were a pale blue. His hair was brown at the root and blond thereafter. He was somewhere between the ages of thirty-six and sixteen and smelled of rose attar.

I wondered if the water fountains in that building were fed by an earlier, slightly flawed version of the Fountain of Youth.

"Mr. Beard?"

"Yes." Even if he was a hired gun, I figured I still had the advantage; the wadding in my coat was laced with Kevlar.

"Follow me."

He turned and gestured for me to go before him. I ran point down a useless hallway, finally coming to an opulent room that had three desks with a beautiful woman behind each one.

You can tell a lot about an employer by the makeup of her or his staff.

From the feminine bodyguard to the three office workers (all of whom were of a different race), I could tell that Antrobus was a sensualist.

There was a small oil painting of a bathing nude above

the central desk, where a broad-faced and striking Asian woman sat. I would have given even odds that that canvas was an original Degas.

"Mr. Beard?" the woman said. Her name tag read HATIM.

"Yes."

"What is your business, sir?"

"Private between me and him."

"You must tell me or you won't be meeting him."

"Then," I said with a shrug, "I guess I won't be meeting him."

I turned and the young-like lad in the violet suit got ready to block my exit. I decided that I'd have to shoot him if bad came to worse. My disguise was solid. I doubted if anyone would be able to identify me in a lineup.

"Mr. Beard," a markedly masculine voice boomed.

I turned and saw a man who fit this voice like a fist in a Siberian mitten.

He was tall with broad shoulders and a big belly, wearing a three-piece bright green suit that had gray pinstripes. His shirt was pearl gray and the clasp at his throat was a bright red-and-green garnet. The mane of hair was gray, but the drooping "oilman mustache" was white, almost blue.

Augustine Antrobus's face was a granite bunker, big with squinty eyes that might have been green. This was the sensualist who had hired the fay violet thug and the women of beauty.

"Mr. Antrobus," I announced.

"You have something to tell me?"

"The buffalo have come back from extinction and soon there will be pioneers raping the fields of Mars."

Antrobus's laugh was a weapon. In it was all the strength of some wild creature.

"Come on in," he demanded.

I took a step and the violet thug did too.

"Not you, Lyle," the master said. "Mr. Beard and I will meet mano a mano."

The corridor behind the room of women was set between a wall and a series of slender windows that looked down on Central Park. The striation of shadow and light made me feel as if I were on a safari behind an as yet unsuspecting lion.

Antrobus's office was all dark wood and royal blue fabric, bookshelves with only hardbacks, and no computer in sight. There were two plush chairs set side by side in front of his grand piano–size mahogany desk. The chairs were turned ever so slightly toward each other, like old friends sharing cognac and confidence.

"Sit," the master ordered.

I did as I was told.

When his bulk was situated, he put his hands on the clawed armrests and snorted.

"You talk about buffalo and dress like a buffoon," came his first salvo of words. "You were obviously christened in America but go by the name Beard, which means you have a sense of humor and are anything but a buffoon."

"I appreciate the attention, Mr. Antrobus. Most of the time I spend hidden . . . even in plain sight."

"You are even now."

"I come to you with intelligence and maybe a chance to do a little business," said the man I was pretending to be.

"I like the word *intelligence*," Augustine said. "Even a fool can bring intelligence if he's been given the right words."

I could feel my heart beating again. This larger-than-life

man scared me. He came out of one of the storybooks of old, designed to frighten children into understanding how the world really worked.

"I'm a private agent who does work for those who need to stay in shadow," I said. "Somebody representing a man named Stuart Braun hired me to bring him hopefully incriminating information on another man—William James Marmot."

The masculine chatter stopped then. Antrobus studied me with his slitty eyes and nodded ever so slightly.

"For what purpose?" he asked when my question was almost forgotten.

"He said that Marmot was leaning on him and that he needed leverage."

"What kind of leverage?"

"That I do not know. I met a man named Porker who told me that he knew another man who said Marmot worked for you."

"A man who knows a man who knows about me?"

"That's the way it is in my business."

After a fair length Antrobus asked, "And so why come here just because a man told a man that the man you're stalking might have something to do with me?"

"I wanted to see if you were as serious as I heard."

"And am I?"

I smiled, wondering what my new face looked like with that expression on it.

"I don't need to do any more stalking if you and I can come to an agreement."

"You say," Antrobus parried, "that someone representing Braun hired you."

I nodded without smiling.

"Who is that?"

"Someone calling themselves Lacey."

"A lacey beard?" he asked.

I refrained from smiling again. You can often identify a man by his grin.

"What do you want, Mr. Beard?"

"Six thousand dollars in cash and Mr. Marmot falls off my radar."

"Hardly a fair business practice," Antrobus observed.

"I'm not applying for a position."

Antrobus roared with laughter.

"Do we have a deal?" I asked.

24.

SUNSET CAME BEFORE 5:00 at that time of year. The ferry moved peacefully through the dusk toward the Saint George dock. I was standing in my bulky and bulbous costume at the front of the boat, enjoying the stiff breeze and thinking that I had done a good job of putting myself off the scent for an afternoon.

I had killed a man that day, and the amoral stench of that action hung about me. There were sixty-six hundred-dollar bills in my right front pocket, proof that Stuart Braun was going to have to deal with me sooner or later—if he survived.

A short man with a broad chest came out on the mostly abandoned deck and stared at me for all of forty-five seconds; then he turned away.

Maybe I looked like someone he knew.

In Saint George I made a pay phone call, then boarded the commuter train and sat at the south end of the center car, looking back and wondering why I felt so calm. Life was coming down on me like grain filling up an empty silo, but there I was moving backward in a modern marvel of technology. Life was like the miracle of a tiger on the hunt, only no one around me seemed to appreciate this fact.

Then the door at the far end of the car slid open, and the short white guy with the broad chest who had eyed me on the ferry came through. He wore jeans and tennis shoes, a maroon wool sweater under a loose pale green sweatshirt—its hood thrown back.

He saw me and moved with purpose toward my throne of wonder.

"You the niggah they call Cueball," he said when he was maybe three steps off.

The other people around me moved away. All except for an older gentleman directly across the aisle. He was also white, wearing a dark blue pea coat, black work boots and pants.

I noticed the brave older gentleman while feeling a little stunned by the short stranger's language.

I tried to remember the last time someone had called me nigger. Even my black male acquaintances had mostly given up that tag.

I put my right hand in a yellow pocket and stared.

"You heard me?" my antagonist asked. He was powerful, no doubt. And he was as mad as hell about something; probably had been most of his life. The only thing left to know was if he was a fool or not. There was a gun in that pocket, and I'd already proven to myself that I was unafraid to use it.

Usually when a man reaches in his pocket to threaten a

would-be attacker he's bluffing. But I have found that if you don't say anything the threat seems more real.

"Well?" the short man said.

I said nothing.

He took a step.

"Junior," the older man said.

The racist turned his head and saw the older man, maybe for the first time—that day.

"Ernesto," he said, his voice trying and failing to express both anger and respect.

"You see the man doesn't know you," the brave oldster explained. "You see he's about to kill you. Leave him alone. He's not Cueball."

The man's words carried weight, and after a moment of contemplation, Junior decided to retrace his steps back to some other car.

When he was gone I asked Ernesto, "What was that?"

"Boy lost his girl to a black man named Cueball," he said. "Bald, you know? Junior thinks the guy took her from him. He don't see that the last time he put her in the hospital was the day she stopped bein' his friend."

"Well," I said, "thanks for gettin' him off me."

"I don't give a fuck about you, man. Junior too stupid to understand you got a real gun in there. I could see his death in the corner of your eye."

Pleasant Plains was seventeen stops from Saint George. Ernesto went the whole way and beyond. We didn't talk anymore, and I was on the lookout then for others who didn't celebrate the Underground Railroad of Staten Island.

*   *   *

Mel was waiting at the station. Pay phones still had some use.

We walked up to each other and shook hands.

"Almost didn't recognize you in that getup," he observed.

"Looks like you got a friend. Can't be too careful these days."

I turned and saw the angry young white man whose fists were still crying out for satisfaction.

I gave Mel an abbreviated account of what had happened.

"Wait here," he said, and then he strolled over to Junior.

A few sentences passed between them, and Mel took out a cell phone. He entered something, said something, and then handed Junior the phone. The younger man had a brief conversation at the end of which he shook his head as if indicating to whomever he was speaking that he did not wish whatever had been suggested. Then he gave Mel back his cell, turned, and hightailed it to whatever bar he used to assuage his feelings of inferiority and loss.

We walked fourteen blocks from the train station to the church and didn't speak until we were both seated in a kitchen set behind where the choir once praised God.

"Yeah, sometimes it's like that" were Mel's first words to me.

"Like what?"

"Sometimes there's just a black cloud over your head. If there's trouble anywhere near, it will come to you first."

"Like your red bird."

Mel smiled.

"What did you say to Junior?" I asked just to be talking.

"I called a guy named Genaro. He's one of the connected guys on the island. He told Junior to climb back in his hole."

"Genaro knows you're here?"

"On the island. I got an apartment on the water in Saint George."

"There was this guy on the train," I said. "Junior called him Ernesto."

"Used to be an enforcer in the fifties and sixties," Mel said, nodding.

"Now he just rides the trains?"

"It's a peaceful life out here," he said, and we both laughed.

Mel made a tomato sauce with chicken thighs and hot peppers, which he poured over vermicelli. With that we had sweetened Chianti and a salad that any French chef would have been proud of.

I told Mel about the kidnapping and Antrobus, also about Inspector Dennis Natches and how he might have something to do with the frame that bounced me out of my profession.

"You're still a detective," he pointed out.

"But I'm not a cop."

"Yeah," Mel admitted. "When pretty high school girls grow up they're no longer cheerleaders, but they're still pretty girls."

He poured me some more wine and I considered the odd comparison.

"But tell me something, King."

"What's that?"

"Does Braun have anything to do with Natches?"

It was then I told him about both of the cases I was on. He listened quite closely, nodding now and again.

"Now, let me get this right," he said when I had finished. "You're trying to prove a conspiracy against this Free Man?"

"Yeah. Him and me too."

"They have any connection?"

"Other than cops are mixed in with both . . . I don't think so."

"So you're trying to prove Man is innocent?"

"Yeah. But I can't expect you to go all the way with me on this. I mean, I appreciate what you've done, but I'm a fugitive now."

"Maybe not," Mel opined. "There's nothing on the radio about any shooting in Queens. And I don't care anyway. I'd love nothing better than to grab a man off the gallows. Shit, that's a life-defining moment right there. That's Errol Flynn in *Robin Hood*."

From there he asked me about the details of my inquiries. I told him about most of the names and their involvement; about the Blood Brothers of Broadway and Johanna Mudd, Little Exeter and the heroin trade at the old Brooklyn docks. I didn't give him Willa Portman's name.

At the bottom of the second pitcher of wine, he said, "Okay, okay, I get it, what you want about Man. Prove he was being stalked and that his friends were killed and framed by the cops that were on him. Okay. But what about the thing with your job?"

"I want the union to take my case and have me reinstated."

"But do you want the job back?"

"I want to be exonerated." Saying these words reminded me of another obligation. "You got a phone I could use for a few days?"

The burner he gave me was still in its plastic packaging.

I set up the phone and sent a text to my daughter based on a simple code she'd devised years before. Our cypher was the transposition of numbers, where 1 = 4, 2 = 9, 3 = 1, 4 = 7, 5 = 2, 6 = 0, 7 = 3, 8 = 5, 9 = 8, and 0 = 9. I sent the number of my new phone to her stepfather, and then she would get another disposable phone and we could talk.

"So what do you want to do next, King?" Mel asked when I stopped working with the phone.

"I need to get Natches to admit that he was working with Convert to scuttle my career."

"You just gonna walk into his office and say that? I mean, you came outta that ex-cop's building and they tried to murder you."

"I think I might be able to get a little leverage on the inspector. I might even get him to come and meet me."

"You need some help?"

"Hell! I need the whole goddamn French Foreign Legion."

The devil laughed and my phone rang at the same time.

"A.D.?" I said, answering.

"No. It's Monica."

"Oh." I could tell by her tone that I was in for grief. "Hey."

"What the hell do you mean telling us that we had to leave town because of something you'd done?"

Despite my profession, I don't like lying to people. I don't like making them feel bad either. A good cop is a professional who knows how to lie and inflict pain but does not enjoy these things. I was a good cop, but I needed Aja in my life and Monica was at least part of the reason I was in so much trouble. So I had worked out a tale that would protect them while keeping me from blame.

"Not something I did," I said. "Something *you* did."

"Me?"

"When you called Congressman Acres you set a game into play that got me on the radar of some extremely bad men. Government men. Acres figured out who hired me when I didn't even know myself. He reported this to some very dangerous characters who need their business kept secret. Now they're after me and I'm neck-deep in shit, just like when you let them cops keep me in that hole."

After a brief pause she said, "You're lying."

"Did you call Acres?"

"So what?"

"You did and I got men with guns on my ass. I don't give a fuck about you and your boy-toy, but with this trouble I need to know that Aja's safe. You did leave, didn't you?"

"Yes. But I'm not telling you where."

"As long as you're outta state, I don't care. Now, let me speak to A.D."

"Her name is Denise!"

"Hi, Dad," Aja said a few moments later.

"Don't tell your mother about anything I'm doing at work, okay?"

"Did I cause this problem?"

"No. But don't tell your mom that either."

"Okay. Are you all right?"

"Yeah. I'm fine. You didn't use your phone to call, right?"

205

"Of course not. I bought this pay-as-you-go phone at a drugstore."

"You're a smart cookie."

"I love you, Daddy."

"Me too," I said. "Talk to you soon."

There was an upper floor to the onetime house of worship. Little cells for the devout priests or parsons—whatever the denomination was. My feet hung over the edge of the cot, but I didn't mind. The door wasn't locked and through the small window a half-moon shone brightly.

I didn't sleep. Just lay back with one knee up and moonlight on my face. My newly shaved head itched a little and my little girl was safe. I had survived a slaughter and murdered a man. All that and life was still the best it could be.

I got out of bed at around 4:30 and went down to the kitchen, where Mel was drinking coffee at the table.

"Got a car I can use?" I asked him.

"Copper Lexus in the stable."

"Stable?"

"Behind the church. You know this is an old institution."

"You going in to work?" I asked.

"If you don't need me later I will."

"You got a typewriter around here?" I asked.

"Word processor and a printer."

"I guess that'll have to do."

I drove via Brooklyn to Manhattan's Upper West Side before the traffic was a bear. There, on Eighty-Third, I found a coffee shop that made western omelets but had run out of real bacon. So along with the eggs I had strips of turkey pressed, salted, and dyed to look like and taste something like bacon.

There was a storefront across the street that had been rented out on a temporary basis. I dithered over the bad food and weak coffee until a man I recognized walked into the pop-up campaign office.

"May I help you?" a young woman asked. She was quite dark-skinned. Upon her blueberry blouse was a big square button that proclaimed, ACRES IS OUR MAN!

I liked meeting young black Republicans. It meant that some part of the younger generation was thinking. Who cared if they were wrong?

"Mr. Acres, please."

"The congressman is not in yet."

The campaign receptionist had a fortieth birthday party a year or two before. Hers was the kind of plain face that promised something deeper than transient beauty. The blue chemise was silk, and from the thread-like gold chain around her neck depended a yellow diamond that was at least two and a half carats.

"I didn't think Republicans needed to lie," I said.

"Excuse me?" she said in a tone that could have easily turned to anger.

"I was coming here from down the block when I saw Bobby walking through the front door. That would bring him right here to you. Now, I guess you could have been somewhere else, but I find it hard to believe that the first face you meet at a campaign headquarters doesn't know when the candidate is in the house."

"What is your business with the congressman?" she asked coldly.

"Tell him that the man he almost ran into in Jersey the other night would like a few words."

"I'll need a name."

"Believe me when I tell you, sister, that's the last thing the congressman would want."

Five minutes later I was walking into the broom-closet-size office that the candidate had commandeered. There were larger offices, but these were for volunteers who had to spread out and work hard. All Acres needed was a chair to sit in and a phone to yak on.

He ushered me in, closing the door on the blue-bloused woman.

I sat in a simple oak chair and he went around to his seat.

"I never expected to see you again," he said as he sat.

"I'm not here to cause any trouble," I said.

"Okay. Then what is it?"

"I need you to call an NYPD inspector and ask him to meet me at the English Teacup off Broadway, in the nineties, around, um, let's say, two forty-five."

"And why?"

I took a sealed envelope from my pocket and handed it to the candidate.

"Mimi Lord told me that you got in touch."

"Yes."

"I want you to tell Inspector Dennis Natches that I gave you a sealed envelope to register with the Library of Congress."

"Should I read it?"

"I wouldn't suggest it. In your position, ignorance is better than the apple."

"And who shall I tell Mr. Natches that he's meeting?"

"A man named Nigel Beard. You can say that you have no idea what the letter contains but that I said to say it had to do with Detective Second Class Adamo Cortez."

"And this won't cause me any trouble?"

"It will not. And you have my e-mail address, Congressman. If you ever need my kind of help, just drop a line and I will be there."

25.

THE REST OF the morning I sat in a congested watch-maker's shop on Cherry Lane in the Far West Village.

Melquarth and I worked out a security plan for me and my meeting with the high-ranking police official.

"Suppose he sends cops to take me down?" I asked at 10:58 by the Bavarian cuckoo clock on a high school.

"I don't think heroin-dealing cops use honest Joes for business like this," the expert in evil replied. "Anyway...if somebody tries to get at you, they will feel my wrath."

I felt bad exposing one of my brothers to a madman like Mel, but it was pretty certain that Natches was at least aware of my kidnapping, and I doubted if my murder would have lost him any sleep.

I was at the English Teacup at 1:00. I told the waitress that my appointment was going to be late but that I would order lunch then and get a high tea when he arrived at 2:45.

Somewhere outside, Mel was in a specially designed van that had pretty good firepower. I also placed a quick-drying plaster that hardened like old chewing gum under the table where Natches would sit.

Prepared for victory or death, I took out an old copy of *Steppenwolf* by Hesse. Since meeting the young woman on the subway I had a yearning for the old German's romance with the life of the mind.

I had a proper English breakfast with sausage, grilled tomatoes and mushrooms, beans, Canadian bacon, and fried toast. I ate even though I wasn't hungry while reading through glasses that did nothing for my eyesight.

At 2:15 a hale-looking white man came in. He was about my age, wearing a light gray suit. He sat three tables away from me and ordered coffee.

At 2:45 exactly Inspector Natches walked in wearing a dark blue suit. He was both bulky and tall; though he was twenty years my senior, I was sure that he had some fight left in his sinews. He said a word to the hostess and she led him to my table.

He stood over me a moment or two, staring intently. He knew who I was. He might not have pierced the disguise, but Congressman Acres's message was a clear proclamation.

"Have a seat," I said.

He hesitated but sat.

"I don't know who the fuck you think you are, but this little game of yours is not going to work."

"Tea?"

"No, I don't want any fucking tea," he said, a few decibels above the proper volume.

People around turned their heads. Natches's brows furrowed.

The waitress came with the preordered platter of sandwiches and pastries.

"What kind of tea would you like?" she asked Natches.

"Whatever," he said, at least keeping his voice down.

"I'll have Irish Breakfast," I said.

"We only have English Breakfast."

"Then that'll have to do."

We waited for the service, Natches fuming and me feeling like a cop again.

After the woman—who was straw-haired, forties, and quite comfortable with her body—poured our tea and retreated, Natches sat up straight.

The man in the gray suit sat up also.

The tinkling bell at the top of the front door sounded and Mel walked in. He wore black trousers and a herringbone sports jacket. He took the lay of the restaurant and asked for a table quite close to the gunsel in gray.

"Look, man," I said to Natches. "I've been beaten, scarred, disgraced, imprisoned, and had my marriage torn apart by you motherfuckers without even a word of explanation or warning. People have tried to murder me, and you sit there on your ass like you're Boss Tweed or somethin'. Understand me—you are not safe."

"You think I'm scared of you? You think just because you can string a sentence together that I'm gonna make you a police again? I wouldn't have a half-assed disgraced cop like you shine my shoes. I sure the fuck will not kiss your feet."

He was angry. Maybe, like the short cuckold on Staten Island, he was always angry. But I believed this passion was anchored in fear.

"If that's true," I said, "then why are you here?"

It was an honest question, and how he answered would inform my next moves.

"Don't fuck with me," he said.

"The fact you're sitting in front of me with a bodyguard a few tables away means I'm already fuckin' with you, brother. What I want to know is why Paul Convert framed my ass. What I want to know is why you motherfuckers tried to murder me—twice."

The inspector's hazel eyes were suddenly filled with questions and revelations.

"You're crazy," he said in a voice that was trying desperately to take the higher ground.

"Why go through all this shit?" I asked. "I mean, okay, ten, twelve years ago I was on a case. I might have been bullheaded and tried to take down whatever you had going on the docks. You felt that you had to stop me. I could see that. But now that I know the game and the players, why don't you just let me back in?"

Asking these questions, I realized that this was what was most important to me.

Keeping me in the dark, maybe even putting me in the grave, was what was most important to Natches.

I looked up and noticed that Mel had gotten to his feet. He walked over to Natches's gray guardian and took the seat across from him.

"You don't know a thing," Dennis Natches said to me. "A little man like you could go out like a candle sitting on the windowsill. We should have taken care of you back then, when you were a cowboy."

"Why didn't you?"

The answer was in his eye, but it wouldn't make it to his lips.

"I'm finished with you," Natches said. He pushed his chair back from the table.

"You should finish your tea," I said.

"You're dead and don't know it," he said with a grin that couldn't help but be evil.

"You mean like your friend over there does?"

Natches glanced over and saw smiling Melquarth Frost and his own man looking both serious and defeated.

"I learned a lot since I was a police detective thinking he could do it on his own," I said. "I learned that reading is important, that law is an ever-changing variable equation, and that a man is a fool if he works alone."

Natches settled back into his chair.

I continued, "I learned that anyone can be brought low no matter how high or powerful they are. I know that if I die you will too. You should know that, Dennis. Your man over there with my man's gun on him should know that.

"Now get your ass outta here and remember that your heart can stop beating too."

He took his time standing from the chair.

I looked over to see that the bodyguard was also on his feet.

They both tried to intimidate us with their stares, but we knew that two cops couldn't open fire in a New York place of business, and they couldn't trust that we wouldn't. After all, there was already one dead man across the river in Queens.

When Natches and his man were gone, Mel got up and sauntered over to me. I told the straw-headed, zaftig waitress to bring the bills for Mel and the bodyguard to me.

214

"You think they're laying for us out there?" I asked Mel when the waitress went away to do my bidding.

"I hope not," he said, "for them. But it doesn't matter anyway."

"Why not?"

"The reason I chose this place is that it has a little-known exit to the building next door, and that building has an exit on the alley behind.

"But even if that wasn't true, I got three guys outside with all kinds'a firepower. I sent them photos with my cell phone and they're the kinda guys that know when an ambush is set up."

I smiled and told him about the conversation.

"He's already in somebody's crosshairs," Mel pronounced.

"But who?"

Mel's cell phone sounded.

"Yeah?" he answered. Then: "All right. Thanks."

He put away the phone and said to me, "Nobody's out there. The inspector and his man left in the same car."

I picked up a crustless cucumber sandwich and took a nibble.

"You got a place to stay, King?"

"Storage unit in the West Village."

"Huh."

"Look, Mel, I appreciate your help. But right now I'm gonna look into some stuff. I'll call you later on and maybe, if you got the time, you could help me again."

"You sure the fuck need it."

26.

THERE'S A BEAUTIFUL high-rise apartment building on Forty-Second Street a block or so east of Tenth Avenue. It's constructed from plate glass and steel girders with a thirty-foot-high atrium for an entrance.

"May I help you, sir?" a caramel-colored, red-jacketed man asked. He was standing behind a four-and-a-half-foot-high green marble counter.

"Miranda Goya," I said, happy to have at least one sentinel treat me with decorum.

He picked up a phone receiver, but before bringing it to his ear he said, "Your name?"

"Joe Oliver."

Making all the right moves, the man said into the phone, "A Mr. Oliver for you, Miss Goya."

He was younger than I by at least five years and had generous lips that were exactly the same tone as the rest of his skin. This unusual aspect gave the guardian a kind of specialized, almost synthetic, air.

"Twenty-eight thirteen," he said to me.

"Thank you."

The elevator was large and my only companion was a woman, probably in her eighties, who had mastered makeup well enough to take at least fifteen years off her appearance. She had a small black-and-white dog on a leash that was straining to get at me.

I like dogs. If some evolutionist had told me that men had descended from canines I would have believed her. All the brotherly passion, fang-baring hunt lust, and fear I feel on a daily basis I see in dogs.

I was a dog. I'd been told that my entire life—by men and women alike.

"I can't let him greet you," the lady said. She was wearing a fox wrap over an emerald cashmere sweater.

"He bites?"

"Pisses. He pisses on any man's foot that gets close enough. He's a bad boyfriend, but I love him."

I nodded and felt real empathy.

"You in a new play?" she asked then.

"What?"

"The mustache," she said. "And those silly sideburns."

"How can you tell?"

"This is an actors' co-op," she explained. "Everyone here knows makeup, camera shots, and about hundred thousand lines of bad writing."

"Just came from a dress rehearsal at BAM," I said. "A play we're debuting in Cincinnati. Right now I'm going to run some lines for another project."

"With who?"

"I'd tell you, but I don't think her husband would like it."

The older lady with the dead fox around her neck smiled and bowed her head ever so slightly.

Dog lady got off at the fourteenth floor and I traveled alone to twenty-eight.

I walked halfway down the hall of doors to my left and pressed the button on the jamb of twenty-eight thirteen. There was no faraway sound of a bell or buzzer, but I didn't want to seem impatient and so refrained from following up with a knock.

"Who is it?" came a woman's voice.

"Joe Oliver."

"You don't look like him."

I wondered if Lamont had somehow taken a cell phone picture of me or if he just told her what I looked like.

"I put on the mustache and shaved the head because I didn't want anybody recognizing me on the case. I could call Mr. Charles at the Aramaya if you want."

After a brief pause she pulled the door open.

Miranda Goya was one of the most beautiful women I, or the dog in me, had ever seen. She was in her late twenties but had the stance of a veteran. Her knee-length dress was composed of equal swirls of purple, red, and green. Her figure denied the garment and, I was sure, had betrayed her again and again from the age of thirteen. Her face was heart-shaped and haughty; the blended color of ethereal rose-gold and earthbound bronze informed her skin.

I crossed the threshold and she moved to the side.

She bit her lower lip as I took off the bulky coat.

"That coat makes you look fat."

"Thank God for small blessings."

"Go on in," she offered.

It was a small studio with a diaphragm-high wall separating the kitchen from the living room. The wall was mounted by a flat, two-foot-wide Formica-covered plank that was both her dining room and desk. A glass double door formed her outer wall; this led to a tiny terrace that looked north toward Harlem. Next to the glass door was a huge bird-of-paradise in a ten-gallon clay pot sporting eleven of the gorgeous orange-and-blue blossoms.

"Mr. Oliver?" she said.

"Yes?"

"Is that your real name?"

"Yes, it is."

I took out my wallet and handed her my PI's license. She took the laminated card and compared it to the bald man standing before her.

"This looks like the man Lam told me about," she said. "What do you want with me?"

"I'm looking into the defense of A Free Man," I said. "And ever since then people been on me. I decided that if I look different maybe I'd get a little deeper without gettin' shot."

Miranda took a deep breath and pursed her lips to express her empathy.

"Have a seat, Mr. Oliver," she said.

There were two padded wicker chairs facing each other right at the veranda door. Between them was a green-glass box that stood in as a table.

I sat and she asked, "Whiskey?"

"Scotch or bourbon?"

"Sour mash," she said with a pleasing sneer.

"Darling, you have just become the favorite person of my day."

The laugh didn't make it as far as her throat, but it was real mirth from a dark place.

From the kitchen she said, "Ice?"

"No, thank you."

When she sat down across from me I started to think about Aja. My daughter was a beautiful woman with curves and class and a smile that made you happy.

This trick worked. My heart slowed down and I emptied the generous dram of whiskey.

"You want another one?" Miranda asked.

"Yes, I do, but, no, I won't."

That smile etched her lips.

"Lam said that he thought you might be all right," she shared.

"That's unusual?"

"Every time somebody come talk to him about Manny he calls me from a pay phone and tells me what they look like and when they were there. Lam don't talk about Manny to just anybody. Especially if that anybody is a cop."

"Ex-cop," I corrected.

"Once a cop, always a cop."

I laughed and felt the whiskey spreading mildly over my brow.

"Okay, Mr. Ex-cop," Miranda said. "What did you want me to talk about?"

"A Free Man."

"What do you want to know?"

"I have heard that there was a conspiracy against him and all the Blood Brothers and there are still people working to make sure his story is silenced."

The beautiful woman looked toward the window.

She turned back to me and said, "Your mustache is comin' loose. Up on the left side. Not that much right now, but people will be able to tell after a while."

I touched the side she mentioned and felt the looseness.

"You want me to touch it up?" she asked.

"Say what?"

"That's what I do. I'm a makeup artist. After Manny freed me, the Blood Brothers aksed me what I wanted to do an' sent me to school."

Without further discussion she went to a closet near the front door, pulling out what looked like a fisherman's box and a collapsible stool. She set up in front and to the right of me, putting the box on the green-glass coffee table.

"Move your head back."

I did and she studied the false hairs.

"Somebody did a pretty good job of this. Your girlfriend?"

I explained the class I took and the reason I took it.

"That's really smart for a straight man," Miranda said. "You know most men only know about tits and ass. They couldn't even tell you the color of somebody's eyes."

"Detectives do it for a living."

"What you wanna know about Manny?" she asked as she went to work on the semidetached lip hair.

"Lamont says that Mr. Man pulled you out of a bad situation."

"Not only me."

"I'm talking to you, though."

"Yeah." She dabbed a strong-smelling ointment across the top of the mustache. "I was deep in it and one day Manny walked in a room and took me out. That was it."

I was slowly becoming a reluctant fan of Leonard Compton / Free Man.

"And it wasn't just me," she repeated. "There was a hundred children at any one time doin' all kinds'a shit for them."

"Who?"

She had to take a breath before saying, "Valence and Pratt."

"Were there others? I mean others working with them."

"Yeah, but I didn't know their names."

"Policemen?"

"I'ont really know." She concentrated on the hairs a little more and said, "They had this piece'a paper with a price list for sixty-seven things we had to do if they paid for it. Nasty things. Anything."

"So they were full-out pimps and Mr. Man took you away from that," I said.

"Not only pimps. They killed people too. Murdered 'em."

"You mean the Blood Brothers."

"Them . . . kids tried to run and family wanted to free 'em and anybody got in their way."

"These murders are on record?"

Miranda pressed against my whole upper lip with at least six fingers, then she sat back in her chair. She took in a deep breath and watched me with eyes that, like her skin, were not quite brown.

After maybe three minutes she said, "You know I love Lamont. He treated me like a real woman and never even once tried to take advantage. You know a girl like me make men wanna take advantage and we hardly even know it.

"I love Lamont and I can't even tell you how much I feel about Manny. I was in the back room of a massage parlor on Thirty-Ninth with this white man got his fist up my ass felt like all the way to his forearm and A Free Man come in with a gun. Shit! That white man messed himself and ran like some kinda dog. And nobody has done nuthin' to me I ain't said yes to since that night.

"Now Manny's up on death row and I cain't do a damn thing to help him. He won't even let me come visit 'cause he don't want me to get in trouble.

"All that and I'm still scared shit to talk to you."

My temporary phone beeped and I took it out. Mel had texted me a name and an address.

"Thanks for the cosmetic work," I said. "How much I owe you?"

"You don't owe me nuthin'. I offered."

I stood up and said, "Thanks for your help, Miss Goya. I'm sorry to bring up such painful memories."

"That's it?" she said.

"Yeah. I'm going to try and prove the things you said, but I can't promise that someone might not figure out if you told me things that nobody else knows. I never met Mr. Man, but I don't think he'd appreciate me trading your life for his."

Her eyes opened wide as if she'd remembered something.

"Burns," she said.

"Huh?"

"He was with me that day Manny busted in. Manny took him outta there too."

"His name is Burns?"

"They call him that but his real name is Theodore."

"Why they call him Burns?"

"He had a client liked to burn him after every time they fucked. And he fucked Theodore once a week. He got all these scars on his face and left arm."

I'm pretty sure that that was the turning point for me. It might have been what Miranda had experienced in the massage parlor. Maybe if I had not heard what happened to her there I could have overlooked Theodore's experience. I don't know. But from that moment on I wasn't merely solving one case or another...I was as serious as a slave who said *no more* to his chains.

"What about Theodore?"

"Before Manny got us, he used to work with Valence and Pratt pretty close. I mean, they had him fuckin' people too, but sometimes he helped them with the heavy lifting."

"Can you tell me anything else about him?" I asked. "A last name?"

"He only goes by Burns."

"Anything else I should know?"

"He's on heroin," the beauty said with an ugly sneer. "He don't wanna give it up. He says the only way he stays alive is to be high."

"You try to get him some help?" I asked. I don't know why.

"No," she said, flat and low.

"Why not?"

" 'Cause he right," she said, her tone a dialect sliding all the way back to that massage parlor. "Gettin' straight would kill him for sure."

27.

AS I WAS leaving the actors' co-op, my head was as light as a helium balloon, and my feet felt as if they were forged from lead. There was an abscess of evil out in the world and for some reason that was my responsibility if not my fault. A Free Man was on death row. No cop, judge, or average Joe was going to put up their hand and say, "I have a doubt."

Before that afternoon I had often wondered how men and women became traitors. How could they one day wake up and say, "Everything I believed was wrong and now they have to pay."

I never even considered for one moment that Miranda Goya was lying; me, a man who didn't even trust his own clients, a man who had experienced betrayal on almost every level.

I walked down to Port Authority and stood on the corner of Forty-Second and Eighth trying to feel my way back to Montague Street and its mild indictments of big business and human nature. I wanted the worst problem to be my daughter's choice of dresses or some traumatized white man thinking that I was abusing A.D.

"You okay, sir?" someone asked. The words were friendly, but the tone was not.

It was a beat cop who patrolled the sidewalks surrounding the giant bus station. I didn't recognize him. I *did* wonder how he picked me out of all the junkies, pickpockets, prostitutes, and runaways.

"Yes, I am, Officer," I said. "It's just that I had to stop a minute and put my head together."

"Can you walk?" the shorter, white cop asked.

I smiled, nodded, and then moved away from the big building that made humanity seem like the last dying colony of prehistoric ants.

I could have taken the subway, but instead I walked up to Eighth and Seventy-Third. Down Seventy-Third, about half a block, stood a seven-story brownstone apartment building that was very old.

I climbed the stoop, pulled open the outer door, and then searched the list of names for Thurman Hodge. I pressed the button for twenty-seven, Thurman's designation, and waited.

"Who is it?" a gravelly voice asked over a staticky intercom connection.

"Smith," I replied.

The address and the names Thurman and Smith were all sent by text to me by Melquarth. The fact that I was there meant that I had abandoned and very possibly betrayed the world I'd known.

"Be right down," the rough voice told me.

The vestibule smelled of mold. Some people might have been put off by the odor, but for me it was a pleasant reminder of the apartment building where I lived with my mother, brother, and sister after our father was sentenced and before I was old enough to run away.

"Yeah?" a man said from the other side of the apartment building's windowed door.

He was five eight in shoes, with coarse salt-and-pepper hair that he brushed equally to either side. Wearing a paint-stained, once-white artist's smock, he looked like some villain from *Dick Tracy* in the old newspaper comic strips: Flattop, or maybe, because of his scowl, Gruesome.

"I'm here for the bargain basement," I told the beady-eyed comic strip villain.

He squinted a little harder and then opened the door.

"Follow me," he said.

We walked down a slender corridor to a flight of three steps, out a door that led to an especially small courtyard, and across the yard to another door.

While Hodge, if that was his name, searched a large key chain, he said, "You can tell Moran that this is the last time I can rent the place. The owners want to put some kinda IT center down here and ain't nuthin' I can do about that."

I had no idea who Moran was, but Mr. Hodge didn't need to know that.

He found the key and worked it on the lichen-crusted white-enamel-painted door.

He gestured for me to walk in and turned on the light after I realized that there was a series of stairs leading down. I stumbled only slightly but was reminded of the day before, when, on a similar set of stairs, I shot a man in the head.

Fifteen steps down, I found myself in another cellar. This one had been transformed into a studio apartment designed for men and women on the run. This reminded me of Mel's connection to the Underground Railroad; made me think that I was fighting a war beyond the laws that once claimed my allegiance.

"No TV or radio reception down here," the man who might have been named Hodge said. "The hot plate works, but there's no good ventilation so don't cook anything you don't want to smell for the next few days. The space heater works. And here's the keys for the apartment and the front door. There's a bell for the super up front, but don't call her. It's me you deal with."

I nodded and handed Mr. Hodge one of the hundred-dollar bills that Antrobus's purple-garbed goon had given me. Hodge took the tip with an expression of surprise.

"Anything you need," he said. "Just ring."

"Do you get cell phone reception down here?" I asked before he could depart.

"Not unless Jesus Christ gave you the phone."

Two blocks away I found a coffee shop that served glazed meat loaf and sour mash. I got the taste for the whiskey at Miranda's apartment and wanted to follow it down a ways.

"Hello?" Andre Tourneau said.

"Hey, brother."

"Joe. How are you?"

"Feel like I went to sleep on the ground and woke up in a coffin."

"I get that way every time I go home to Port-au-Prince. What can I do for you, my friend?"

"Call Henri and tell him to call this number from a pay phone."

"You're not gonna get my boy in trouble, now, are you, Joe?"

"I remember why you bought that pistol, Mr. Tourneau, don't you worry about that."

The meat loaf tasted better with every sip of whiskey. I was feeling almost jocular when the cell phone sounded.

"Hello?"

"Joe," Henri Tourneau said. "You still hiding?"

"I called Natches."

"And what did he have to say?"

I told him as much as was necessary and added, "I think he might be able to figure out our connection so I wanted to ask you if you had some friend who could look up a street name for me."

"Anything, Uncle."

The familial endearment touched me. I don't think it was just the whiskey. The days I followed down my expulsion from the police and the Man conviction I was also learning that I had a multifaceted life with many planes of beauty to it.

An hour later I received a text that said a junkie called Burns was a regular at the Bread and Bees Homeless Shelter on Avenue C in the East Village.

When I got that message I was already on Seventh Avenue at Christopher in the West Village. There I was waiting outside a nameless fortune-telling parlor.

Through the glass wall facade was a shallow room done

all in reds. There were various crystals and two plush chairs, a calico cat, and the framed photograph of a large-nosed man with a receding hairline.

I walked in and was assailed by a sweet brand of incense that I recognized but could not name. The electronic announcement of my entrance was the sound of a solitary lark calling out for an old friend or a new love.

Through red curtains came a plump woman with pale skin dressed in a green wraparound that was festooned with tiny round mirrors.

"Yes?" she asked.

"Lackey," I said.

The woman's face didn't have far to go for the glower she gave me.

"Tell him it's Seamus from the Southside."

She sneered but went back through the curtains.

I waited there wondering what kind of prison time I could expect after I'd finished with my investigations.

The woman opened the curtains without entering the spiritual consultation room, saying, "Come."

We passed through a short dark hall into a bright kitchen where two women and three children were either cooking or eating. One dirty-faced little girl looked up from the dining table, smiled, and stuck her finger in her nose.

The frowning woman took me through another door into what I could only call a sitting room.

There were two stuffed chairs therein. One was yellow with big dark blue polka dots. It was of normal dimensions and looked quite comfortable. The other chair was twice the size of its little sister and might have been black. I couldn't make out the full design or color because

230

they were obstructed by the impossibly fat man who sat there.

Kierin Klasky weighed well north of four hundred pounds. He could have willed his face to be sewn into a basketball after he died; it was that large and round. The features of his physiognomy were mostly just fat, as were his bloated hands and ham-round thighs.

Kierin was a white man in a blue suit wearing a red tie. There was a black Stetson on the table next to his sofa-size chair. I wondered if he ever donned the hat and stood up.

"Joe!" he bellowed.

"Kierin."

"I heard you got fired."

"That was eleven years ago."

"I'm still here," he said. "What do you need?"

Back before my dismissal from the force I saved Kierin from a bust that would have put him away for years. He had information I needed about the heroin connection at the Brooklyn docks and I got a friend in records to taint his most recent arrest report.

"Can I sit?" I asked the fat man.

"Please do," he said and gestured. "Maria!"

A woman blundered gracelessly into the room. She was young and wearing a peasant dress that might be found anywhere in Eastern Europe a century ago. It was made from strips of differing fabrics dyed in bold colors.

Her face was both beautiful and haunted.

"Yes, Papa?" she said.

"Bring our guest grappa."

"Yes, Papa," she said and then lurched away.

231

"She's a beautiful thing," Kierin said. "But her mind is always somewhere else."

"Looks like she doesn't need to pay attention," I said.

"Why are you here, Joe?"

He was older than I, but in our business age hardly mattered. I was his inside asset for three months when he really needed it.

"Do you know a junkie named Burns?"

Maria came back carrying a delicate water glass three-quarters filled with clear hundred-and-ten-proof liquor.

She waited for me to take a sip. When I didn't gag she smiled and left.

"First or last name?" Kierin asked.

"Nickname. They call him that because he has burn scars on his face and left arm."

"Oh, him. Yes. A very troubled young man. Do you need to find him?"

"I can do that on my own. I just wanted to know anything you could tell me."

"He's a good customer when he's got money. Must have found a new connection, though. I haven't seen him in months. Maybe he's dead."

"What's his habit?"

"Used to get two hits at a time. For a while there I was seeing him three times a day."

"Two at a time?"

He nodded.

"Then that's what I need you to sell me."

Bread and Bees Homeless Shelter got its name from the beehives Arnold Fray kept on top of the building. He used the honey to feed his homeless, wino, and addict population.

"Honey," Arnold would say, "is the food of God."

When Arnold died, his daughter, Hester, took over management of the retreat. She was big like her father and tough like him too. She maintained the apiary and baked the bread.

I strolled up to the desk of the men's shelter and said, "Hi, my name is Joe Oliver."

"The cop?" Hester asked, standing up from her walnut office chair.

"Last time I saw you, you couldn't have been more than sixteen," I said. "And I don't look anything like I did."

"I got a long memory," she said. "You need it in this calling."

She wore a long black dress that completely hid any figure she might have had.

"What else you remember 'bout me?"

"All I need to know is that you're a cop."

"Not anymore. I was fired more than a decade ago."

Her smile was unbidden.

"I came to see if I could find a guy called Burns," I said.

"And you expect me to help you?"

Her eyes were gray and, I knew, mine were brown. We studied each other, looking for a reason to trust, but there was nothing there.

"I'll promise you that I have no evil designs on Theodore and on top of that I'll donate a thousand dollars to the shelter, in cash, right now. I'll agree to meet him under your supervision too."

28.

AFTER THE FINANCIAL transaction Hester summoned a wraithlike young black man to lead me to a shed up on the roof, near the beehives. He had gray eyes like hers.

The shanty-shack's door was secured by a padlock. After the impossibly thin young man had used his key, I asked, "What's your name?"

"Mikey."

"Give me the lock, Mikey."

He did so and I attached it to the eye of the latch so that the door would have to remain unlocked.

"I'll take the key too."

He almost balked but then acquiesced.

Inside he found the pull chain that flooded the one-room work shed with at least four hundred watts of yellow light from a single bulb.

"She'll be up in a while," he said, looking everywhere but at me.

I called Mikey a black man because that's the term I use for people who come from our so-called race. But he was actually a shade of gray that was tending toward black, where his eyes were a similar shade headed in the opposite direction.

He turned away, leading with his shoulders, and left me to the chilly shack. I had *Steppenwolf* in my overcoat pocket, but before I could take it out, I spied an old textbook of first-year Latin on the cluttered worktable. All around the old russet-colored hardback were tools that had to do with bees and their honey.

Reading the editor's introduction to the book (which had been published in 1932), I learned that there had been something called *The General Report of the Classical Investigation*. This university study had recommended a new way for learning the ancient language, a way that took a historical and also a cultural approach.

I skimmed through the author's preface, then delved into the meat of the book. I had just learned that "Vergil called his countrymen *gēns togāta*, which meant toga-clad people," when the unlocked door swung open and black-clad Hester walked in. She was followed by another slender man of color who wore a yellow-and-green sports jacket, stiff jeans, and no shirt at all.

"Theodore," Hester said, "I'd like you to meet Mr. Joe King Oliver."

The fact that she knew my middle name was truly a shock.

"Hey," the man I would always think of as Burns said.

I closed the book, stood, and took his proffered hand. His face was a deep brown, but all along the left side there were craters and calloused, scarred skin. His left hand was also mutilated and defaced. The skin was scabrous and scaly.

While I studied the details of his disfigurement he stared at me. I was sure he couldn't see my scar, but somehow I believed that he intuited it.

"Mr. Oliver wants to ask you some questions," Hester said.

"Have a seat," I said to both the young man and his chaperone.

The worktable was against an unpainted pine wall and there were five backless stools along it. We each took a stool.

Hester was staring at me, prepared at any moment to end the interview.

Burns was the epitome of what I understood to be a junkie. He was afraid of me but at the same time wondering if there might be a profit in our interaction. He was always looking for the next fix. Maybe he could smell the packets I scored from Kierin.

"It's good to meet you, Theodore," I said.

"You too." He nodded.

"Miranda told me to tell you hello."

"You know Mir?"

"I met with Lamont out on Coney Island and he sent me to her. She told me her story and said I might want to talk to you."

"Mir didn't know I was here," Theodore said with suspicion. Hester swiveled her shoulders as if she were about to pronounce judgment.

"She told me you used, so I asked a friend on the force to

look up your nickname along with Theodore. They knew you came here sometimes."

"All the time," Hester said. "He's trying to get his head together."

"Why you go from Lamont to Mir to me?" Burns asked.

"Because I was hired to prove that A Free Man was hunted and conspired against by members of the NYPD; specifically Officers Valence and Pratt."

Both Burns and Hester had the same frown on their faces.

"Manny?" said Burns.

I nodded.

"What does Theodore have to do with that?" Hester asked.

"I have no idea," I said truthfully. "I talked to Miranda and she pointed me here."

"Like a gun," Hester said to Burns.

But he wasn't listening.

"You wanna help Manny?" he asked me. It seemed as if he saw something important and lasting in the intention alone, like a burning bush or a resurrection.

"That's what I've been hired to do."

"Hired by who?" Hester asked.

The burned man's eyes echoed the question.

"Nobody official," I allowed. "I'm not working for the cops or the state, and the person paying me really wants Mr. Man to be released. But I can't give you a name. That would violate client confidentiality."

"How do we know you're not lying?" Hester asked.

"You don't," I admitted. "But I've paid the shelter the money for this meeting and you don't know anything about the case."

There was an agenda to my answer. If Burns knew that I had money to pay for information he was more likely to want to deal with me.

"This meeting is over," Hester said. But she was already too late.

"No," Burns interjected. "No...I believe him. I know why Miranda send him here."

Hester's shoulders sagged then. She knew Theodore. She knew that he knew that I had what he needed.

I remembered something that my grandmother would say.

"You cain't protect a wolf from bein' a wolf. That's like tryin' to say it's midnight when it's really high noon."

"We should probably talk alone," I said to Burns.

"No," Hester proclaimed.

"Yeah, we should, Auntie H.," Burns said, a note of authority in his voice. "You don't wanna know nuthin' 'bout what got to do with Manny and them, and them cops."

"You can't do this," Hester said to me.

I stood up from my stool. Burns followed suit.

"I'll give you the money back," Hester offered, realizing too late that her greed for the shelter was, in its own way, a betrayal.

"I'll bring him back tonight," I said.

"You'll get him killed."

"He's no use to anyone as a witness, Miss Fray, and I won't tell about our conversation if you don't."

"He's vulnerable," she said in a whisper.

Vulnerable. With that one word she was able to explain the pain of his prostitution and the need for self-destruction; his addiction coupled with the inability to escape any part of the suffering rained down upon him by a life not of his making.

There were hundreds of thousands, maybe millions of young people like Burns stumbling down the streets of rural, suburban, and big-city America. They each had the same affliction, but they could only be saved one at a time.

"No, I'm not, Auntie Hester," the scarred man intoned. "Not even a captain in the Green Berets could survive one day in the life I got to live. I'm strong. I could take it."

Hester Fray was defeated by this claim. I could see in her eyes that she was in love with her job and her people. This passion made me want to know more about her, but there was no time for that kind of recreation.

"I got to score before we do anything else," Burns told me on the street.

"I got what you need," I said.

"What?"

"Kierin sold me two hits," I said. "He said two was your base buy, so I got one to cut the pain but at the same time keep you able to talk. I'll give you it right now. After we talk I'll give you the other and two hundred dollars."

"Kierin from up Harlem?" Burns asked.

He delivered the question as a foregone conclusion, telling me that he was a canny junkie whom I had to be careful with.

"You and I both know he works for the Gypsy in the West Village."

"Let's see what he give you."

"Is there somewhere we could go?"

Burns's grin was missing a brown tooth or two, but there was still mirth and real satisfaction there.

We went east a couple of blocks, crossed a concrete park, and entered a street I'd never been on; I call it a street, but it was closer to being an alley.

Halfway down that block was a three-and-a-half-foot space between two nondescript buildings blocked by a padlocked Dumpster. Burns and I pushed the can aside and made our way maybe fifteen feet when we came to a door that looked to be locked too but was not.

On the other side of the door was a chamber no more than six foot square. I could see this because there was a small lightbulb dangling from a socket overhead that Burns turned on by twisting it. It wasn't inside, but then again it was walled off and roofed away from the outside. The floor was asphalt. The only furniture was a three-legged wooden stool.

There was no trash or garbage on the ground. As a matter of fact, there was an old broom leaning in a corner that had seen quite some use.

"What is this?" I asked my informant while taking the wallet from my pocket and the heroin from there.

Burns took the little fold of cellophane and studied it carefully.

"That's Kierin all right," he mumbled. "He step on this shit hisself."

It felt odd that we shared knowledge.

"What is this place?" I asked again.

"You ever hear of Juaquin de Palma?"

"Yeah." De Palma was a socialite addict who would give wild parties for like-minded people of all classes. He was slippery and dangerous, attracting artists, musicians, and debutantes to his "cause." He was finally murdered by a man named Tibor whose daughter had OD'd at one of de Palma's raves.

"I used to hang with him. This was his place he'd go when he just wanted to get high and be alone. And then when he died it was mine's alone."

While talking, Burns put together his fix. He sat down on the stool, filled the spoon, cooked the aitch with water from a bottle in his pocket, and used the simple hypodermic attached to a red rubber bulb.

The seclusion, dim light, and ascetic nature of the "room" made his actions seem holy.

I was hoping he didn't die.

For one very long minute after the injection Burns stared at the ground. Then he looked up at me.

"I could use another one."

"And so you shall have," I promised, "but first we have to talk."

"I like coffee after my fix," he said, reminding me of a much older man.

29.

IT WAS MAYBE eight blocks from the unique shooting gallery to Cafecino Caprice on Lafayette. The coffee shop was open twenty-three hours a day, at least that's what the sign said. It was late enough that the place wasn't completely crowded. We settled at a round corner table with our two paper cups of black coffee, which cost $2.95 each, plus tax.

Burns was breathing easily, only sipping at the coffee now and then.

"Kierin's shit sets down hard and keeps it goin' for a good long time," Burns said. "If I had two hits I'd be well till lunchtime tomorrow."

"Ms. Goya says that you can help me exonerate Mr. Man."

"I thought you wanted to get him off death row?"

"Not execute," I explained. "Exonerate. Prove he's innocent."

"Oh." Burns snickered. "I know a lotta words, but sometimes they get a little mixed up 'cause I ain't never been to school. Not really. I was in elementary school for eight years, but then, when I just couldn't graduate an' I was fourteen they sent me on my way. My moms was already dead an' I only went 'cause she wanted me to, but then she died and they let me go....My moms was a nurse one time and she loved roses..."

I wondered if he was playing me.

"I need you to concentrate on what happened to Man," I said.

"Yeah," he said. "I could exorate him for ya. I mean...I know what happened and what they planned."

"Who?"

"Valence and Pratt."

"You knew them pretty well?"

"Pretty well? I had to suck Pratt's scrawny dick at least once a week. And he would tell me every time that if I told Valence that he'd kill me. He'd hold the gun to my head while I was suckin' him. I was always afraid he'd bust a nut and pull the trigger at the same time."

"I thought Miranda said that Man took you out from them."

"He did. He did. Three times. But you know I had that junk in my veins, and everything that the brothers had for me needed you to be straight. I tried. I really did. But you know bein' high's the only way things make sense in my head. Valence and Pratt knew that. They knew how to keep me right."

"I don't think the courts would take something like that as evidence," I said.

"No, they wouldn't. No one takes a junkie seriously. Even if I told 'em I was the one set up Manny for gettin' killed they wouldn't believe it."

"You set up A Free Man for Valence and Pratt?"

When Burns looked up at me there was a smile on his face and tears streaming from his eyes.

"Them cops come to me and say that Manny was gettin' in their business too bad and that they needed to talk to him. That was a code. They knew I didn't wanna hurt nobody and so they'd say *talk* when they meant *kill*."

I was sitting right in front of him, but he was looking to the right, at a blank wall.

"You did this for them more than once?" I asked.

"They said they wanted to talk to Manny," Burns continued, ignoring the question. "They said they'd gimme a hundred dollars and I'd be free'a them if I'd tell Manny I had dirt on them and to meet me at the Seagate Pier down on the West Village side.

"I made 'em gimme the hunnert up front and then I called Manny and said exactly what they wanted me to."

"Did you go there too?"

"Naw. I was at Auntie Hester's sleepin' in that same shed where I met you."

"So you're the one who set up Mr. Man for the ambush in the West Village?"

"Yeah. Out near the crypt."

"There's no crypt around over there," I said, realizing that I was beginning to talk like the junkie.

"Not no tourist trap fake plaque sayin' that this was where they buried George Washington or nuthin' like that, but you better believe that there's a sure-enough graveyard just a couple'a blocks from where Yollo an' Anton had me lead Manny."

"And you just told him to meet you even though you knew they planned to kill him."

Burns turned his head to face me. His eyes were still crying while the smile had subsided into a wry grin.

"Yeah."

"And you say you did this more than once?"

"A few times they had me steer people their way, and once I had to help them carry Maurice Chapman down there."

"Show me."

It was a long walk for the junkie, but he made it in his own fashion. At times he'd stagger, and now and then he came to a complete halt. He didn't talk much. I got the feeling that this mission was more serious than just the one hit of aitch could handle.

There was an abandoned church a block north of Christopher on the West Side Highway. This made me think of Mel and the evil where only good was supposed to exist.

There was a metal door behind a stand of holly at the north wall of the defunct house of prayer.

"See that brick with the black spot over the door?" Burns asked.

"Yeah."

"Reach up an' pull that suckah out."

The iron door was tall and wide. I could barely reach but finally managed to tease out the loose stone. On the inside plane of the brick there was taped a sophisticated key that fit the lock set in the corroded but still strong metal door.

I pulled the door open and was about to step through when Burns said, "Hold up, ex-cop."

He reached inside the doorway and flipped a switch to

turn on a spotlight that illuminated a brick courtyard. The inner square was teeming with rats of all shades and sizes. There were hundreds of the rodents disturbed by the sudden flash of intense light.

In the meanwhile Burns found a handful of Ping-Pong–ball size rocks that he threw in among the swarming carpet of fur.

The rats scattered then. Dozens flooded through the doorway, over my feet and between my ankles. They skittered and screeched loudly, decrying the invasion of their nest.

"Come on quick," Burns said, hurrying through the doorway. "You know street people can smell it when a door's open somewhere."

We made our way into the spotlit courtyard. Burns pushed the iron door shut and threw the bolt to secure it. I noticed that the hinges were well oiled for such an ancient entrance.

"You still got that key?" he asked.

"Yeah."

"It's that green door across the way."

Maybe fifteen feet away was another metal door; this one was made of copper and had turned the green of scum atop a stagnant pond.

"Hurry up an' get it open," Burns said. "We don't want no cops seein' the light."

Using the same key, I unlocked the door, pulled it open, and immediately Burns turned off the anti-rat spotlight. He moved around me, turned on another light in the vestibule we'd entered, and closed the door behind us.

It was only then that I noticed the acrid-sweet scent

of death. It was mild considering what a human corpse might be.

We descended a long stone staircase and came into a room piled with the corpses of at least a dozen souls. It was like my solitary cell, or the cellar in Queens where assassins meant to bury me, or the underground apartment that Melquarth had gifted for my time on the run.

Most of the dead had been that way for quite some time. They were desiccated and shorn of almost all flesh by meat-eating rats.

But the topmost corpse, a smallish body, was still decomposing. There were two of the rodents in the hollow of the rib cage tearing at the rotted flesh. Without thinking I took out my revolver and shot them.

The reports were quite loud, but we were underground and in an abandoned building.

"Are you crazy?" Burns yelled. It was the only time he'd raised his voice.

Looking at the partially exposed skull I saw a golden upper front tooth gleaming there.

"Johanna Mudd," I murmured.

"You knew her?" Burns asked.

"Who were they?"

"Kids that caused trouble," Burns said. "Enemies, ODs that would be better not founded."

"And you carried some of them in here?"

"You gonna shoot me like you did them rats?" he asked.

There was no fear in his voice. He was like an old-time condemned Soviet prisoner, sentenced to death but never told when the bullet to the back of the head might come.

"Let's get out of here," I said.

Up the stairs we went and out into the rats' courtyard. We passed through the iron door and secured it. I kept the key.

We stood at the entrance a moment or two, maybe experiencing the silent exercise of unconscious prayer for the dead. On each side, in the sheltering holly, dozens of red eyes of rats watched us, willing us to leave.

"What you gonna do with that key?" Burns asked.

"Throw it away," I said. "If they can't get in, maybe somebody'll bring out a body and get caught."

At Christopher and Hudson I gave the remaining cellophane packet and two hundred-dollar bills to Burns.

"Thanks!" he said like a gleeful child. "I thought you might be lyin' about another one."

"I try not to lie to people who help me."

Burns nodded, patting the pocket where he'd deposited the drug.

"Did Valence and Pratt work with anybody else?" I asked.

"Not usually. I mean, they had pimps and kids do some pretty bad things but they was always in charge if that's what you mean."

"Any other cops?"

"No. Never."

"Nobody?"

The only thing that Burns wanted was to get somewhere where he could inject his escape. But he didn't want to be rude to his benefactor so he stood there concentrating.

"One time they gave me a envelope and told me to meet this guy down by the United Nations."

"What kinda guy?"

"Just a short prissy faggot."

"White? Black?"

"White guy in a—in a pink suit smelled like roses. I remember because I usually can't put a name to a perfume but his was definitely roses."

"What was in the envelope?"

"I didn't open it 'cause Anton give it to me an' I was only gonna get paid when I got back."

"That's all?"

"Why you wanna know anyway? Anton an' Yollo is dead and all the businesses they had is ovah."

"That was a fresh body in the tomb," I said. "It couldn't have been there more than a few days or so. Somebody who knew the dead cops' business used it to bury that woman."

"Maybe I'll remember more later," Burns speculated. "You know, after I shoot up and then sleep, sometimes in my dreams I put things together that were far apart before."

"Yeah," I said. "Okay. If you remember something Hester has my number."

"Maybe we could make some kinda deal?"

"Maybe . . . if you remember something I need."

We stood there a moment or two in silence.

"You gonna get Manny outta that prison?" Burns asked.

"One way or another." I didn't know what the words meant—not yet.

The junkie took it as his cue to leave.

I stood there on the corner. It was nearly 3:00 a.m. The impact of the mass-murder gravesite manifested as a shudder in my chest and forearms.

30.

I KNOW I slept because all night long I heard that unnamed prisoner threaten to rape and murder my wife and
child. I felt the dank coldness and the crawling, hairy legs
of insects over my skin. Men cried out in pain and mad-
ness, and there was the continual sound of tramping feet:
men pacing in cells only two and a half steps in length.

None of this could have been real because, even though
I was in an underground cell, I was not anywhere near the
sounds of suffering. There were no rats keening for love or
blood, or footsteps destined for nowhere.

I would have done better staying awake and planning my
next move.

I woke up exhausted, with no appetite and little hope.
But I knew what I had to do next. I knew where to go and
how to get there.

My first destination was Ray Ray Wanamaker and Company
on the south side of Central Park at 11:45 a.m.

Ray Ray's brother, Brill Wanamaker, was a bus driver for

the city of New York. He worked hard and had many commendations from the city, his union, and private commuter organizations that judge public transportation and those who deliver it.

Brill was a bastion of good, but his brother, Ray Ray, was just bad. His first stint in prison was for drug dealing. His second conviction was for attempted murder, and his final period of incarceration was for stealing an ambulance; no one, not even Ray Ray, it seemed, could figure out why he stole that emergency vehicle. When he was in for the third time, Brill decided to save him. He bought a fleet of five defunct buses and worked diligently rebuilding them while Ray Ray languished in Attica.

Upon the career criminal's release, his brother presented him with a ready-made business that would ferry family and loved ones directly to the prisons where their blood, kinfolk, and friends were interned.

Love is a powerful tool. I believe that Ray Ray rehabilitated not because he had a good-paying business but because of the idea that his brother worked all those years just for him.

Ray Ray got a license to drive a bus, hired a staff of mainly ex-cons, and worked seven days a week transporting spouses, family members, and other lovers to see their unlucky kinsmen for a minimal price.

I took off my fake facial hair, donned a yellow hoodie, and made my way to the makeshift bus stop that the NYPD had been ordered to let operate so as not to incur political rancor from proponents for prisoner rights.

Most of Ray Ray's clients, to most prisons, were women and children, mothers and now and then a brother or father. But Bedford Hills Correctional Facility was the only maximum-security female prison in the New York penal system. So there were a good number of husbands and boyfriends sprinkled in among mothers, grandmothers, grown daughters, and children. When I climbed up into the entry well of the old-time bus I had my $17.50 in hand, ready to pay and ride in relative anonymity.

"Joe?" the driver said.

"Lenny."

"You got somebody at Bedford?"

"Private now. There's someone I need to talk to."

"You lucky Ray Ray don't drive this run," Lenny the Lookout said. He was a skinny white guy with dirty blond hair and skin something like an albino crocodile hide.

"Why's that?"

" 'Cause you busted his ass more than any other cop. He told me that you could never get on this bus."

"And?"

"I won't tell if you won't. That'll be seventeen-fifty."

"You goin' ta see ya wife?" a plump black woman with a beautiful face asked me. She had the window seat and I the aisle.

"A friend of a friend. He can't be seen up there and so I deliver the message."

"Conjugal visit?"

"I don't think my friend would appreciate that."

"He don't have to know," the brown-faced Aphrodite explained. "I mean if her man can't come up and give her what she needs he should be happy he got a friend that'a do that for him."

"If he could be happy about that, then he wouldn't be in so much trouble that he can't be seen."

"He don't have to know," she said again.

"Leonard Pillar," I said, extending a hand.

"Zenobia Price," she replied, accepting the proffered hand. "I been up to see my sister's husband in Ossining five times. She in jail for the same robbery up here."

"What would you do if your man came up to service your sister?"

She thought a moment and then grinned. The gap-toothed smile reminded me that the letter from Minnesota had re-sexualized me.

"I'd cut off his dick, take Athena's kids, and move to Lake Tahoe—the Nevada side, where I could deal cards for a livin'."

Before we got off the bus Zenobia gave me her phone number and I gave her one that might seem like it was connected to me.

Bedford Hills Correctional Facility was a group of old brick buildings separated from the world by high wire fences and enough razor wire to protect Fort Knox.

I let Zenobia enter before me because I didn't want her to hear my real name. I lied about who I was going to see and my name because I wanted to linger someplace with Zenobia Price. I wanted to smell her sweat, but I knew that I had to hold back some or soon I'd be in some deconsecrated crypt, stacked with strangers and eaten by rats.

"Name?" the front-gate lookout asked. Even though she was sitting, I could see that she was tall; her skin, white like aged ivory. The sentry did not smile within the confines of the prison, but she didn't seem dour.

"Joe Oliver."

"Inmate you're coming to see including her number and the number we gave allowing your visit."

"Lauren Bachnell."

The officer, who had not been looking at me, raised her head.

"There is no inmate here with that name."

"Not an inmate," I said. "The assistant warden."

"And who are you?"

"I already told you that."

The sentry was confused. The words I gave her didn't have a corollary in her rule book.

"Step to the side," she said to me. "Mary! This man needs assistance," she called to another woman sitting behind a metal desk maybe fifteen feet away.

Mary had broad shoulders, and when she stood up I had the feeling of being faced by a man. She was very upset to have to deal with hoi polloi like me. I imagined she was once the custodian on duty for visitation and now she had risen to a more supervisorial rank.

"Yes?" she said to me. Rather than calling her a black woman, I would have used the descriptor caramel-buttercream. Together her fists would have been the size of my head, and I had no doubt she was close to using those hams on my jaw.

"My name is Joe Oliver and I'm here to see Lauren Bach-nell."

"Assistant Warden Bachnell has a secretary and a phone."

"And yet here I stand, talking to you."

"I can't help you."

"I'll tell Lauren that when I call from the phone booth outside."

Mary didn't like me. Most people don't. I push them and then make them do things that insult their sense of independence. Since my own stint in prison I especially enjoyed making prison guards into pretzels.

"What's your name again?" the woman named after our savior's mother asked.

I told her.

"Wait over there," she ordered, waving at a battered pine bench made for no more than two.

Sitting there I wondered about my life up until that moment. Those many years I had progressed steadily but always on the wrong path. As a lone-wolf cop and a resentful PI I was spry of step but blindered.

It occurred to me that my whole life had been organized around the guiding principle of being completely in charge of whatever I did. Gladstone understood this; that's why he helped me become a PI.

The problem was that no man is an island; no man can control his fate. No woman either, or gnat or redwood tree.

There I was at a women's prison, looking for answers I didn't want, propelled by forces I could not control. For some reason this revelation made me smile. It was as if a great weight had been taken from me. The question was no longer *if* I might fail but when.

"Mr. Oliver?"

I looked up to see Mary and a smaller woman who had bronze-red skin. Mary's uniform was dark blue and imposing, where the smaller guard's costume consisted of a tan blouse and black trousers. She wore a belt that had a truncheon and pepper spray hanging from one side and a walkie-talkie attached to the other.

"Yes, Mary?" I said.

She frowned, then glowered, then said, "The assistant warden will see you. Riatta will show you the way."

The short guard walked me to an iron gate, opened the door with a keypad combination, and then led me down a long brick hallway that had no doors. We came to another door that needed deciphering and then crossed a grassy courtyard where three prisoners were doing gardening work.

The inmates wore gray uniforms that, for the most part, hid their figures. They looked at me with interests that ranged from come hither to stay away.

The guard named Riatta did not speak to me or anyone else on our journey. We passed maybe eighteen prisoners, three women guards, and two men. Finally we came to a door that had both a sentinel and an electronic lock. Riatta passed both tests and then shepherded me through and to a gray-green elevator door.

When we got there the door opened, revealing a chamber that no more than three bodies might inhabit.

"Get in," were Riatta's first and last words to me.

I experienced a sudden pang of fear. I was no longer in New York City, but for all I knew there was a warrant out on me for murder, and here I was in a state prison.

The door closed and a motor hummed. The chamber moved at a pace that was so slow I didn't feel it. Two minutes later the door slid open and there before me stood a familiar face.

"Hello, your majesty," she said.

Lauren Bachnell had been a green recruit in the halcyon days of my police career. Her hair could be called either red or blond, and her gait was graceful if not quite feminine. She was tall for a woman, her face was broad, and her skin as pale as any Scandinavian's.

Her body, in a uniform-like dark blue pants suit, was a bit wider than when I last saw her, but I was not fooled. I had seen her lay low an angel-dusted six-foot man with one punch.

"I'm just a civilian now," I said.

She turned with military precision and I followed.

We went into an office that had large barred windows set within three of its walls. The desk was pale green, constructed from plastic of some sort. There was a computer on a side table and a blue blotter with not even a pencil in sight. Laur—that's what I called iher when we worked together—had always been inordinately neat, maybe even a little obsessive.

She sat behind the desk and I took the hot seat across from her.

She gave me a big smile.

"What brings you out here, civilian?" she asked.

"Looking for a woman."

"You always were."

"Work," I said.

Lauren liked me. I never saved her life or even taught her very much, but I treated her like a partner, and not all men did that on the force in our day—today either.

"Name?" she said.

"Lana Ruiz."

Lauren cocked her head to the side like she used to when we were partners and my voice modulated when talking on the phone to a lover or at least a potential lover.

"No," I said to her unspoken question. "She has information about something that I need for a job."

"What?"

"Believe me, darling, you don't want to know."

Lauren let a beat or two pass and then reached into a drawer, from which she extracted a phone receiver. Beyond my line of sight she entered a few digits and then said, "Have Lana Ruiz brought to my meeting cell."

She put the phone away and considered me.

I honestly had no idea what she was thinking. Even though I love the company of women, I can't claim to understand them very well.

"My husband left me over you," she said after quite some time of silence.

"Say what?"

"He said that every time I came off a shift with you I was all sexy and did things that I never had before. He said he didn't realize it at the time, but after you and I were reassigned to new partners he said I hardly even touched him and when I did there was no feeling to it."

"Is that true?" I asked.

"You made me realize something about myself, Joe."

"What's that, Laur?"

"Well." She hesitated. "It's like this. I'm definitely a heterosexual woman. I like men's parts and how they use them. But the world that men imagine themselves living in has nothing to do with the world I know. Their football games and physical violence are just stupid to me. And even though you were one of those men, when we were together in that cruiser I could imagine a life in a world maybe a hundred years from now where my ideas and some man's might be the same."

Our eyes met and the phone sounded. Lauren picked up the receiver, listened, and then put the phone away.

"Get in the elevator and it will take you to Lana. When you're through, knock on the door and the guards will take you back to clearance."

"What about what you were telling me?" I asked.

"That was then," she explained.

"And this is now," I argued.

"My new husband has given me a daughter," she said with a friendly look on her wide features. "And as many times as I imagined you when I was with George, I'd never upset Cynthia's applecart."

I nodded and stood.

"No one will be watching or listening in on you and Lana," Lauren assured me.

Moving as slowly as it did, I couldn't tell if the lift was taking me up or down. But when the door opened I found myself facing a riveted metal portal guarded by two women, both of whom were equipped with sidearms and batons. One was brown and the other near black.

"You here for Ruiz?" the darker-skinned guard asked.

"Yes."

The questioner's partner unlocked the metal door and pulled it open. I walked through into a room similar to Lauren's "meeting cell." The only furniture was a solitary table and two chairs.

A young woman in a gray uniform was looking out the barred window, over the tops of trees.

She turned, saw me, and frowned.

"What is this?" she asked.

"My name is Joe Oliver," I said. "I'm a private detective investigating the conviction of A Free Man."

"You think they could kill him two times?"

"I'm trying to prove that Detectives Valence and Pratt had targeted the Blood Brothers of Broadway and finally got killed trying to bushwhack Mr. Man."

Lana was five five with dark brown skin and hair that was straight and coarse due to hard water and substandard hair products. She was handsome the way beautiful women get after they pass the age of forty. But she was a young woman, in her late twenties, aged by prison and a life that charged more than it gave back.

"Come have a seat," I offered.

She sneered and then wondered, finally taking one of the battered wood chairs at the sad and slender table.

Sitting down across from her, I noticed that she'd bitten her nails. She saw what I did and put her hands in her lap.

"Manny," she said. It might have been a mantra. "How did you get here to me?"

"I got your name from a court document," I said. "But before I came here I met with Lamont Charles. He sent me to see Miranda Goya and she pointed the way to a guy named Theodore."

"Who?"

"Burns."

"Oh." A twinge of sadness crossed her features. "That kid was a sad case. How is he?"

"So high he could peek into heaven."

The phrase brought a smile to her face. She sat back in the chair and assessed me.

"What you want?"

"Can you give me anything that might put a bright light on what Valence and Pratt were up to?"

"Not if I evah wanna see my little girl again."

"Um..."

"Cecilia," Lana said in a rolling Spanish lilt. "She's four now and with my mother. Yollo Valence told Billy Makepeace that if I stayed quiet I'd get outta here before she gets to high school."

"Valence is dead."

"Yeah, but him an' Anton had connections that want all that shit they did kept quiet."

"Can you tell me who?"

"I don't know no names, but even if I did I wouldn't be sayin' 'em."

"Who's this Billy Makepeace?"

"A cop I was bangin'."

"He was your lover?"

Lana smiled at me.

"If it was nothing, then why would he help you with a dangerous man like Valence?"

"He couldn't come with a condom on and sometimes we'd get a little high so maybe I'd let him."

"And then came Cecilia."

"Manny didn't want me seein' no cop, but I needed things that Billy wanted to give me. He paid my rent half the time and fooled himself to think he was in love with me. After I had the baby he had the test done and he didn't want his daughter's mother killed."

"He knew about what Valence and Pratt were doing?"

"Everybody knew," she said, as disgusted with the human race as Laur had been with men.

"You think he'd consider making some kind of testimony about that?"

"Would you?" she sneered.

It was such a good question that I fell out of my role as investigator for a moment or two. In order to be a cop, a good cop, you have to be ready to put your life on the line at any moment. Most cops had families and futures to think about. They acted as if those who broke the law had put themselves in jeopardy. But that wasn't the case with me. Melquarth could tell that; so could my daughter.

"They don't have no cameras in here," Lana said.

"The assistant warden told me."

"You wanna do it sittin' in that chair?"

The question on my face made her smile. She stood up, sat on the table, and spread her trousered legs.

"We could do it like this if you want?"

"I'm old enough to be your father," I argued in spite of the sweat at the back of my neck.

"You could be my baby daddy too."

"What about Billy?"

"He ain't here."

"I don't have a condom."

"They got this thing called the Family Centered Program at Bedford Hills. If I get pregnant I get nine months' care and then get to spend at least a year with my baby. Cecilia need a little brother or sister. After that I be out in less than two years.

"Billy's marriage went dry," Lana coaxed. "He cain't say nuthin' 'bout me gettin' laid. Shit. Do you know what it's like up in here?"

I certainly did. My breath came funny and I was certainly aroused. But the thought of Aja kept my zipper up. I *was* old enough to be Lana's father—and I would act the part. I took seven hundred dollars of Augustine Antrobus's money and handed it to the young woman.

"I have a daughter," I said in answer to the confused frown on the Blood Sister's face. "I love her more than this life or the next."

"We could do somethin' else if you want."

"How about telling me how to get to Billy Makepeace."

31.

"MR. MAKEPEACE," I said when he answered the phone.

I was seated in the last row of the bus in a solitary seat across the aisle from the toilet.

"Who is this?" a man said. "How did you get this number?"

"Lana wondered if you had gone to see Cecilia."

"Who is this?" William Makepeace demanded.

"A friend of A Free Man."

I imagined that in the barrier of silence Billy was wondering if he should just hang up.

"Tell me who this is."

"I want to know if you're willing to testify against two dead men, set the mother of your child free, and maybe keep an innocent man from getting executed."

Another spate of silence.

"Whoever you are," he said, "I am an officer of the law and your threats constitute a crime."

"Not if you know about a private graveyard maintained by Officers Valence and Pratt. Not if there's even a shred of a suspicion that you knew what they were up to."

"Who is this?"

"Like I said, a friend of Manny's."

"What about Lana?"

"She asked me to ask you about your daughter when I said I wanted to know why she wasn't dead like the rest of her friends."

"I don't know anything about what you're saying," he said flatly. Then he hung up.

I pulled up the window and threw the phone onto the highway.

There's a liquor store five blocks from the underground bunker on Seventy-Third Street where I was hiding. There I bought a liter of Hennessy, extra old, and then I made my way into the sleeping crypt.

On a shelf in the studio I found a turquoise plastic drinking glass that held maybe three ounces. I filled it with cognac, drained it, then filled it again.

After four drinks, my lips and fingertips were tingling. I stumbled up the stairs and out of the hideaway into the street.

I walked, almost without a misstep, down to the Theater District, where I found an electronics store that sold disposable phones. I bought three of these.

At a popular coffee shop chain store I ordered a huge cup of dark-roast coffee, which I had no intention of drinking. I jiggered one of the temporary phones to life and started making my late-night calls.

*　　*　　*

"Hello?" Aja-Denise Oliver said in a tremulous, sleepy tone.

"It's me."

"Daddy."

"You okay?"

"Uh-huh. Tomorrow we're gonna go to Disney World and Coleman says we could all go fishin' if we want."

I was relieved that she was so far away.

"You aren't calling your friends, are you?"

"No."

"Nobody?"

"This one guy I met at the roller rink in Dumbo called my real phone. I told him I was down with relatives in D.C. for two weeks. Nobody knows I know him, though."

"I love you, girl."

"Mama's here. She wanna talk to you."

There was a rustling sound and then: "Joe?"

"Hey, Monica."

"Are you all right?"

Rage sparked at a place very near my dinosaur brain. There was a time when my wife could have shielded me from the terrors of Rikers. She could have put up the money and I might have escaped the brunt of my late-night terrors.

"Joe?" she asked again.

"I'm fine."

"Can you tell me what's going on? Did my call really bring all this down?"

"Not completely. I mean, I could'a become a plumber," I said. I just didn't want her angry with me. There was no need to torture her, no matter how deep my pain.

"Why are you calling?" she asked.

"Because my little girl's voice is like penicillin for my

wounds." I felt a little eddy of giddiness twist through my mind. The alcohol was increasing its hold.

"We're fine," Monica said. "Coleman is protecting us."

I sent two texts after saying good night to Aja. Twelve minutes later my temporary phone rang.

"Hey, Effy."

"Joe?"

"Yes, ma'am."

"What's this phone?"

"I'm in a little trouble."

"You need me?"

There was something in the tenor of her question that sent a chill through me. It was something beyond love all the way back to when humanity was a group animal connected by experience deeper than any memory.

"I been thinkin' about you," the cognac in me said.

"What?"

"You don't owe me anything, Ef."

"Only my life, baby."

I stood up from the small table and walked toward the front door of the coffee emporium. People, I felt, were staring at me. I think I was able to walk in a fairly sober fashion but the liquor was getting stronger.

"Maybe so," I said into the tiny receiver. "But you kept me from crash and burn whenever I called. I needed a woman to be there and there you were."

She was silent for a moment or two, and I was trying my best to walk a straight line up Eighth. People were moving in sober gaits all around me. I was worried that some cop might see me and bring me down.

"Where are you?" Effy asked.

"Nowhere."

"Do you need me to come there with you?"

"I love you, Effy" was all I could say.

She gasped over the airwaves and into my soul.

Damn, I was drunk.

It took four blocks to explain that I wanted a new relationship; that I loved her and maybe we could be friends. She told me that at first I saved her from prosecution and then, when I let her in when I was down, she was able to use me like a life raft through her own troubles. Together we had navigated into safer waters.

We disconnected when I got to the front door of my hideaway.

Ensconced in the apartment, I poured another glass of cognac and drank it at the sink. Then I served up another and went to sit on the single-mattress cot that passed for a bed.

The ceiling of the underground room was low. I could feel it pressing down on my head. The room was spinning, but that wasn't too serious a problem; I could ride that whirlwind too. But there was a certainty in my mind that I was going to die in the morning or maybe the day after. Someone was going to kill me.

I remember feeling nauseous. I thought I was going to throw up and tried to lurch from the bed. But instead I fell sideways into an unconsciousness that contained entire scenarios of me shot, killed, drained of blood, and bunged into a coffin.

* * *

The ringer on the temp phone started at a note in the lower register and then climbed higher and higher for sixteen tones. The last, and longest, chime was a little piercing. I know the musical scheme so well because it rang three times somewhere after 4:00 a.m.

The first series of notes reminded me of a stream making its way across the floor of my underground cave. There were fish in there and a mountain lion somewhere above looking to take me down if I tried to drink water.

The second call was a shimmering wall of lights that resonated with the tinkling sounds.

Halfway through the third attempt I sat up straight, snagged the phone from the floor, and cried, "Who the fuck is it?"

"How's it comin', King?" Melquarth Frost murmured in my ear.

"Mel."

"You okay?"

"That might be a little optimistic. But I'm not dead."

"How's the room?"

"I expect a big red devil to bang the door down and take my soul any minute. Why are you calling me?"

"You the one texted me your number."

"It couldn't wait till the sun came up?"

"I was working on this spring-driven wooden clock from the seventeen hundreds when it hit me."

"The clock hit you?" I was just talking, trying to keep from throwing up.

"If you crossed the line and the cops are after you I got a plan."

"Plan for what?"

"For you."

I thought about standing, realized I couldn't, then leaned back against the cold brick wall behind the bed. The chill went some way toward rejuvenating me.

"Talk on," I said.

"Man is dead no matter what way you look at it. And the police department is never gonna admit to cops as bad as Valence and Pratt. Neither will they admit to framing you. You're a bug to them, and we all know what happens to a bug when he get between a rock and the hard place."

"Doesn't sound like much of a plan, Mel."

"I know a dude down in Panama could make a whole baseball team disappear. All I need is a plane and that's just some money."

We talked longer, but I don't remember what was said. I hadn't been that drunk in a very long time. And I hope never to go that far again.

32.

LANGUISHING IN THE darkness of semiconscious-
ness, creeping danger, and certain death, I felt the splash
of a drop of water on my forehead. If I were the Wicked
Witch, that would be the sign of my undoing. I would die
and the war of flying monkeys would be over.

My gut felt like a flagging dirigible and the pain in my
head was a brick wall: solid and everlasting.

Another tiny splash.

That was one of the tears on my neck when Aja hugged
me after I'd been let out of Rikers. I cried too because I was
so happy to be loved.

"Are you okay, Daddy?" she asked. It felt as if she were in
that room with me and we were crying together.

The next drop brought to mind the rainstorm I was
caught in, in the third grade walking home from school.
It had been gray all day, but no one had told me it might
rain. I gave up protecting my homework and my books.
The spring rain soaked through my clothes. It was cold and
set me to shivering on the cot where I lay.

I remembered slogging through the downpour toward my grandparents' house. There was no other choice. When I got there my grandmother put my clothes in the dryer so that when I put them on again I'd be warm and toasty.

There must be a leak above the bed; that's what I thought. I didn't want to get up in the middle of the night to fix it, so I turned on my side and moved closer to the wall. All I wanted was unconciousness.

The next drop landed in my left ear. I shot up straight voicing a wordless complaint.

When I opened my eyes I saw that the lights had been turned on and that the leak was actually a man with an eye-dropper torturing me like some minor demon from Dante's hell.

"Glad!" I cried. "What the fuck, man?"

He'd pulled a chair up next to me and used one of the blue plastic juice glasses for his store of torture drops.

"At first I thought you were dead, brother," my oldest cop friend claimed. "Then I smelled the XO."

"How'd you find me?" I noticed that he was wearing all black.

"I put out the question on my Facebook and got a mes-sage from Lauren Bachnell that you had just left Bedford on Ray Ray's commuter line. All I had to do was set up across the street and wait for you."

The hangover that I thought would never leave drained out of me in less than sixty seconds. It was a matter of life and death in that room with Gladstone— mostly death. It all came clear to me right then. I under-stood what happened to me and why. I knew what the verdict was too.

I looked at my brother in black and asked, "Are you here to take me out?"

"That's what they said. Not for the first time either."

I considered attacking him but knew better. He could have put a bullet in my skull rather than those drops on my head.

"You were in league with Little Exeter and his crew?"

"Not me. They just called me up and said that you were a dead man."

"Why call you?" I asked, even though I knew the answer.

"Nowadays I'm kind of a clearinghouse under the new mayor and chief. They wanna clean up the past and start the future with a blank slate. But back then there was a kind of a club that shared all that money swirling around. My nephew was in law school, and I bought my wife a house in Miami. I had told my friends back then what you were up to and they decided to make you die."

"But you gave them a better choice," I said.

"I knew you and the ladies, Joe. I knew we could put a frame around you with a cute young white girl. Worked beautiful. But Convert is a pervert. He made it so Jocelyn Bryor got the case and turned Monica against you. I had it so you'd make bail and then I'd talk you into accepting what had happened. But after you got slashed I just put you in a hole and let the powers that be do what they did."

"So you destroyed my life," I said. "Just like that."

"I saved your life, Joe. Don't you ever believe anything else."

"But now you're gonna come in here and kill me."

"When I saw you come in this building, I knew you had taken Mr. Thurman's hideaway," he said. "We've

273

known about this place for a while. How'd you know about it, anyway?"

"Are you gonna kill me, Glad?"

"Do I have to?"

"I'm a cop, man. I saw something bad and I took steps. Your people wrecked everything."

"You're an ex-cop, Joe. And who knows? Maybe if you stayed on the job you'd'a gotten shot down in a firefight or somethin'. It could be I saved your life twice."

"It was wrong what you did."

"Maybe," Gladstone Palmer admitted. "Maybe. But you have to understand, Joe, the brass now is all new. The people I worked with are off the force."

"Paul Convert's still around."

"He's not gonna be a problem long. After he messed up in Queens he's in more hot water than you."

"You knew about Queens?"

"After the fact." Glad's smile was friendly if sad. "The force can't afford a scandal, Joe. The people dealing on the docks are either retired, dead, or reformed. Not even the mayor would stand in the way of your demise."

Gladstone had a way of revealing the truth. I could see that I'd never be exonerated, much less reinstated.

"And there's another thing," my friend said.

"What's that?" I asked. A wave of exhaustion passed through me.

"This thing with Free Man, Leonard Compton."

"How you know about him?"

"I'm lookin' for you, and in a whole other precinct you're kickin' up dust over a cop killer. You know the left hand speaks to the right even on the dark side of the force."

"Valence and Pratt killed over a dozen people, Glad."

"I know."

"You do?"

"Everybody knew about Valence and Pratt. But nobody kills a cop unless it's the last resort. And you know those boys made a lotta money. They could grease the wheels of machines half the way to Albany."

"That's wrong, man."

"Yes, it is, but that's not the question."

"Then what is?"

"Do you need me to kill you right now?"

There was no smile on my old friend's lips. I couldn't remember him ever without at least the hint of a grin somewhere on his face. I took the question seriously, and from somewhere in the depths of my mind an answer rose to the surface like the carcass of some long-dead deep-sea creature.

"No," I said. "No."

Sleep came with my last negation. I don't remember whatever else Glad might have said. I don't remember him leaving my subterranean cell. I just passed out, unable to defend or save myself.

But in that deep repose the answer to my quest remained in light.

I couldn't repair my career. I couldn't achieve a reprieve for A Free Man. All I had was the truth and the certainty that I had to do something about that truth. If that meant breaking the law, I was ready. If it meant missing my child's graduation, that would have to be.

33.

THE HANGOVER RETURNED with consciousness, but it wasn't nearly as bad as it could have been. The only aftereffects were jitters in my extremities.

I got out of bed, used the water-closet toilet, and sat in the chair that my old friend and near assassin sat in to sprinkle water on me.

It all started with a letter from the Midwest. My life was in shambles, but sometimes you had to break things down to see what was wrong.

I knew what to do and half the way to do it. It wasn't so much a plan as it was a suicide mission aimed at the heart of enemy territory. I was now an enlightened terrorist planning to show the all-powerful enemy that I could hurt them, that I could take away their shiny baubles and false judgments.

"Mel?" I said when he answered the phone.

"My liege."

It was 10:16 a.m. and I was at the coffee emporium again. This time I drank what I bought.

"Am I right that you sit around workin' on timepieces all day; that and thinking about stickin' it to the law?"

"Every hour of every day," he said. "Rain or shine. Sound asleep or wide-awake."

"I like your plan about that baseball team escaping to Panama. But I need to add a little to it."

We talked for more than an hour, during the first thirty minutes of which my new best friend was quite leery. But by the end I had brought him around to my way of thinking. Around 11:30 he expressed an excitement that could only mean that something bad was bound to happen.

It was chilly that morning, but I still had my heavy disguise coat so I wandered down until I came to a Times Square street that the previous mayor had blocked off so that touristical pedestrians could stroll freely and sit on benches placed here and there.

He answered the call on the first ring.

"Hello?" His tone was anything but confident.

"Mr. Braun," I said. "Tom Boll here."

"Boll?" he whined. "What do you want now?"

"I misled you in the beginning, Mr. Braun. I wasn't hired to find Johanna Mudd but to prove your case that A Free Man was innocent. My clients had heard that you were backing off and they wanted to keep that engine running."

"Man?"

"Yeah. I found Johanna too. She's dead on top of a heap of dead bodies provided by the cops your client killed."

"I had nothing to do with any of that."

"You sent men to kill me."

"Marmot told me he was going to threaten you, that's all."

"And you believed him?"

"You don't understand what you're doing."

"No, sir, I do understand. You might not like it that I passed the black mark back to you by telling Marmot's boss that you hired me to indict him—but that doesn't make me ignorant. All I did was turn the focus on you."

"Not me, you idiot, my daughter."

"What about your daughter?"

"The reason I backed off the Man case was because they took my daughter. They have her somewhere and they said unless I do as they instructed that she'd be hurt and then killed."

"Marmot said this?"

"Yes."

"And Antrobus?"

"I don't know that name. But now that you told them you're looking into Marmot for me, they say they're going to kill my little girl."

The bane of police work is innocent bystanders. You try your best, but unseen events, ricochet bullets, and false arrest are a part of the job.

"I'm sorry to hear that, Mr. Braun. I mean, all I knew was that you were about to wreck Man's case and then you set me up to meet two assassins. If I knew about your child I would have done something else."

He was quiet on the line.

"I have some questions," I said in a mild tone.

"Why should I answer?"

"Because I'm probably the only hope you have of getting your daughter back."

He took in and released three breaths, then said, "What do you want to know?"

"How old is your daughter?"

"Seven," he said, and then he cried some.

"I will get her back for you if you set up a hearing for Man in Manhattan. It'll have to be sometime next week."

"How can you get my daughter?"

"How did I get to you?"

"I'll do as you say if you agree to free my daughter *first*."

"No, Mr. Braun. This is the deal—you set up a meeting between a group of people of my choosing and Man. After that we will bring your daughter to you."

"Who are you working with?"

"Deep talent, Mr. Braun, deep talent."

"I can get a court date set," he admitted, "but I've been told, by people who know, that it will be impossible to change the verdict unless I prove that he didn't pull the trigger. And I don't care how much you investigate, Mr. Boll, you will not prove that. I grieve over Ms. Mudd, but you cannot save her either."

"I appreciate your honesty, Mr. Braun. If I'm about to partner up with somebody, I expect honor. But don't worry, sir. All we need is A Free Man in a downtown holding cell. You won't be required to prove the impossible or raise the dead."

"I'll try to set the hearing for Monday. I know a judge who owes me a thing or two."

"I'll be in touch."

"All I care about is Chrissie, Mr. Boll."

"I understand. I have a daughter too. I can't even imagine how you must feel. But you stay true to me and you two will be eating ice cream sundaes by Wednesday night."

The outside bench was getting chilly so I walked over to Grand Central just to warm up. I went upstairs there to the steak house and ordered a porterhouse steak, medium well, with thick fries and French beans.

"Hello?" a jaunty voice answered on the other end of my third and final phone call.

"Was that you last night or just a dream?" I asked.

"Was I handsome and witty?"

"I guess."

"Then that was me. What can I do for you, Joe?"

"What do you know about Augustine Antrobus and William James Marmot?"

"This is that Free Man thing, right?" Gladstone Palmer surmised. "Joe, you cannot exonerate a man who killed two cops. Sherlock Holmes couldn't do shit like that."

"I know," I said. "And I accept it. But you know I stepped on a few toes before you enlightened me, and now I have to do some housekeeping."

"You'll stop trying to get Man exonerated?"

"If Convert stays off my ass."

"I'll send you what files we have by e-mail. But, Joe."

"What?"

"I can't save your ass every time you step out of line."

* * *

The files came before my steak. I couldn't read them on my cheap phone, but that didn't matter. I forwarded them to Mel with a note and started on my steak.

They seated me next to the outer wall of the dining area. From there I could look down on the rotunda as thousands of commuters, civilians, cops, and some crooks passed through. There rose a senseless, very human hubbub from below while I ate my red meat and plotted against the state.

"Ferris," he answered on the third ring.

"Hello, Mr. Ferris. Joe Oliver here."

"Hello, my boy. How are you?"

"It's the fifteenth round of an old-time boxing match," I said. "I've lost every minute of every round up till now, but I think I finally see a way to get my hook past his defense."

"It's hard to find the torque to hurt a man that late in the fight," the world-wise multibillionaire opined.

"Don't I know it."

"What can I do for you, son?"

"Is there some music event going on tonight that you'd like to see with my grandmother?"

"There's an invitation I have to hear three of Mozart's four-handed sonatas in the upstairs chamber at Carnegie Hall."

"If you want I'd be happy to go with you and bring my grandmother along."

"That would be wonderful."

"Then it's done," I said.

"And what can I do for you?"

"A huge favor for me," I said. "I hope not so much for you."

We discussed an impossible task for all of four minutes, at the end of which Roger Ferris said, "I've been a crook all my life, Joe. It's nice to know I could use that talent to do something right."

"Can I come casual to the event?" I asked. "I have a chore or two before the performance and I might not be able to make it back to Brooklyn in time to change." While I was saying this I heard three tiny beeps in the receiver.

"Do what you can."

After disconnecting I saw that the beeping was a text from Mel.

Set!

"I suppose this means that he's doin' somethin' for you?" my onetime sharecropper grandmother said.

"Yes, ma'am."

"You know if I go to this thing I got to get my hair done."

"And I know how much you love sittin' in Lulu's chair."

"Roger called over to her after he talked to you, and she's comin' here."

"I guess he really wants this date."

She harrumphed and then said, "I guess. Are you bein' careful, Joey?"

"Better than that, Grandma...I'm doing what's right."

34.

IT TOOK AN hour and a half to get to Pleasant Plains, Staten Island. I called on the walk over from the train station. Melquarth met me at the gate of his unholy home.

"How ya doin'?" he asked while shaking my hand.

It was a rhetorical question. My host expected a nod or maybe some noncommittal phrase, but instead I stood still, considering his words.

"What?" he asked.

"Tell me something, Mel."

"What's that?"

"I know why I'm here at your door. My world went crazy a dozen years ago and you are the only one crazy enough to help me through."

"Okay."

"You say that I was the only one ever, like that red bird you saw, to do what was right by you, but that feels like, I don't know, a little weak."

"For you it is, Joe." It was the first time I could remember that he used my first name. "I mean, you weren't raised as the demon inside a house of piety. You never had a rapist father and a mother who hated you for it. But take my word... You didn't shoot me and then you didn't lie; and those few years where we played chess you just sat there like the brother I never had, the friendship I could take for granted, or the father who led me by the hand.

"In my world, in my mind, that was the treasure I longed for."

"What about that watchmaker?"

Melquarth smiled sadly and then nodded. "One day I'll tell you about him."

I'd hit a nerve in a man who didn't seem to have nerves.

"Okay," I acceded. "Let's go."

"You didn't answer my question."

"How'm I doin'?"

A friendlier smile with the same nod.

"Got cold stone instead of a brain and a hornets' nest in place of a heart."

"Then we're ready to begin."

On the other side of the unbreakable glass wall stood a tall man in a light tan three-piece suit. On the floor next to him lay a metal folding chair that Melquarth had set in the otherwise bare white cell. I figured that the man was William James Marmot and that he had used the chair to test the unbreakability of the opaque glass wall. Now he was pacing nervously, looking everywhere for a way out.

The blood from Porker's torture had been cleaned away.

"How'd it go?" I asked my self-assigned friend.

"I used a partner, nobody you have to worry about. William James had two bodyguards, so I needed a hand. He came along peacefully when they went down."

"Anybody see your face?" I asked.

"Naw."

"How should we do this?"

"You say that Antrobus knows you," Mel offered. "That means if we let this guy live that he shouldn't see your face, or your skin color for that matter."

"Why didn't you grab Antrobus?"

"I asked around about him. He's a dangerous man, a very dangerous man. I wouldn't mind going up against him, but first I figured we could play with Jimmy here."

Mel was wearing blue jeans, a blue T-shirt, and the white mask of a Greek god. In his left hand he carried a long-barreled .22 pistol.

Prisoner was on the other side of the cell when the bad man walked in. Marmot was a shade taller than Mel. He listed forward before Mel raised the pistol. This gesture set the security expert back a step and a half.

"What do you want?" Marmot asked Frost.

"I need for you to tell me where Chrissie Braun is."

"I don't know what you're talking about."

"An eye for an eye," Mel explained.

Marmot's lips parted.

"I told you that I don't know—"

Mel lowered the pistol and shot the upright man in the left foot. Marmot yelled, fell, and at the same time threw himself at Mel. For a moment I feared for my cohort, but Mel sidestepped the attack, pistol-whipping Marmot on the side of his head as he passed by.

On the ground the man turned into a child crying as he held his bloody and shod left foot.

Mel reached into his pants pocket and pulled out a cloth bandage roll and two thick wads of cotton. These he threw at his victim.

"Take off your shoe and sock and wrap yourself up before you get blood all over my floor."

Marmot did as he was told, blubbering the whole time.

When he was through, Mel said, "I got another bandage in my other pocket. I hope you don't need to use that too because the next bullet goes in your left hand and you know it's a bitch to tie on a bandage with just one hand."

"What the fuck do you want?"

"Where's Johanna Mudd's body buried, and where are you holding a living Chrissie Braun?"

"If-if-if you don't let me go, my people will kill her."

Mel lifted the barrel of the gun so that it was leveled at Marmot's face. The man cowered.

"If that's true you're as good as dead."

"Mudd is buried in a church down in the West Village. It's a—it's abandoned and the cops I worked with used it to hide the bodies they made."

That proved Marmot's collusion. I reasoned that Porker and his friends planned to bury me in that rat-infested pit.

"What about the child?"

"How do I know you won't kill me after I tell?"

"First," Mel said, gesturing carelessly with the pistol, "I can't kill you right off because you might be lying, or maybe the girl got moved while you were crying like a baby on my floor. Second, I've been employed to find a dead woman and a live girl. You don't mean enough for me to kill."

"I don't believe you," the conniving child who lived in Marmot's heart said.

"Believe this," Mel replied, now aiming the pistol at our prisoner. "If I don't have the address and situation of the child in the next three minutes, I will start putting holes in you until either you give me what I want or bleed to death."

It was an address in Yonkers. If we were to believe Marmot, the girl was guarded by two women he knew. When he'd finished the confession Mel thanked him and walked out of the cell.

"Are we gonna kill this one?" he asked.

"Not unless the girl's dead or he lied about where she is."

"You see? If I stay working with you long enough, I might work off nine, ten percent of my sins. I'll be right back."

Mel left the room while I stood sentry. After maybe five minutes Marmot made it to his feet, picked up the folding chair, and limped to the door. There he stood waiting to ambush Melquarth.

I hated the man for what he'd done, but still I identified with him. Just days before I was in a similar situation, desperately struggling to survive.

"At least he's still kickin'," Mel said from behind me. I was so concentrated on Marmot's silent monologue of survival that I didn't hear my friend come in.

He was carrying a small beat-up oak table, resembling a nineteenth-century child's writing desk; that and a paper folder.

"You need some help?"

"Nah," Mel said with a shrug. "I like to use my words when I can."

287

With that Mel entered and then closed the outer door. Marmot heard something because he raised the metal bludgeon-chair.

"Back away from the door and put down that seat," Mel's slightly altered voice said.

Marmot hesitated.

"You got sixty seconds and then I'm'a shoot you through a hole in this door."

I fingered the scar on my cheek.

Marmot threw down the chair and backed away from the door.

Mel walked in, put the desk down so that it faced the window, and said, "Now pick up that goddamned chair and sit down at this table."

When our prisoner did as he was told, Mel placed the paper folder on the tabletop and flipped it open. There was a small stack of white paper with a yellow plastic mechanical pencil hooked at the spine.

"You know you don't go to somebody's house and throw their furniture around," Mel said. "Now, I want you to write a confession for the murder of Johanna Mudd, the kidnapping of Chrissie Braun, and the subsequent extortion of her father. In there I want you to name everyone you worked for and all those that worked for you. And you better include your boss and those bad cops."

Marmot began to shiver.

"What are you waiting for?" Mel inquired.

"I can tell about the cops and my men, but I can't say who I worked for."

"Even if I kill you if you don't?"

"I'll be dead anyway."

"Not if they put your boss away."

"That will never happen."

Mel couldn't get the name Antrobus out of Marmot. The dark-side security expert gave the details and the whereabouts of the kidnapped child. And he named everyone else. Porker and his friends, Valence and Pratt. Marmot facilitated the drugs and the sex slaves distributed and afforded by the cops. He threw a wrench in Man's appeal just to keep all that quiet. His men murdered Mudd and took the child. Marmot was willing to implicate everyone but his boss. He knew that a coerced confession would never make it to open court. But if he even breathed the name of Antrobus, that would be the end of the line for him.

After the confession was written, Mel had Marmot handcuff himself to the chair. Then he got behind the man and pulled his hair until his neck was exposed. He injected Marmot just like he'd done to the thug who worked for him.

"What was that?" Marmot said.

"Just a little cyanide to help you sleep."

Just as the dread entered Marmot's eyes he passed out.

"You didn't really kill him, did you, Mel?"

"Nah. I just like seein' how scared a man gets when he thinks he's about to die."

35.

I LEFT STATEN Island, headed for Carnegie Hall. Mel had promised to leave the unconscious crook in a place where the cops would find him first.

"And I'll pin the confession to his vest," he added. "They'll get the girl and find that graveyard too."

"He won't go to prison, though," I said.

"If everything I hear about Antrobus is true, you won't have to worry about our boy living till spring."

The concert was lovely. My grandmother wore a red gown that sparkled from glitter and clear plastic scales.

"I didn't know you even owned a dress like that," I told her.

"Roger thinks his fancy gifts will get him in my pants," she replied with not a hint of shame.

After the event was over we went to a private gathering in an oval room that had a heavily patterned picture window for its roof. When my grandmother excused herself for the toilet, Ferris took me aside and said, "The item is on hold for you starting Monday morning. You got someone who can handle it?"

"Yeah. I have a friend who has a friend."

Despite her protests, my grandmother was swayed by the rich white man's attentions. But I don't think it had anything to do with his money. Be it a red gown or a red ribbon, at some point the expressions of love are all the same.

"Hey, babe," I said on the phone to my daughter the next morning.

"Hi, Daddy. How are you? Are you okay?"

"I think maybe I might be the best I have ever been in my life."

"Really? Is the trouble over?"

"For you it is. For me it's just beginning."

"Are you gonna be okay?"

"Like I said . . . the best. Tell your mother and Coleman that I say the coast is clear for them to come home whenever they want."

"But what about you, Daddy?"

"I'm gonna be fine, girl. I have figured what to do so that I don't stare out that window anymore, whining in my mind about jail."

"Did you prove them wrong?" she asked. Aja-Denise refused to accept that I could be guilty of anything.

"That will never happen. But I know now how to turn my back on all that."

"How?"

"I'll tell you on the day you graduate from college."

"That's too long."

"After all I've been through, it's just the blink of an eye."

"Can I come to work Monday?" she asked.

"A week from Monday."

"Why till then?"

"I have work to do."

"Can I see you?"

"I'll call as soon as I can. How's that?"

"I guess."

"I love you, Aja-Denise."

"I love you too, Daddy."

"Good-bye."

I was lying on my back with no blankets on the bed of my third-floor Montague Street apartment. In my life I'd been slashed, stabbed, and shot. I'd broken bones and had bruises that went so deep they never fully went away. But I was feeling as young and hopeful as my grandmother in her red gown.

The next call rang eight times before she answered.

"Hello?"

"Willa."

"Mr. Oliver? Is everything okay?"

"Perfect."

"Do you have any news?"

"I need you to come to my office at one this afternoon."

"Does it have to do with what happened to Mr. Braun?"

"Tangentially."

"Okay, I guess. Is it good news?"

"More like a challenge that might bring the news."

"I'll be there."

*   *   *

I'd already talked to Mel so the next call would be the trickiest.

"Hello." An old persistent bluster was already back in the lawyer's tone.

"Mr. Braun."

"Mr. Boll."

"I did that."

I was referring to the headlines of most of the papers, all except the *New York Times*. The discovery of the unconscious body of William James Marmot on the downtown doorstep of the NYPD was too tawdry for top billing in "all the news that's fit to print," but it did make the lower right corner of the front page.

"They brought my daughter back last night. She's unharmed if a little scared."

"I know. They found your friend Marmot with a note pinned to his chest that led them to the house of two women in Yonkers. Did you do as I asked?"

"First I'd like to know what your plans are for Mr. Man."

"No."

"What do you mean, no?"

"The police know that Marmot was trying to pressure you, but they don't have evidence that you were actually abandoning your client. They don't know about Johanna Mudd."

"I had no idea what they were planning to do," he claimed. "When I realized what had happened I got sick."

"She got dead."

That put a cork in the lawyer's whining.

"I have enough evidence to put you in deep shit, but that's not why you're going to do as I ask."

"No?"

"No."

"Tell me."

"Marmot was a minnow in the waters around Valence and Pratt. If I suggest to the man who employed him that you know his name, the tables will be turned and Chrissie will be missing an old man."

"I do not bend to threats," he said with a certainty he did not have.

"Make sure he's in downtown holding and make plans for five visitors Monday in the morning and afternoon."

"What visitors?"

I listed the people I had in mind. One or two of them surprised him. He asked about them, but I gave him no answers.

"You do what I ask," I told him, "and Chrissie will grow up believing she was visiting with her cousins in Yonkers and that you are the greatest man in the world."

I went down the rope ladder to my office after bathing in the big iron tub. I had slept eleven hours and the world had moved ever so slightly off its axis. People were milling down the avenue unaware of the mad machinations I was hatching over their heads.

My time in the prison cell, Gladstone Palmer's betrayals, even the loss of my shield no longer had a hold on my soul.

I picked up *All Quiet on the Western Front* and read without a break until the buzzer of my office door sounded.

Willa was wearing a blue dress reminding me of the femme fatale of one of my favorite novels. Her hair was up, and seeing her red lips, I realized that she hadn't worn makeup at our first meetings.

"Mr. Oliver."

"You look gorgeous."

"Thank you."

"Come on in."

I sat at Aja's desk and Willa took the seat across. She was looking very good and I wondered why. Was this an attempt to make sure that I helped her one-night lover?

"I read the in-depth article about Mr. Braun in the paper this morning," she said. "I had no idea that his daughter had been taken."

"That's why he was backing off."

"He called and said that he wanted me to meet with Manny on Monday at noon."

"That's what I want. He was just the mouthpiece."

Willa got the joke and smiled.

"I'm going to ask you to go off the reservation," I said.

"What does that mean?"

"In a little while a man will come here and he's going to give you a note that we want you to bring to Man. There's an item in the note that is vital to his case."

"Vital in what sense?"

"I can't answer because of…what do you lawyers call it? Oh yeah, plausible deniability. Just bring him what my friend gives you."

"They search you too closely for something like that."

"My friend has been smuggling contraband for his entire life."

"In prison?"

I nodded and a hint of concern entered her eyes.

"I love him," she said, connecting the fear with this revelation. "I don't want him hurt."

I smiled.

"You find that funny?" she asked, the woman she'd become echoing in her tone.

"You got a man with his comrades mostly slaughtered and him sitting on death row for the murder of two cops. His lawyer has betrayed him. Judges in the high court are whispering that he will most certainly die. And here you think I might be the one to bring him pain."

"What . . . what about his wife and child?"

"What about them?"

"Shouldn't they be made aware of your plans?"

"I will not share my plans with you or anyone else, but if everything works out, Mr. Man will be able to make his own decisions."

I could see that she was about to ask another question and many more after that, but then the buzzer sounded.

I didn't even look through the peephole.

Mel was standing there wearing a corn-colored suit with a black shirt underneath.

We didn't speak. I walked him over to the desk and Willa stood. She was both fascinated by and afraid of this man. He looked at her like an evolved tiger might, through self-imposed bars.

Mel pulled up a chair.

After her usual hesitation, Willa sat too.

Those few days held the most potent experiences in my life up until that point. It was as if every nerve had the volume turned up and every perception had a dozen meanings—all of which I understood and profited from.

"This is going to be a short meeting," I said. Then, turning to Willa: "My friend here is going to give you something and you will take it into that room for private meetings with lawyers. You will give him the packet and say that you got it from a friend. Don't tell him any names. Do not indicate anything about us, including gender, knowledge we might have, or about any investigation. He will take the item and make up his own mind."

"What will the note say?" Willa asked.

"That has to be between us and him," Mel said in a surprisingly soothing voice. "That way everyone is protected."

"They search you down to your underwear when you go in to visit a death row inmate."

Mel reached into his pocket and came out with a small box with the name A Summer's Day printed over a field of windblown grasses. It was a popular feminine hygiene product—a packet of three tampons. He handed the box to the young lawyer and she took it.

"The seals are intact and the price is stamped on the bottom," he said.

"But I won't be having my period Monday."

"Then it must be coming on," he said with an irrepressible wolfish tone.

"Just give him the packet," I said. "The note is inside."

"Tell him to keep it hidden and tear it open when he's back in his cell," Mel added. "If you follow these instructions to the letter, he will have a fifty-fifty chance of being saved."

"What does that mean?" she asked, looking directly into my friend's dead eyes.

"If I told you I'd have to kill you."

Her nostrils flared and I wondered if she was turned on by the power pulsating behind those words.

"Okay," Willa said to me. "That's it?"

"That's it."

After she was gone I took out a very old port and served.

"You think she'll do what we said?" Mel asked.

"I'm pretty sure. He's a man she loves and we're the only show in town."

"The only one," Mel agreed. "Now, how about this place?"

"It's called Treacher Admitting on Maiden Lane just a couple of blocks east of Broadway."

"I've never seen it."

"It doesn't advertise. They mostly serve rich patients from Wall Street, but they have a deal with law enforcement; free medical attention for certain protections." I paused and then asked, "What about the powder?"

"It's what they call a derivation of the shigella bacteria," Mel explained. "Targets the appendix but has a short life span, just long enough for our purposes."

"Not that I'm complaining," I said. "But how does a self-educated heist man turned watchmaker get his hands on something like that?"

"Whenever I get put away I try for the sentence to be carried out in a prison where there's a lotta Russians. They always have the most organized gangs and they're connected to people from the old country and Eastern Europe in general; those people often have ties to intelligence. This little poison comes straight from the defunct laboratories of the KGB."

"Damn." I was impressed. "I'll give you the plans to the clinic. Their security is not so strong seeing that they rely on the cops and the fact that nobody knows they're there. Because there's so many cops I need to stay away as long as I can."

"I got that covered."

We finished our wines and then poured two more.

36.

I SPENT SUNDAY morning wondering how I kept my lawless side down for so long. That train of thought brought me to the realization that I no longer missed being a policeman. I'd been a good cop in my own estimation, but that shit nearly got me killed.

I wasn't a criminal, not exactly. But those flexible rules of law could not bend as far as I was willing to go; as I needed to go.

The Internet news told of how William James Marmot had a crazy story of being kidnapped, shot, tortured, and then made to write the confession pinned to his chest. Under the threat of death he merely wrote what his masked captor dictated. He was a victim and not a criminal mastermind. Marmot was put in a hospital, but sometime after midnight, he evaded his police guard and effectively disappeared.

I went to a reinvented old-time boxing gym in Dumbo at noon. There I lifted some weights and did a dance with the heavy bag for an hour or so.

When I got back to the office there was a message on my office line.

"Mr. Oliver, this is Reggie Teegs. I'm an unofficial representative of the parties that you've been negotiating with. We would all like to keep this matter outside the legal system, and so if you call me we can meet and I will offer you a settlement on behalf of my clients."

He left a phone number that I was sure could not be traced.

I considered calling Mel but decided that I shouldn't rely too heavily on him. I thought that maybe it would have been prudent to wait a week or so before responding, but that didn't feel right either. Something about Teegs's request sounded like an immediate threat.

"Mr. Oliver," he said upon answering.

I had walked all the way to Park Slope to call him from a phone booth in a small restaurant I frequented. It could have been a call from anybody, but he knew that the only ring that line would be getting had to be from me.

"So?" I said. "What is it?"

"We have to meet."

"I haven't been very lucky with clandestine meetings in this century," I said.

"You choose the place."

"Columbus Circle mall, fourth-floor wine bar," I said, "in thirty minutes."

"Done. You'll know me because I will be the only man there wearing a herringbone jacket with an orange bow tie."

*   *   *

I reached the fourth-floor, inside, open-air wine bar in twenty-eight minutes. He was drinking cognac from a snifter and looking about him like some kind of humanoid alien examining the rituals of an alien species in a forsaken corner of his cosmic domain. Preternaturally thin, he was what passed as a white man, but his coloring was olive and his black eyes were startling, even from a distance.

I told the hostess that I saw my friend. She smiled and moved aside. As I walked toward him he took no special notice. This told me that he wasn't armed with a photograph.

"Mr. Teegs?"

Due to his slender build and finicky attire, I expected the professional middleman to be shorter than I. But as he unfolded himself from the chair he rose and rose until I was looking up into his void-colored eyes.

He took inventory of me: my Crayola-blue suit and black canvas shoes (worn in case I had to run). I had to concentrate to keep my hands from writhing nervously. This strange man unnerved me.

His smile revealed very bright but tiny teeth.

"Mr. Oliver," he greeted, holding out a hand. "So glad you decided to come."

I shook the hand and took the chair across the small circular table from him.

The wine bar—it had no name I knew of—wasn't very crowded. We sat next to the outer wall, looking down the atrium to the entrance hall three floors below. I chose that particular place because no matter the economic state of the nation, or the world, that mall was always crowded because it catered to the upper classes, who, it seemed, were never at a loss for disposable income.

We were sitting in an isolated corner, so my host spoke clearly and at a decent volume.

"There was a regrettable decision to end your life," he said as if talking about a small dog that had taken a shit on my rosebushes. "We apologize for that lapse in judgment."

This answered my first question: Teegs worked for whoever it was who used Gladstone to frame me back in the days when I was cop.

"Whatever happened with that?"

"The agent, who took the unconsidered decision upon himself, has been dealt with. You don't have to worry about him anymore."

"What about his accomplices?"

"One has moved on and the other has simply gone away."

I liked the way Teegs talked. His references could be either vague or rock solid.

"Why would you apologize if it was Convert who took it upon himself to do what was done?" I wasn't as accomplished a conversationalist as Reggie Teegs.

"If a man represents another man, then the man in charge has to take responsibility. That rule is what Western civilization is based upon."

"And are you the man in charge?"

Showing his small-toothed grin again, he said, "Heavens no. I am merely a fulcrum, the man who attempts to achieve parity among the parties involved."

"I could have used somebody like you a long time ago."

"As I have said, there have been mistakes made."

"You talk about this shit like you stepped on my toe or brought me a black coffee instead of one with cream."

"Come on now, Joe," the Fulcrum said reasonably. "Men have died in this arena. I'm here to offer you recompense."

"What kind of recompense?"

Teegs reached under the table, pulling out a dull buff-colored leather satchel.

He said, "Four hundred and fifty thousand dollars in un-traceable bills."

If I was still a cop I would have walked away right then. Even if I had just considered myself loyal to the clan that abandoned me I would have said no. As merely a responsible citizen the negation was on the tip of my tongue.

Teegs saw this and said, "Before you make a rash decision, Mr. Oliver, let me say that the people on the other side would feel quite nervous if you were to refuse their offer."

I could send Aja-Denise to college with money like that. And there were the costs that the next day's jobs would incur. The most I could hope for was some kind of payoff, be it from a judgment or from the conniving of some lawyer like Stuart Braun.

"Your pain is undeniable," Teegs said, trying to drive the point home, "but, despite our lapses, you are still alive."

"If I take that satchel the people you represent will back off?"

"Like the darkness at the break of day."

"And if I don't take it?"

"I have no words for that consequence."

I returned, that evening, to my office, with the pigskin satchel and more money than I'd ever had. I put on a duet by Charlie Parker and Dizzy Gillespie. They played those horns like maniacs finally released from the asylum of humanity.

I listened to the piece over and over, thinking about the victims whom I'd uncovered and to some degree whom I had avenged. I thought about the truth that undergirded the lies circulated by the institutions of governments, large and small. That was, I knew, my excuse for taking the payoff.

37.

AJA CALLED ME in the morning. They were back from Florida and she wanted to ditch school to meet me for lunch. I was her father and should have said no, but instead I agreed and called the school, telling them that I was keeping her out for the day.

We met at noon at our favorite pizza place across the avenue from Lincoln Center. There they made simple pizzas on the thinnest crust imaginable.

"What happened to your hair?" was the first thing she said.

"I thought I'd take up track," I joked. "Cutting off my hair makes me aerodynamic."

She wasn't amused.

"Are you okay now, Daddy?"

Instead of answering, I hugged and kissed her; then we sat at a window table.

"Almost."

"Why only almost?"

"The best thing I can ever teach you, honey, is that the truth will kick you in the ass."

306

She giggled; then the waitress came to take our order.

"Are you getting kicked at by the truth?" Aja asked me when the server departed.

"Yeah."

"Can I help?"

"You know how I was gettin' on you about how you were dressed?"

"Yeah?"

"Whenever I do something like that you should listen to what I say but do what you want."

"I usually do," she said.

"Don't I know it?"

"But you're almost always right, Daddy."

The concern on her face made her look older and, in my opinion, even more beautiful.

"I was real worried about you when we went away," she added. "I hardly slept at all. One night I woke up and found Mom sitting on the couch in our suite."

"You had a suite?"

"Coleman said that we should have it so that we were together. He was pretty scared."

"What about your mother?"

"I told her how worried I was about you and she said that she was too."

"Really?"

"Uh-huh. You know what she said?"

"I couldn't even imagine."

"She said that she shouldn't have abandoned you all those years ago when that policewoman showed her the tapes of you with another woman."

"She told you about that?"

"Just about that she saw you with somebody. But she said that you were a good man and she knew it, but she was just so mad that it was like somebody else was there making her turn her back on you. She said that she was still mad, but now she knows that that shouldn't have mattered and she should have had your back. She said that you guys should have worked it out and maybe you wouldn't be in so much trouble today. I told her she should tell you all that when we got back, but she said that she never could, that it would be wrong for a married woman to say something like that to another man."

"Whoa. Then why are you telling me?"

"Because usually when Mom doesn't want you to know something she says not to tell. That's how I knew she wanted you to know how she felt."

The waitress brought our pizzas and salads, giving me a respite in which to think.

"So?" Aja asked when our server, whose chipped blue name tag read MARYANNE, had gone again.

"So what?"

"Are you gonna ask Mom to get back together?"

That was the perfect moment for me to do what I had come there for. I reached into my inside jacket pocket and came out with a small brown envelope made from tough plastic. The letter was sealed, and I handed it over to the person I loved the most in the world.

"What's this?"

"If I am ever hurt or in big trouble I want you to open this and do what it says. Put it away somewhere safe, somewhere where neither your mother nor Coleman will find it."

"I know a place," Aja said with convincing certainty. "But what does it say?"

"You will probably never have to find out."

I didn't want her worrying, but three hundred thousand dollars of my bribe money would be in a safe-deposit box where only she and I were signatories.

"What about you and Mom?" she asked, putting the envelope in her purse.

"Aja-Denise, do you really want me and your mother under the same roof after all these years of fighting?"

I could see her imagining what that union would be like. After a moment her eyes opened wide and then she smiled.

"Never mind."

38.

I MET MEL at a diner called Clown's Carnival four blocks away from the semisecret clinic. It was a few minutes past eight. I had on my fake facial hair just in case there was some errant CCTV feed lurking above.

Mel was all in black. I was too, under my bulky umber overcoat.

"Your layout of the place is a little out of date," he told me after we'd greeted and I ordered coffee.

"Yeah? How'd you find that out?"

"Building permits. City has a website for all construction work. They weren't hiding because the cops keep it on the down low like you said. They installed all kinds of security to keep people out up front, but the back of the building is the same as it always was."

"There is no back of the building," I said. "Treacher's shares a back wall with Kershaw and Associates."

"Au contraire," the sophisticated demon argued. "There's a two-foot space between the clinic and Kershaw, after the sixth floor. And most of the fancy security updates are on the ninth floor. There's only one hospital bed up on that level. All we have to do is make it up there now, break into the floor, and then wait nearby until they bring our guy in. Once that happens, and we see how the guards are placed, we decide on how to get him out. Only thing I wanna know is if you're willing to use deadly force."

"You mean kill a cop?"

Mel didn't even nod.

"No, man. This is about not murdering."

"Okay. I got ya. I know how to spin it. But considering on how things might go, it could make it that much more difficult to get through."

There was a side door to Kershaw and Associates. Mel had been in and out of the building over the past few days and had put together a plan for us to enter unnoticed. That particular side door had no camera on it, and he had fixed the lock so that it only appeared to work properly.

We made our way in and up to the eighth floor. There we jimmied the locks of the offices of Myer, Myer, and Goldfarb. I couldn't tell by their walls or desks what business MM&G were in, but it didn't much matter. The eighth stage of the Kershaw building was halfway between the eighth and ninth floors of the building that housed Treacher Admitting.

I had brought a go bag with all the tools a burglar might need. We had to completely remove the unused window that looked out onto the slender divide between the two buildings. I had two crowbars for that job. We wedged a metal chair between our window and Treacher's wall. From there, one after another, we crawled up high enough to make it through the hospital room window. We had to break the lock, but Mel put it back together well enough that it looked okay if you didn't inspect it too closely.

Then we used a half-chewed piece of gum to attach a tiny transmitter under the hospital bed and made our way back down to MM&G.

That was our time to wait.

We had a tiny speaker receiving a continuous feed from the transmitter in the room. When something happened there, we would hear it.

So for the next three hours we sat in darkness and silence.

It was a fairly simple plan. The note hidden in the tampon, printed in block letters culled from the Internet, told A Free Man that if he wanted to be free he should take the powder folded in a small cellophane envelope that accompanied the note, at any time between 11:00 at night and 2:00 in the morning. This would give him abdominal pains and a fever. He should call a guard at the first signs of these symptoms and that's all he had to do.

We waited. I don't believe either of us uttered a word in that time.

But even though I didn't chatter, my mind was filled with excitement, fear, and even some remorse.

I was not an extortionist-rapist even though I *had* had sex with the woman calling herself Nathali Malcolm. A Free Man was not a murderer even though he had shot and killed the two policemen who had betrayed their oaths and tried to murder him. We were both mostly innocent men slated to take the fall for the real criminals. We would never receive justice from law enforcement or the courts, and so the only thing that could be done was to take the law into our own hands.

This decision frightened me. Taking these steps brought me to a place I had never been, a place that I had always thought was wrong. And it was wrong. My demon friend and I were executing an honest-to-God prison break.

For a man with my history, that was just about as bad as you could get.

There were butterflies all through my body. I felt as if I were damned. But still I knew that this was the only course left open to me.

"Bring him in here!" a woman commanded over the small speaker on the desk between us.

The time was 1:57 a.m.

There were sounds of squeaky rubber wheels on the linoleum floor and the squealing of metal frames moving and sometimes bumping into other objects.

"Put him on the bed," the woman said.

"Lift!" a man said.

Then we heard the less definable sounds of a body being hefted and moved, probably from a gurney to the bed.

"You don't need to restrain him," the woman complained. "He has a fever of one oh three."

"Ma'am, this here is a convicted cop killer. As far as I'm concerned we could have let him die in his cell. But as long as he's here he will be chained to this bed."

There were more sounds and some conversation. Mel and I were on high alert. I no longer worried about right and wrong because it was a time for action.

"He has all the symptoms of appendicitis, but that's not what I'm seeing," the woman said.

"Should we take him back?" a man I had not heard before asked.

"No," the woman doctor said. "I want to observe him for twenty-four hours at least. If this is some kind of communicable infection I'd like to isolate it before it spreads through your jail."

"You mean we could catch this?"

"I don't know. But I'd like to see what happens."

"Arkady," the first man who spoke said.

"Yes, sir."

"Set up outside this room and don't go to sleep."

"What about if it's catching, Sergeant?" Arkady asked.

"That's why God invented medical insurance."

The doctor and the cops talked for a while more. Most of the police left. For the next twenty or thirty minutes we could hear someone, probably the doctor, moving around the room. And then, for thirty-four minutes, there was silence.

As quietly as he could Mel climbed out on our ladder-chair and lifted himself up to look through the hospital room window. Then he opened the window and climbed through. I followed as soundlessly as possible and clambered into the dark room.

We'd been wearing gloves since entering the Kershaw building. Before we crossed over to the clinic the first time we had donned dark ski masks.

A drawn and unconscious Free Man was chained to his hospital bed. His dreadlocks were tangled and there was a twist to his lips.

I had a bolt cutter and so used it on the restraint that chained Man to the bed frame. In the meanwhile Mel was fashioning a shoulder harness from thick rope that he intended to use to lower the unconscious Mr. Man from one building to the next.

I hefted the tangle-headed Man up into a seated position, and Mel began to loop the jury-rigged harness around the left shoulder.

That was when the door burst open and the light came on.

Time froze for a moment there. Officer Arkady had taken on too much what with opening the door and turning on the light. He probably heard something and thought it was Man trying to get out of his cuffs and so had not drawn his weapon. He did, however, reach for his piece when he saw us.

Mel was faster. The habitual offender swiveled to the right and fired five shots, which sounded like no more than pops. Arkady was hit in both legs and both arms. Then Mel rushed the faltering cop and hit him in the center of his forehead with the barrel of the gun.

The cop, who was portly of build, hit the floor like a dead bull and Mel was quick to use the man's own handcuffs to restrain him. I thought that this was going a little overboard when I noticed there was no blood coming from Arkady's extremities.

Mel noticed me looking and said, "Rubber bullets."

Then he took a metal hypodermic from a pouch at his side and administered what I figured was some kind of knockout concoction.

While this was going on I ran out into the hall and located a wheelchair.

When I came back in my cohort asked, "What you plan to do with that?"

"No sentry. We could take the elevator."

"What if they got cameras?"

"This place is for VIP clients. They don't want electric eyes following them."

Mel's grin actually filled me with pride.

"I'll go back down to Kershaw and take our stuff out of there," he said. "You got those whiskers on so don't have to wear no mask. Once you get out head west toward Broadway. I'll grab the van and snag you on the way."

It was the right plan, but I felt like a rat in a trap waiting for that elevator and then taking it down. Even when I made it to the delivery exit on the bottom floor, my heart was going at a triple rate. Mel had handed me his pistol, but that didn't give me any solace. I'd spend the rest of my life in prison if I was captured. All of that said, there was a feeling of elation in my fast heart that I never had before . . . or since.

On the sidestreet sidewalk I began pushing the wheelchair. All of the clinic's security was aimed at keeping unwanteds out. No one was expected to try to escape.

Even though Man was sedated when we found him, Melquarth had given him a shot of his tranquilizer.

"You had two hypodermics?" I asked.

"I got a gun with real bullets too. Same reason you brought along those crowbars, to get the job done."

We had strapped the thin, long-haired Man with restraints that the chair provided. I looked down through his dreadlocks. His dark brown skin could have been mine.

The handsome slant of his face might have belonged to a radical historian college professor.

It was cold outside; I could see that in the mist from my breath. But I didn't feel it. Up ahead I saw the red and blue flashes of a police car. These passed by the intersection of Broadway and Maiden Lane.

"Hey!" Mel called.

He'd pulled to the curb just behind me. His van was middle green and there was a sign on the side that read HOBART AND SONS CONSTRUCTION.

We left the wheelchair at the curb and lay Man's inert form on a mattress on the floor.

I sat back there with him while Mel drove.

We made it through the Holland Tunnel to Jersey City and then took 95 to 78 past Newark International and on, twenty miles or so past Elizabeth, arriving at a private airport. I spent most of that time making sure Man didn't bounce around too much.

The elation was flaring inside me. I had done something, something real. This meant more to me than anything other than the birth of my daughter.

We were allowed in by a security guard at the gate to the airfield. He was a short white guy with a huge face.

"Who are you?" he asked Mel, the driver.

"Lansman," my friend said. It was the code name I gave to my grandmother's billionaire boyfriend.

"Your pilot is already here."

The pilot was a tall, very handsome Hispanic man who told us to call him Jack. The three of us carried Man into the small jet and strapped him into yet another chair.

My only interaction with A Free Man was with his unconscious body. It was as if, I suppose, I was his dream. An apparition that he'd never remember but that changed his life.

"I know Jack here," Mel said to me while the pilot made ready at the controls. "I'll go down with him to Panama City and make sure your boy's settled in."

"I should go with you."

"You been talking to people about this guy, right?"

"Yeah."

"That means you should be living your normal everyday life in case anybody wants to look at you. Also we need to get this van away from where your friend's airplane is to keep you out of that. I mean, we don't know if maybe somebody saw us drive away. Don't worry, Joe. I didn't go through all this to trick you now."

He was right. And I really didn't want to go away just then.

"You brought my duffel bag down from that office?" I asked.

"Yeah." He rummaged around the back and gave it to me.

I pulled out the leather satchel that Teegs had given me.

"There's one hundred and fifty thousand dollars in here. Twenty-five is to cover your costs. After you pay the pilot the rest is for Man."

Mel took the satchel and smiled.

"You see that, Joe? A man like Mr. Man here is one'a my people. And there you are on the other side of the wall doing what's right."

"You better get outta here before we start kissin' or somethin'."

* * *

I parked the van in the long-term section of an automated underground parking lot. I had a hat and my whiskers and hope in my heart that there was no camera to see my disguise. Then I took the train from Newark back to Manhattan and the A train, which ran local after 10:00 p.m., to High Street in Brooklyn.

39.

I GOT TO bed by noon and slept for nineteen hours without even getting up to urinate.

In the early morning I read all about the daring prison
escape. Stuart Braun had set up seven visitors for his client.
The man's wife, three doctors, Willa Portman of course,
Stuart himself, and a Catholic priest for prayer. All were
questioned. None were held. The investigation would go
on for decades, if I was lucky. Even if Willa told about the
package we gave her she had no proof of what was in it.
Our note told Man to destroy and discard the note and
packaging after taking his powder.

I should have been afraid, but there was nothing but joy
for me that morning.

In the following days Aja came back to work. The only
thing she said was that she knew what happened and we
never had to talk about it.

On Friday Mel dropped by and gave me a small memory
chip.

"I gave him what money there was," Mel said. "He

recorded a message for his wife. I watched it and heard what he had to say. He didn't mention a thing that would get him or us in trouble." He took a slip of paper from a pocket and handed it to me. "Here's his mother-in-law's address. Print out a note that says 'For Honey Mama and Lil Sugar,' and she will make sure it gets there."

Later that day the buzzer to my apartment sounded.

"Yeah?" I said into the intercom.

"It's Gladstone."

I hesitated but then decided that whatever my ex-friend had to say I should hear him out.

We were sitting at my table-desk drinking Irish whiskey that Gladstone brought.

After some small talk he said, "I hear that they made a settlement with you."

"Maybe."

"That guy Teegs is a trip, right?"

"Why are you here, Glad?"

"I know you feel like I sold you out, Joe, but the way I look at it I saved your life. I couldn't have stopped them from doing something. I tried to tell them to pay you off then, but they said they couldn't take the chance."

"They were probably right," I said. "Back then I was blue all the way to the core."

"And you aren't anymore?"

I took in a deep breath and looked at my friend.

"It's okay, Glad. I get it now. Back then I didn't understand. I thought I knew the rules, but now I see that the rules don't cover every damn thing."

My eternally smiling friend frowned a little then.

"You still wanna be in that poker game?"

"Sure I do. After all you did, I should let you win a little of that money. And you're right, you did save my life."

Late that night I put the memory chip into a reader connected to my computer. An icon appeared on the screen and I clicked on it. Immediately the image of A Free Man appeared. He was wearing a loose shirt of a yellow hue. His dreads were tied back and then piled up at the back of his head. His smile seemed to want to lift up off his face and fly around his head.

"Hey, babe. I went to sleep a condemned man and woke up in freedom. I'm in the bright sun and as happy as a man could be. I can't tell you where I am or how I got here, but you and Lil Sugar have to know that I love you and we'll be together as soon as I can make that happen. I will be in touch and if you need to get to me all you have to do is remember that North Blue thing we used to do.

"Hi, Lil Sugar! I know you're there too. I love you and I never did anything wrong. Don't listen to what they say. Your heart knows the truth."

I felt that I was set free along with Man. It was a deep grinding feeling that hurt but at the same time felt like the hand of some momentary apparition of God.